Across My Dreams With Nets Of Wonder

JOHN HOWARD

Fisher King Publishing

To my English teacher, Mr. Leach, who told me to, 'use that imagination of yours and write.' And to my art teacher, Miss Shaw, who told me to, 'never be afraid of being different.'

Prologue

Butterfly Cottage in Turnham Green, London, a pretty red-brick detached bungalow, built in 1961 and bought that year by Dr. Braintree and his wife, Alice. The Wedgewood-styled name plaque on the gate reflected her love of the exotically-patterned butterflies which inhabited the garden during their first Summer there. The house was the last one of six in The Green, a charming, leafy cul-de-sac just five minutes' walk from the tube station.

The land had been bought by a local builder, Ernest Franklin, who'd knocked down the large derelict mansion, Lockton Manor, which had stood there since the 1800s. The Lockton family had been residents since it was built but, so the story told by the older locals went, by the early 1920s the surviving Lord Lockton, a rather eccentric carefree bachelor, 'had a breakdown of some sort and deserted the place.' It was rumoured that Lockton had, before leaving, released all the butterflies from a sanctuary he had built beside the manor, which explained the many unusual varieties which still fluttered around The Green.

After Lockton had left the manor, 'a rather spooky Gothic pile' according to one neighbour, it was bought by an elderly couple in 1922. The bohemian pair, whose names were now forgotten in the mists of time, didn't stay long, mysteriously disappearing one morning in 1924, leaving no forwarding address.

The place fell into disrepair but was requisitioned by the army in 1940. The men shored up enough of the building and roof to make it basically habitable for the duration of the war. After they left in 1945, it slowly became a dilapidated relic.

Franklin bought it from the council in 1959, his plans to demolish the mansion and build the bungalows being hastily approved by a relieved council committee. Their one condition of sale was that an area of parkland would be created behind the bungalows, and the marble fountain which had stood in the grounds of the old manor, boasting a wonderful metal sculpture of nymphs and angels playing with a dolphin, which had once spouted water from its mouth, would remain, renovated to full working order. The council also insisted that a laurel hedge be planted along the bungalows' back walls to ensure privacy for the residents.

Many of the windows at the front of the house were arts and crafts-designed stained glass, featuring various plant designs. Franklin saved them all, using six panes for the front doors of his new bungalows, and the rest in a block of flats he built in Kew.

Chapter One

Arthur and Alice Braintree were in their mid-fifties, wanting a smaller house after their four children had grown up and left their three-storey Edwardian home in Twickenham. Butterfly Cottage fitted the bill perfectly. With its pretty privet-hedged front garden, split in two by a crazy-paving tiled footpath up to the front door which boasted an attractive stained glass insert featuring a red and cream butterfly resting on a Buddleia, the bungalow possessed enormous kerb appeal.

A bright hallway led to a double aspect sitting room on the left, the main bedroom opposite that. Next to it was the bathroom, with the second bedroom opposite, next to the sitting-room. Finally a kitchen/dinette at the back led out to a large flint-walled garden.

The bungalow came with a large plot of land, a sizeable front garden and two good size side areas which led to half an acre out back. Dr. Braintree had laid it to lawn and planted a variety of shrubs along the borders, creating a wrap-around garden.

At the bottom of the back garden, he had built a brick summerhouse, clad in tongue-and-groove wooden slats and painted a pretty shade of duck-egg blue. With a matching wood-panelled interior and slate roof, which looked silver when it rained, Alice fell in love with its cabin-in-the-forest look and the quiet solitude it offered.

"It looks so American," she declared to Arthur. "You'll have to learn to play the guitar and serenade me as we sit on the veranda drinking Southern Comfort each night."

Arthur, as he always did when responding to Alice's fanciful imaginings, just smiled and said, "Maybe one day, dear."

One morning, Alice was watching Arthur pruning the roses and mulching the beds, as she worked on one of her books beneath the dappled shade of an old silver birch. Although none of her novels found an interested publisher, one of Alice's short stories, a romantic tale featuring time-travel adventures and a handsome hero, did make it into Woman's Realm.

Waiting for inspiration to emerge out of the ether, she reflected on how she had longed for a perfect little home like this for years.

Bringing up four children in a large draughty old house, full of the noise of others, had unsettled Alice. She never embraced the joys of having a young family running and laughing around her. All she ever longed for was peace and quiet. She had actually dreaded four o'clock in the afternoon, when the three eldest kids had come running in from the car, excitedly reporting the events of their day. She'd done her best to appear interested, always being sure to give them a hug and make them feel loved, but while she thought she'd succeeded in achieving that, she was never far from the feeling that it had been simply a duty. So, now, Alice could finally tell herself that she was happy; the guilt gradually fading, the feeling of inadequacy evaporating, the morning sun warming her new life.

Mulling over all this and admiring the Autumn colours of the silver birch's leaves as they gently drifted to the ground, 'like a final sigh', she heard from behind the wall a scraping sound, followed by exertive grunts and obvious efforts to climb up it. After listening for a few moments, she went to the edge of the veranda to see what or who was there.

A small boy emerged, peering over the wall as he held on for dear life with his elbows, his face a bright red from the effort.

Alice smiled at him and said,

"Hello there, what's your name?"

His mouth fell open, his eyes widened in shock and he promptly jumped down and scrambled through a gap in the hedge behind the bungalows. Chuckling to herself, Alice sat down and reflected on the young lad's very attractive blue velvet outfit, reminding her of Little Lord Fauntleroy. She wondered if he was from the nearby school, which a neighbour had told her was rehearsing a Victorian play.

Arthur had just finished hacking at a particularly verdant shrub, standing up and wiping his brow so Alice called him over. As usual, when she told him about the mysterious child, he gave her one of his looks

"He was *there!*" Alice insisted, pointing at the wall. "I only saw him for a few seconds before he ran off through the hedge."

As his wife smiled dreamily into the distance, Arthur sighed.

"Oh, Alice dear, let's not start all that again."

"Start all *what?*" she protested.

"Seeing things, seeing people, you know how it upsets Alistair."

"Well Alistair isn't here, so it can hardly upset him."

"He's actually on his way, he should be here in about twenty minutes, I imagine. Please don't mention this disappearing boy to him, he'll only…"

"Of course not. Alistair would only grimace and groan," Alice said. "His favourite occupation."

John Howard

"Exactly, and you hate that. So - just relax and tell him how much we like it here. Okay?"

***

Alistair Braintree stood in the front room of the bungalow, pulling one of his faces, which Alice had always hated. It was a mixture of puzzlement, annoyance and distaste, which he adopted whenever he was accusing his mother of 'being daft'.

"I've never understood why you and Dad wanted to live in such a poky little house," he told her, staring round the walls like they were coming in on him.

"We wanted a smaller place," Alice replied, trying not to sound tetchy and, as usual with Alistair, not succeeding. "Your father and I were sick of constantly paying for the upkeep of a house which was far too large for us, full of rooms we never used."

"But *we* used them when we visited," Alistair wailed, trying to wander round in an expansive way and failing. "The kids especially *loved* that house."

"Exactly. And I got increasingly fed up being treated like a free weekend B 'n' B."

Alistair looked wounded.

"Oh, you know what I mean, darling," Alice said, stroking her son's arm and feeling him flinch. "I've always hated cooking and entertaining, you know that, and now there are *hordes* of you, all expecting me to wait on you hand and foot whenever you decided to 'come over for a break'. The last straw was when you assumed we'd be putting on Christmas dinner for god knows how many of you. That was the moment I knew we simply *had* to move. We put the house on the market, accepted an excellent offer within two weeks and found this, our perfect little bungalow."

Alice went to the window, sighing at the view of the peaceful little street, which led to tree-lined walks she and Arthur enjoyed every morning.

"I sometimes wonder if you've actually enjoyed being our mother," Alistair said behind her.

Alice spun round, partly in anger but also a little shocked that her son had sussed her out.

"Arthur and I brought up the four of you very well," she said, her voice shaking. "We gave you security and as much love as you needed, but you're not children any longer, Alistair."

Feeling the argument gradually coming back to her side, she continued.

"Our responsibility ended when you left home and found your successful careers and better halves, with whom you produced your own children to worry about."

"You mean your *grandchildren!*" Alistair almost shouted, his eyes popping out and his face going red.

"Who I never asked you to have, sweet though one or two of them may be. I certainly have no intention of becoming their carers whenever you feel like a weekend away without them."

"Well, you've certainly made sure that can never happen again," Alistair said, resisting the urge to stamp his foot. "There's just one spare bedroom here, which Dad has filled with his clutter."

"And why shouldn't he? One of the reasons your father and I fell in love with this house is that it's impossible for anyone to come and stay. The house is *ours*, no-one else's. That's the whole point of getting older, finally having the chance to be independent again."

"You sound like a teenager."

"I *feel* like a teenager," Alice replied, throwing her arms in the air. "And I am *loving* it."

She marched out to the kitchen, talking as she went, forcing him to traipse behind her like a little boy who'd been promised a sweet. Then, out of the blue, she turned and stroked his face.

"Darling, you know I love you, all of you, in my way, but this is now mine and Arthur's time. This house will give us the peace and quiet we have longed for, *our* space."

She stroked the blue Formica work surface like a pet cat.

"I absolutely *love* this house. It has something about it. It feels like a friend."

"It's a house, Mum, how can it 'feel like a friend'?"

"I have no idea, but I sensed it as soon as we viewed it. There are good spirits here."

Alistair guffawed unattractively then looked at the stove which was ominously not switched on.

"Are you not making us any lunch?"

"No. Your father's taking you to the pub and I am staying here to, well, to mull and plan."

"Plan? Plan what?"

Ignoring Alistair, Alice began busying herself at the sink.

"By all means, come and visit anytime for afternoon tea," she said, drying a couple of plates.

She put the plates away in a cupboard and turned to face her son.

"But, do take note, Alistair, I am *not* cooking meals for the army anymore. Arthur enjoys banging a few pans together in the kitchen much more than I do anyway. He does a splendid pesto pasta and his salads are to die for."

Alistair looked shocked.

"Daddy? *Cooking*?"

"Yes darling, how terribly radical of us."

Alistair was about to reply when Arthur came in from the garden.

"Here's your father," Alice said with relief. "Go and have a nice natter over a steak and kidney pie and a pint."

Alistair looked like he'd been ordered to go and play rugby rather than stay in and read. With hunched shoulders and reddening face, he followed Arthur down the hall, disconsolately realising that this new decade had completely ruined his life.

As Arthur drove off in the brand new mini, Alice imagined her son complaining about the lack of leg room and asking why they'd want to get rid of 'the good old Austin Cambridge' in which the family had taken trips to Cornwall every summer. Doing his best to look like a trapped animal and waving weakly at his mum as the car pootled off down The Green, Alice mused that, for someone so young, and a successful solicitor in the West End, Alistair was terribly old.

Simply accepting that the 1950s were over was a real challenge for him. Whereas, for Alice, the 1960s promised youthful energy, an exciting modern outlook and god-sent labour-saving appliances in every home. It was, she thought, as she emptied a tin of Heinz tomato soup into a pan and heated it up on the small but perfectly formed electric hob, truly liberating.

***

Washing up her bowl and spoon and putting them on the draining board, Alice decided to do a bit of dusting while she had the house to herself. Going into the sitting-room she randomly picked up family photos off the radiogram, and sprayed the pine teak with Pledge. She smiled at the one of the twins, Michael and Miriam, sitting in their double-pram in the park. They'd come along a couple of years after Alistair and, although they'd been cheerful, bonny babies, they'd grown into clones of their brother, in terms of temperament and expectation.

Michael graduated with honours from medical college at the age of twenty-two, eventually specialising in geriatric care. Alice always wondered just how sympathetic, and indeed empathetic, Michael would be with the aged, having such a disconnected personality himself.

Alice then picked up a photo of Miriam, taken when she'd got her first job at the *Twickenham Herald* and gave it a quick dust. Like Alistair, her eldest daughter was emotionally blinkered, and, like her brother, harshly judgemental and incredibly selfish.

It hadn't been a surprise when Miriam had gone into tabloid journalism at The Sun, where a 'scandal-scoop' about someone else's misery was more important than considering the feelings of the people involved.

When she'd challenged Miriam about one of her articles, which had even shocked Arthur, her daughter had replied, "Oh, Mummy. Don't be so bloody naïve. It's called life."

And then there was Verity. Alice involuntarily smiled to herself as she wiped the small bronze sculpture Verity had created of her mother shortly after she and Arthur had moved into the bungalow. Verity had been a true love-child, not expected at all. Alice had been feeling run-down and even suspected an early menopause, so

Arthur had arranged an appointment with a specialist he knew, who sent her for scans. They revealed that little Verity had been quietly growing within her for the last two-and-a-half months.

It had been a difficult pregnancy, Alice nearly losing the baby twice, and being born at just twenty-seven weeks meant the poor little mite spent several more weeks in an incubator. It was 'a case of wait and see', as the doctor put it, but Verity fought against all the odds and finally, on the day she'd been originally due, Alice and Arthur took her home.

Alistair was ten when Verity was born, the twins nearly eight and all three of them had viewed her as an intruder, an unwelcome addition to their perfect unit.

Alice on the other hand loved Verity to bits; she was funny, charming, generous to a 'T' and extremely talented. From a tiny child she loved making things, always winning prizes at the local fete for her handicraft pieces. This naturally made her three older siblings even more resentful - and her mother constantly protective of this little gem in their midst.

As Verity reached her teens it became clear all her crushes were on female teachers. They never lasted long but she'd become especially besotted with the new art mistress, whose own specialty was sculpture.

Verity attended all of Mrs. Benson's twice-weekly night classes, and one evening brought home a small clay figurine she'd made. It was of Mrs. Benson, Verity proudly told her, and it took Alice's breath away. It showed a near naked woman looking up to the sky, both hands holding her head as if overjoyed at what she saw. Arthur was particularly concerned about the attention to detail of Mrs. Benson's voluptuous figure, which of course Michael sniggered about.

However, Verity's parents were much happier after they'd visited the teacher one evening after school. Firstly, they'd been surprised at how slight Mrs. Benson was, not at all bosomy, quite boyish in fact, and clearly blissfully married to her enormous rugby-player husband Eric, who came to pick her up after the meeting.

"Verity is extremely talented, a real individual with a marvellous imagination," Mrs. Benson told them, Arthur saying under his breath 'she certainly has an imagination'. "Please don't worry about her," Mrs. Benson continued, flashing a quick look at Arthur, "just encourage her and she will shine."

And shine Verity had. Now in her twenties, her sculptures were catching the attention of some influential art critics, one Guardian reviewer of a recent exhibition of her work extolling 'the joyous freedom of unbound movement in all of Verity's impressive creations'.

So, while Alice was reluctantly fond of Alistair, Michael and Miriam - she was their mother after all – and admired their ambitions and career successes, she was especially proud of Verity, her 'little fighter' as she called her.

**

Alice had been saying for a while that she would like to photograph the butterflies in the garden, so, for her sixtieth birthday, Arthur bought her a Nikon-F camera. While he viewed it as a fond indulgence of another of his wife's occasional passions – the exercise books had been quietly tucked away in an upstairs drawer – he was unexpectedly impressed with her first attempts.

Alice took to photography like a natural, achieving a wonderful stillness as she focused on a butterfly gathering pollen from one of the roses, never disturbing the creatures as she clicked away, then slowly backing off and moving to another beauty which had caught her attention.

Arthur took Alice's first roll of film to Boots The Chemist in Chiswick High Road. A week later, when he went to pick up the prints, the pharmacist smiled and said, "May I say, sir, you have a great eye."

"Oh, they're not mine," Arthur said, taking the bulging wallet of photos from him. "My wife took these."

"She has a genuine talent, sir," the pharmacist said. "I look forward to developing more of her photos."

Arthur took one of the photos out and stared at it, astonished.

"My *word*," he said, a sudden surge of pride making him feel a little emotional. "This is really good, isn't it?"

"Yes, quite lovely," the pharmacist replied, "exquisite, in fact. I can get one or two of them blown up if you wish?"

"Yes please," Arthur replied. "I would like that very much. But, er… could I ask you to choose, say, six of the photos? Maybe one of each butterfly?"

"Your wife photographed nine different species," the pharmacist said.

"Then let's say nine photos."

He handed the wallet back over the counter, deciding to tell Alice that the photos weren't ready yet as Boots had been 'inundated with holiday snaps' during a particularly hot spell.

***

"Oh my *god*!" Alice exclaimed, staring at the photos Arthur had just collected from the chemist's. "Did I take these?"

"You did, my dear. The pharmacist was most impressed."

He watched with delight as Alice's face slowly went an excited crimson, admiring the blow-ups and laying them out on the coffee table.

"I can't believe I took these. They're... well, they look like professional photos."

"The pharmacist suggested you should send one to a magazine – what about that one who published your short story?"

"The Woman's Realm? Yes, I could. It's a while back, so they may not remember me but... Joanna, the editor, she and I were on very good terms. I'll send one to her. You never know."

Two weeks later, as Arthur was busily preparing scrambled eggs on toast in the kitchen, Alice ran in waving a letter in the air.

"They're publishing my photo!" she said, excited as a child at Christmas. "Woman's Realm are publishing my photo. *Look.*"

She gave the letter to Arthur.

"This is great, darling," he said, sitting down at the kitchen table.

A few moments later, he looked up at Alice over his glasses.

"Have you seen this bit at the end, where Joanna asks you to tell her what species it is, so they can add it to the credits?"

"Yes, I read that," Alice said, looking worried. "But I

have no idea what it's called."

"In that case," Arthur said, as he got up and put the letter by the hob, "after we've eaten, we're off to Smith's to get you a book on butterflies. That way, you can name all the ones you've photographed."

He winked at her.

"And while we're in town, we can pop into Woolworth's and choose a frame for your soon-to-be-published photo."

***

A few days later, Arthur was in the sitting-room reading Ian Fleming's *Octopussy & The Living Daylights*, when he heard his wife shriek. Imagining all kinds of disasters, he ran through to the hall where Alice was staring at a letter in her hand.

"Woman's Realm have asked me if I could send them a butterfly photo *every month,*" Alice said, in a kind of daze. "For their new feature, 'Braintree's Butterfly Corner'."

Arthur, who wasn't a particularly demonstrative man, took Alice in his arms and hugged her.

"I am so proud of you, dear," he said. "My beautiful wife is an acclaimed nature photographer."

"I *know,*" Alice said, loving her husband's acclaim more than the magazine's. "Who'd have thought it?"

Alice's magazine feature lasted twelve months, until Joanna left to run a lifestyle monthly in New York. Her replacement had decided that the butterfly feature, 'while cute', would not fit her new vision.

"We must appeal to a younger, more go-getting generation of women," she said, in her rather brutal letter to Alice, "the kind of women who go out to work and have no desire to stay at home flicking through pictures of babies, knitting patterns and pretty insects."

Alice continued to take photos, Arthur duly having them framed and named and added to their summerhouse gallery, but eventually, she decided that they had far too many wallets of photos stuffed into drawers, unlooked at and forgotten about.

The Nikon was passed on to one of her grandsons, who had shown an interest in photography after seeing Alice's collection.

"I want to take photos of dragons," he declared, reading out the names of the butterflies he liked the best, the Gatekeeper and Black Hairstreak sounding like something from one of his comic books.

Alice and Arthur continued to live very happily at Butterfly Cottage, Alice throwing herself into several short-lived hobbies, the results of which usually ended up in a trunk in the loft, when she'd tired of them and moved onto something else. Arthur pottered about in the garden, enjoying occasional forays into his greenhouse where he'd tend the tomatoes, radish and lettuce, which all helped create the salads he'd become so adept at putting together.

In 1990, Dr. Braintree suffered a massive stroke while he was weeding the borders listening to The Archers, as he did every Sunday morning. He was found by his wife, who'd popped out to tell him that the oven had reached temperature for a joint of beef he was planning to cook. As she checked for a pulse, Alice heard Jenny Aldridge calling out, 'Coffee, Brian!', and cursed the radio lying on its back against Arthur's lifeless head.

***

Alice insisted she was quite happy to stay on at the bungalow on her own, while Alistair felt it would be far better if she moved into the annex of Carstairs Lodge, the five-bedroomed house in Gunnersbury he'd bought in the '70s to accommodate his growing family. Informing her that she was no longer capable of looking after herself simply increased Alice's resolve to stay where she was.

One morning, while Alistair was visiting his mother to 'discuss' her moving into the annex, Alice settled him in the sitting-room with a cup of tea, said she was just taking Verity's sculpture of her into the kitchen 'as it could do with a bit of a polish', and was never seen again.

It was assumed she'd been confused and wandered off, mainly due to Alistair telling the police that she had become 'very fuzzy' after his father had died, and a month-long search with house-to-house enquiries was undertaken.

Alistair was briefly suspected of having a hand in his mother's disappearance, mainly because he'd claimed he hadn't heard her walking down the hall and leaving the house. But, after explaining she'd probably used the side gate his father had put in the back garden wall, the investigating officer found him 'without any sign of malicious intent' and 'merely an innocent bystander of yet another missing person mystery.'

Alice's disappearance hit the local news headlines and Alistair was invited to take part in a short BBC Watchdog spot. It featured re-enactments of a dizzy-looking old woman traipsing through the gate and crossing the road towards the underground, ending with a desolate-looking Alistair telling John Stapleton,

"We just want mummy to come home."

It had resulted in several calls of sightings from Devon to Anglesey, which had led nowhere. It seemed that Alice had simply vanished off the face of the Earth.

A few days before her disappearance, Alice had invited Alistair's wife, Sally, to come for afternoon tea, telling her on the phone that she had 'a secret' to tell her. As they sat on the summerhouse veranda, munching happily on slices of a strawberry cream sponge Alice had bought from Scrumptious Seduction on the High Street, she told Sally that Butterfly Cottage was haunted.

"A young man has often appeared, standing by the kitchen window," Alice said, nodding towards the back of the bungalow. "Very handsome; *gorgeous* hair. A mass of golden curls. He looks as real as you do."

Sally licked the cream off her fingers, wondering whether she dare have another slice.

"Does this ghost ever say anything?" she asked Alice, reaching over and cutting a thin wedge of the sponge.

"No, he just appears as though out of the ether, smiles at me like he knows I'd be there and then fades away."

"Did you ever tell Arthur?" Sally asked, moving to hold Alice's hand then deciding it would seem patronising, and anyway her fingers were covered in cream and rather sticky.

"Yes, I did," Alice replied, "the first time it happened – oh, years ago now. He was certain it had been an intruder and called the police. They sent a detective, can't recall his name now, something which suggested speed… Rush, that was it. Entirely ironic as he was rather a slow, methodical man."

The two ladies chuckled, Sally realising once again how much she liked Alistair's mother.

"He was dressed rather oddly too," Alice recalled, looking across the garden as though picturing the detective. "He had on a kind of long caped coat and a large black fedora hat. He even carried a rather impressive silver cane. He looked like a character from a Sherlock Holmes novel, and I found him oddly calming, but he made Arthur very jumpy. Of course, he didn't find any windows or doors tampered with. Why would he?"

Sally nodded, wondering whether Arthur had ever mentioned it to Alistair.

"The oddest thing was, the detective asked me about freesias, if I'd smelt them when I saw the young man. And in fact, I had. I'd assumed it was the ghost's cologne, but of course, ghosts don't wear cologne, do they?"

She looked again into the space kept for memories.

"Or do they? How would we know?"

Sally was wondering that as well when Alice said, "It did seem an odd question, out of the blue like that, and it made me think, 'How would he know that?' How would he know I'd smelt flowers?"

Alice looked at Sally as if expecting an answer.

"Anyway," she said, when none came, "Arthur was very rude to him and showed him out. I felt rather sorry for the poor man. He was very polite, said 'Good day' in an old-fashioned kind of way, tipped his hat and left."

"And this detective, did he ever contact you again?"

"No. Never heard another word. Of course we didn't. There *was* no intruder. But, what really infuriated Arthur was that, just ten minutes after the Detective had left, a young constable turned up, nice-looking chap. Said he was answering our call about a possible intruder. Well, you can imagine, Arthur hit the roof and sent the poor boy packing."

"How often did you see this ghost?"

"Oh, quite a few times," Alice replied. "I haven´t seen him in a while though."

Her eyes rested on a bee buzzing around the honeysuckle Arthur had spent several summers training against the wall.

"I rather miss him," she said, then looked at Sally and smiled a little sadly. "I miss my handsome ghost."

Sally decided this was now the perfect time to hold Alice's hand, sticky or not.

***

On the day of Alice's disappearance, she had gone into the kitchen to give Verity's sculpture a spruce-up. But in truth, it was to get away from her son who'd been, once again, badgering her about moving into the annex at Carstairs Lodge.

Wondering how she was going to tell Alistair, once and for all, that she had no intention of leaving the bungalow, there he was, the handsome ghost.

As always, he was standing at the kitchen window looking out to the summerhouse, but this time he looked older, quite a lot older in fact. His curls had turned grey and were much shorter, and he seemed rather tired.

'I didn't know ghosts aged,' Alice thought, wondering if she should say anything, then deciding that even ghosts must have feelings.

He turned and smiled at her and she suddenly felt very happy, happier than she'd felt for weeks.

"Oh, it's you again!" she said.

Chapter Two

A few months after Alice's disappearance, the four Braintree siblings had a meeting at Alistair's house.

"Now Mummy is officially a Missing Person Presumed Dead," Alistair began, standing, as always, in the centre of the family circle, "I believe it's best to put the bungalow on the market."

Michael and Miriam nodded their heads and asked what Alistair thought it would sell for, while, before Alistair could reply, Verity said,

"What will happen if Mum comes back or is found?"

"She'll come and live with Sally and me, here," Alistair replied, "well, not here exactly, in the annex."

Verity looked unsure.

"If Mum does come back shouldn't we ask her what *she* wants to do?"

Michael and Miriam looked at Verity, 'causing a fuss, as always'.

"The annex would be perfectly comfortable for her," Alistair insisted, "and we'll be nearby, clearly necessary now."

"But would she be happy?" Verity said, implying their mother definitely wouldn't be.

Alistair replied with a dismissive wave of the hand and, addressing just Michael and Miriam, told them the bungalow had been valued at a good healthy price which they would split into four equal shares. As if on cue, Sally brought drinks and snacks in on a tray which everyone dived into, and, after ten minutes of pleasant insignificant chat, she stood by the French windows and invited Verity to come for a walk in the garden.

"Oh, fresh air!" Verity said, throwing her exotically-scarfed head back. "Good idea, Sally."

"Two peas in a pod," Alistair muttered, as his wife and sister walked out onto the perfectly-mown lawn, and swayed like cats together towards the attached woodland.

"Why does Verity always have to dress as though she's about to throw clay and start working on a Braintree Family Group sculpture?" Miriam said, going out onto the patio for a cigarette.

"Because that's how she sees us," Michael said, taking his sherry outside and sitting down. "To Verity, everyone is a potential carved masterpiece."

"But usually of the female variety," Miriam said, pulling a face at Michael's 'Miaow' mime.

Alistair stood in the doorway, watching Sally and Verity walking arm-in-arm up the path into the thicket and sighed.

"I sometimes wonder if Sally and Verity ever were –"
Then he stopped himself.

"Glad you began to say that rather than me, bro'," Michael laughed.

"Now that would make a *great* story," Miriam murmured. "'Famous sculptress and her sister-in-law in romantic tryst'."

"Don't even consider it," Alistair said, waving his finger at his favourite sister.

***

"Do you love Alistair?" Verity asked Sally, as they settled on the large trunk of a sycamore which had collapsed in the storm of '87.

Sally breathed a heavy sigh.

"He's good to me, a good father, I have a good life,

which of course his hard work has given me. It's as near to love as he seems to need."

"And you?"

Sally glanced at Verity, eyebrow raised at a question she didn't want to consider.

"Is that all *you* need?" Verity persisted.

"Anything more would rather unsettle me now," Sally replied. "I couldn't be bothered having an affair. Too complicated."

She turned to fully face Verity.

"And what about *you*?"

"Hm?"

"Are *you* happy? Still single clearly."

"Oh, me, I'm fine. I'm not sure I want to live with anyone, not at the moment anyway," Verity replied. "I have my flings and occasional grand passions, but the idea of waking up with the same person every morning for the rest of my life sends me into cold sweats. I mean, look at Michael and Miriam, both considering second marriages with highly unsuitable people after divorcing highly unsuitable people. It just seems like madness to me. This desperation to belong to someone."

Verity stood up, dusting herself down.

"I think if I had to permanently commit, living day after day with someone, I'd be the one they'd be committing."

"Oh, very clever, dear," Sally said. "You should give up sculpting and take up writing."

"Like Mum. Poor lamb. She loved writing her stories."

Sally got up and linked her arm into Verity's, the two friends wandering companionably off down the overgrown path.

"Alice took up photography as well, didn't she?" Sally said.

"For a while," Verity replied. "She had a real eye, her butterfly photos were lovely. I'm bagsying those if no-one else wants them."

She laughed.

"Alistair would no doubt just throw them in a skip."

"Oh, I wouldn't allow him to do that," Sally said. "But Alice would definitely want you to have them. Her favourite daughter, her favourite child."

"Was I?"

"Of course you were. She loved her other children, of course, but she adored you. You were the only one she actually liked, if truth be told."

Verity went quiet and stopped walking.

"I wonder what happened to her?" she mused. "Do *you* think she simply wandered off?"

"Well, I know one thing," Sally replied, "when your mum disappeared, she took your sculpture, the one you'd done of her. It was the only thing missing from the house."

Verity stared at Sally.

"Do you know, I never knew that."

She remembered the day she'd given her mum the sculpture. She'd just got back from her first trip to New York which her agent, Lexie, had arranged for her.

Verity had visited all the galleries on Lexie's list, but her only offer of an exhibition had been at one of the cute 'corner shop' places in Greenwich Village, which she'd seen by chance and wandered into. 'Shapes of Things' was run by a wiry, hyper little woman called Genevieve who, after browsing through Verity's portfolio, advised her to 'only do sculptures of the people you love and those who inspire you, that is when I see your talent shining through'.

After a rather passionate night together, Genevieve had given Verity her card and told her to contact her when she had ten pieces ready for an exhibition, 'to be entitled, *Love and Inspiration*'.

As soon as she got home to her basement apartment in Holland Park, she got to work creating two table-top pieces of her mother, one of which was a house-warming gift for her parents, who were just about to move into the bungalow.

Both Alice and Arthur had adored it, Arthur particularly loving the pose of his wife standing on a tiny piece of land looking out to the view ahead, with one hand placed as though shading her eyes from the sun.

"'Alice in Wonderland'," her mum had read from the small plaque on the base. "It's utterly perfect, darling. I always knew you *got* me."

Smiling at the memory, Verity heard Sally's laugh cutting through her reverie.

"What's amusing you?" Verity asked her.

"I'm just recalling how put out Alistair was that his mother hadn't taken the framed certification of his passing the bar exam."

"What do you think it means?" Verity asked Sally.

"It means we've now got the certificate on our bedroom wall."

"No, you daft thing, I mean the fact Mum only took my sculpture?"

"Well, darling, it means that she *intended* to leave, and only took the one thing she loved, which had been created by the one person she truly loved, the one living person anyway. It means that she wasn't in any way suffering from, as Alistair put it, 'a complete nervous breakdown.' Or that she was forced to leave. She took her time and knew exactly what she was doing, where she was going... and with whom."

Verity glanced over at Sally as they walked towards the conservatory.

"What *do* you mean?"

Sally smiled enigmatically.

"Alice once told me that she regularly saw a handsome ghost in the bungalow. I think he was the reason she didn't want to leave and come here."

"Apart from the frightful idea of living with Alistair."

"That too," Sally said, and they began giggling like naughty schoolgirls.

"Going off with a handsome ghost," Verity said. "How romantic. Do you honestly think that's what happened?"

"Why not? What other explanation is there?"

"Mum's about the only person I could imagine that happening to," Verity said and beamed at Sally. "That has completely made my day. You are such a tonic, Sally."

From the French windows, Miriam waved at Sally and Verity while saying to Michael and Alistair, "Sapphic love is quite indestructible, you know."

Alistair exhaled loudly, stood up and shouted into the garden, "Sally, are you going to put on the dinner or not? Everyone's famished!"

That night, as Sally and Alistair were in bed reading the Sunday supplements, Sally told him what Alice had said about the ghost.

"What utter nonsense," Alistair huffed, putting down his magazine and taking off his reading glasses.

"Well, she seemed pretty convinced," Sally said. "Didn't your father mention it to you?"

"I don't remember, but Mummy was always fanciful," Alistair replied, "believing all sorts of nonsense. Once Daddy had gone all her airy-fairiness went on the rampage. I had a dreadful dream last night of Mum sitting in a bus stop in Brighton, thinking she was visiting a maiden aunt. I just *wish* I'd been able to get her out of that poky little bungalow and settled here with us, then none of this would have happened."

As Sally leaned over to switch off her light, she thought Alice would probably be very happy sitting in a bus stop in Brighton.

***

After several months on the market and two price reductions after very few viewings, Butterfly Cottage was sold to a young couple, Jack and Ginny Marlowe, in 1992. The estate agent's laminated details said the house was 'in need of major modernisation, with plenty of room front and back to extend and add upper floors'.

The Marlowes saw that most of the other people in the road had done just that, adding large extensions and upper rooms, but were agreed that Butterfly Cottage was perfect as it was.

As soon as they opened the front door and wandered through the house, they knew that they'd found home. Walking out of the back door into the overgrown but massive back garden, they spotted the rather shabby but lovely old summerhouse at the end.

Ginny turned to Jack and said, "I don't think I want to

change a thing about this house."

"The pink bathroom's got to go," Jack replied, grinning at her, "but yes, apart from a bit of redecoration, it's absolutely perfect."

"And I'm going to have a ball with this garden," Ginny said, letting her imagination run riot.

Chapter Three

'My name is Ginny Marlowe-Baker, I am forty-six years old and I run a successful music publishing company, Original Songs, where I've been all my working life, starting out in 1983 at the age of seventeen as a song-plugger.

I was born Virginia Taylor in 1966, named after the actress Virginia McKenna. My parents loved the film *Born Free*, and the fact that the title song was performed by my dad's favourite singer, Matt Monro, made it their favourite film of all time.

I have fond memories of growing up listening to the song on our radiogram, my dad crooning along in his attractive baritone. I think it's probably where I learnt to not only love great songs but to also recognise their connection with people's hearts and souls. Which is no doubt why I moved into working closely with songwriters, whose talents have always been a mysterious wonder to me.

Original Songs was started by Vicki Palmer in 1964, just as the UK pop scene was exploding like never before. In the slipstream of Beatlemania, a host of new British artists were enjoying hits created by songwriters publishers were battling to sign.

Vicki captured, even pre-empted, the zeitgeist perfectly. She was the first female head of a music company, at a time when London may have been Swinging but basically, up to then, only for men. People think of the '60s as the time of 'free love' and sexual liberation, but it was horny young guys on the hunt for a quick lay who were liberated.

Vicki tolerated none of that. Any male employee who tried it on with her or any other female member of staff was instantly fired. It earned her the nickname 'Miss Frostbite' but Vicki rather liked the moniker and even flaunted it. Her office door announced 'Vicki Palmer: Frostbiter-In-Charge', while on her wall was the sign, 'Groping hands and over-enthusiastic members will be chopped off in here.'

She was stick-thin with Cathy McGowan hair, Twinkle mascara and a range of the latest Mary Quant dresses, quickly becoming a fashion icon, chased by every top journalist for interviews and headlines. But, with friends like Twiggy, David Bailey and Ossie Clark, she didn't need press exclusives being offered at every turn. Attending a preview of the latest Hockney exhibition one night, an Yves Saint Laurent fashion show another and the launch party for *A Hard Day's Night*, gave her all the headlines she needed.

As well as being a trailblazer in pop and fashion, Vicki had an innate talent for spotting a hit song as soon as she heard it. She also knew the music business backwards, having been in the female duo The Honeybees, who'd provided backing vocals on hits by Adam Faith, Billy Fury and Marty Wilde and in several package tours with Cliff Richard, Roy Orbison and Connie Francis. They even performed a couple of Honeybees singles on *Thank Your Lucky Stars,* which may have flopped, but it gave Vicki the opportunity to chat to all the stars who were also performing on the show, as well as their managers and publicity officers.

Plugging songs was clearly in Vicki's blood. When John Lennon played 'Misery' to her on the famous staircase at EMI, and told her that he and Paul had written it for Helen Shapiro but her A & R manager, Norrie Paramor, had turned it down, Vicki persuaded Kenny Lynch to record it instead. His version sold well enough to bubble under the Top 75 and gave him the kudos of being the first artist to cover a Beatles song.

In the Autumn of '63, Vicki's Honeybees partner, Trudi Beauchamp – my future mum – said she was retiring to marry Andrew Taylor, who ran an investment company which advised pop stars on how to handle the large amounts of money they were suddenly accruing. It was perfect timing for Vicki. She'd had enough of the recording sessions and the endless weeks on the road, travelling from place to place in an uncomfortable tour bus and staying in pretty basic B 'n' Bs.

Using the contacts she'd built up, Vicki got a job at Chappell Music, as an office assistant. It wasn't as glamorous as appearing on pop shows, or taking part in recording sessions with the stars of the day, but she wanted to learn everything, all the ropes, from the bottom upwards. It was what made Vicki different, and was why she was quickly noticed by the company's Head of Promotions.

He got chatting to her in the kitchen, as she was making coffee and he was on his way back from the loo, quickly realising that she was someone with nous, experience of the business and an innate self-belief. That, coupled with her obvious excitement at the opportunity to find a hit song, made up his mind to offer her a job as a plugger.

Over just a few months, she learnt about publishing contracts, marketing and copyright law, while the vibrant personality her fellow artists had loved quickly began to impress her Chappell's colleagues. She was offered the new position of Liaison Officer, with more independence and freedom to do things her way.

It entailed picking up Chappell's biggest overseas writers at the airport and taking them to their Mayfair Hotel suite. During their stay, she took them to the best restaurants and chaperoned them to any exciting functions happening around London.

This was when her past life as a Honeybee really came in handy. While entertaining the company's songwriters, she'd often bump into pop stars she'd recorded and toured with, the writers then enthusiastically talking about her to Chappell's management.

"She's a natural."

"Music biz to the core."

"Wow, she knows everyone!"

Finally, in the Spring of '64, Vicki threw caution to the wind, and, with a small start-up loan from her bank manager, she set up Original Songs.

Again, her timing was impeccable. *Top of The Pops* had recently begun airing on TV, bringing the British pop scene, and that all-important weekly chart rundown, into millions of homes each Thursday evening. As many of the young new stars in the Hit Parade needed another hit, Original Songs quickly became the go-to publisher for producers.

Shunning all offers from the Big Boys to sell Original, Vicki loved having the freedom to do what the hell she liked, often signing up the writers who'd been turned down by long-standing publishers steeped in tradition and outdated attitudes.

It was Vicki who noticed me, suggesting I join the A & R meetings and go to as many gigs as I could fit in in a week. I´d target new bands who wrote their own songs, and bigged up those I rated to the A & R team. So it wasn´t a surprise when I was offered a job in the department, signing and helping develop writers of my own, and liaising with all the major record labels.

Vicki once said that watching me was like looking in a mirror in the '60s, and she continued to watch me develop at Original until finally choosing me to replace her when she retired in 2001.

"We brilliant girls need to stick it to the men together - *and* stick together," she'd said in her handwritten note of congratulations on my first day as MD. It was tucked into a gift-wrapped bottle of Moet et Chandon which was waiting for me on my new office desk.

Vicki had also been there for me when my first husband, Jack, disappeared on August 31st, 1997, after I'd left him happily singing in the shower. He'd been commissioned to paint Diana The Princess of Wales' portrait and was due to start on it that morning on her return from France, while I was on my way to an early morning preview screening of *Titanic,* having been offered the option to pick up the UK rights to the theme song and incidental music.

As I reached the Hammersmith flyover and hit a traffic jam, I turned on the radio and heard that Diana had been killed in a car crash in Paris. Suddenly regretting us never listening to the radio or watching the TV in the morning, preferring to avoid bad news stories as we began our day, I called Jack on my mobile but he didn't pick up. I left a message on the answerphone, asking him to call me back and cursing him for refusing to have a mobile.

At the screening studio, I checked my phone for messages but there were none, so I rang home again and got the answering machine. I went in and watched the film, not taking any of it in, and, as soon it had finished, went outside and called him again. And again, no reply.

Much to the surprise of several people at the screening, I decided not to attend the lunch, which had been arranged for me to get to know the American owners of the soundtrack. Apart from the fact that everyone was more interested in talking about Diana, I was far more concerned about where my husband was.

I drove home imagining all sorts of disasters, and when I saw his pride and joy, the vintage MG Roadster he'd bought when he got the Diana commission, still parked outside the house, I ran in expecting god knows what.

The first thing I noticed was that the phone messages I'd left earlier were still flashing on the answering machine. In a panic, I looked in the bathroom, worried he may have had a fall and hurt himself, but only the condensation on the walls was evidence that he'd been in there.

In the bedroom, his still damp towel lay next to the outfit I'd suggested he wear to Kensington Palace. I checked the wardrobe and found that his burgundy track suit and matching canvas shoes, which he always wore after a shower, were missing. Maybe he'd gone for a run and had an accident? Maybe he'd been attacked by a mugger? Increasingly worse thoughts began cascading round my head.

I tore round the house, looking everywhere. I ran into the garden calling his name. I ran back into the house and *screamed* his name. But Jack wasn't there, and that awful sense that you're alone and suddenly helpless began to enfold me like a shroud.

I decided to call Isabel, Diana's PA, whose number I found on the commissioning letter she'd sent to Jack. But when she answered, she was clearly too overwhelmed by shock and grief to make much sense. She did manage to tell me through her sobbing that Jack had never arrived.

"We assumed he'd heard the news and was grieving like everyone else," she told me.

I called Jack's mother, Nancy, and immediately wished I hadn't, as I then spent twenty minutes trying to console her over Diana in between allaying her fears that Jack may have been kidnapped.

An hour later, after waiting for the sound of Jack's key in the door, I was beginning to wonder if Nancy had been right and called the police. The desk sergeant was very polite and sympathetic but asked me to wait until the following morning, just in case Jack did return for whatever reason.

"We need to wait a little longer, Mrs. Marlowe," he told me, "before we can treat it as a missing person."

I reluctantly agreed and turned on Radio Four, in case a news item came on about a man found wandering around London in a daze, or a body discovered in a park near Chiswick. I went and lay on the bed, finally falling into a fitful sleep, full of short feverish dreams where Jack was standing in the bedroom doorway or wandering through the hall, explaining where he'd been.

I woke up hours later, Jack still not home. Feeling

inexplicably hungry, I made myself a snack and wandered through the back garden, which I'd planted out into a sea of wildflowers. Bees buzzed around the blossoms, while butterflies sat and gathered nectar with the late afternoon sun warming their wings. All of which would normally have filled me with joy, but as I reached the summerhouse and sat on the veranda, I stared out at scenes from a horror movie which my mind insisted on creating for me.

Finally, as the sun began its slow descent, I decided I couldn't wait until the morning and called Chiswick police station again, insisting that my husband had gone and I was sure something awful had happened to him.

"I'm afraid our forces are rather taken up with what's happening at the royal palaces right now," the lady on the line explained. "It's becoming a little edgy and we're worried that the tension in the air could turn into something rather more concerning."

Her diplomacy was impressive but hardly reassuring.

"I'm sure Mr. Marlowe will return, madam," she said. "Please try not to worry."

It took every bit of steel in my body not to yell at her, but instead I thanked her for her concern while begging her to send someone around as quickly as possible.

"Have you checked with local hospitals?" she asked me, almost as an afterthought.

"Well, no, I haven't, do you think I should? I was advised to wait until tomorrow morning before doing anything so…"

"You live in Turnham Green, yes?"

"That's right."

"Okay, Mrs. Marlowe, leave that with me. I'll make

enquiries for you and call you back if there's any news."

An hour later, she rang to say none of the hospitals in the area had taken in anyone called Marlowe, nor anybody fitting his description.

"But they will call me if that changes," she added.

Feeling both relieved and disappointed, I thanked her for all her help and did as she advised, making myself a large, hot toddy and having an early night. I lay down, held Jack's outfit in my arms and fell into a deep sleep, exhausted by waiting for the sound of the front door opening.'

Chapter Four

Detective Inspector Rush stood in Ginny's front room, admiring a portrait of her on the wall over the fireplace.

"Very striking," he said, stroking his beard with one hand and adjusting his Pince-nez with the other.

"My husband painted it, shortly after we met," Ginny told him, sipping the sweet herbal tea Vicki had made her.

Ginny had called Vicki that morning to explain why she wouldn't be able to make the A & R meeting she was due to chair at ten o'clock. Vicki had immediately cancelled the meeting and driven to the bungalow, arriving just before the policeman knocked on the door.

Now, she sat on the sofa next to Ginny, studying D.I. Rush as one might an intruder, staring disapprovingly at his long caped coat and the silver cane he kept by him. He'd been wearing a large black fedora hat when he'd arrived as well, grandly offering it to her as though she was the maid. That certainly didn't endear her, and as she watched him benignly looking around the room like a potential buyer viewing a property, her patience, never great, was fast running out.

"Aren't you going to organise a search?" she demanded.

Rush turned to her and smiled, as one might at a confused aunt.

"It's a little early for that, Mrs… ?

"*Miss* Palmer," Vicki replied, glaring at Rush. "And I don't think it's early at all. Jack would never have just walked out with no warning or even a note. He *adored* Ginny. They were inseparable. This makes no sense. He's been gone almost twelve hours and you should be out there making enquiries, or whatever it is you do when someone vanishes for no reason."

Rush tucked his cape under him and sat rather heavily in the armchair opposite them, creating a not disagreeable waft of Givenchy in his wake. He picked up his mug of tea and studied the design on it, which bore the bright orange Original Songs logo with the words, 'Where the hits are born' in fluorescent yellow lettering. He smiled at it as though admiring a child's craftwork from school and took a long gulp of his black tea.

"But wasn't there a reason?" he said, shifting his benign gaze back to Ginny. "Mrs. Marlowe?"

Ginny looked up from the floor as though from a daze. Vicki took hold of her hand, glancing much less benignly at Rush.

"Didn't you say, Mrs. Marlowe," Rush went on, ignoring the furious looks from her rather overwrought friend, "that Mr. Marlowe had been due to paint The Princess of Wales yesterday, the day of his disappearance? I mean, her death would have come as a terrible shock to him, a huge disappointment to an ambitious young man about to have such a big break in his career."

Ginny studied Rush for a few moments, then said, "Er - I don't believe I did tell you about Jack's commission, actually."

"But you're not suggesting he'd leave his wife because of it?" Vicki broke in, interrupting Ginny's train of thought.

"Of course not," Rush said, exasperated by this angry woman who had clearly decided she had no time for him.

"He'd have wanted to see Ginny," Vicki went on, "to speak to her, as soon as he'd heard the news. She would have been his safe harbour."

She looked at Ginny, who tried again to ask Rush how he knew about the commission, but was again interrupted by her well-meaning friend.

"She was *not* someone he'd want to escape from!" Vicki almost shouted. "You clearly don't understand true love, officer."

Rush bristled at that.

"*Detective Inspector*, if you don't mind, Madam. And, with all due respect, it is Mrs. Marlowe I am talking to here, not you."

Ignoring Vicki's glare, he paused, seeming to consider what he was about to say.

"Mrs. Marlowe – when were you and your husband married?"

"1987."

"Ah, so ten years, quite a long time these days, and you and your husband were not having any, well, problems?"

"Problems?"

"Disagreements. Resentments. Jealousies? These things can grow over several years together."

Vicki stood up.

"I do hope you're not suggesting –"

Rush looked up at Vicki.

"Do please sit down, Miss Palmer. You'll give me a crick in my neck."

Vicki mumbled something and sat back down.

"I'm not suggesting anything," Rush said, addressing Ginny, "simply making enquiries as to, well, possibilities."

Ginny's eyes widened as what had struck Vicki also dawned on her.

"Surely you don't think I had anything to do with

Jack's disappearance?"

Vicki gasped and was about to say something, but Rush got in first.

"As a matter of fact, I consider it extremely unlikely, Mrs. Marlowe. You and your husband were clearly very close and..."

"So you *have* been making enquiries," Vicki interrupted him.

Rush gave her his best condescending smile.

"There are many things, Miss Palmer, that we in the police service do which the public are rarely aware of."

Vicki harrumphed and shifted her bum on the settee.

Rush waved vaguely round the room.

"You have a beautiful home and rather an exquisite garden, indicating you care about your life here together very much. You are an extremely successful businesswoman and your husband was – er, excuse me, *is* – equally and widely regarded for his obvious talents."

He looked up at Ginny's portrait on the wall.

"I can see no reason and no evidence of the kind of animosity required to kill your husband."

"Kill?" Vicki spluttered, "They absolutely *adored* each other!"

She was actually shouting now.

Rush ignored her and began sniffing the air.

"Flowers. I smell, yes, freesias. Do you have any freesias in the house, Mrs. Marlowe?"

"No. Although my garden does have freesias in it. Sadly, I'm allergic to any flowers in the house. The pollen in a closed room gets me in a sneezing fit every time. A shame really, because I do love them – especially freesias."

"Yes, they are one of my favourite blooms," Rush

said, smiling rather comfortingly at Ginny, who beamed at Rush as though she'd found a soulmate.

Vicki was about to demand what flowers had to do with a missing husband, when Rush took out his pocket watch.

"Ah, I see I have been here for twenty-eight minutes and thirty-two seconds, so I'll take up no more of your time."

He stood up, straightening his cape.

"I think I have bothered you enough, Mrs. Marlowe. I will let myself out. Thank you."

"Is that it?" Vicki demanded.

Ginny gave her a 'Not now' look and stood up.

"You'll keep me informed," she said to Rush, "if you get any news, or sightings… ?"

"Indeed, Mrs. Marlowe. But please be assured that I believe your husband is alive, safe and will return to you, at some point, though I cannot say when. I wish you good day."

He picked up his black fedora hat from off the chair where Vicki had flung it, tipped it at the two ladies and, saying how pleased he was to see a period gem like Butterfly Cottage untouched by 'modern-day nonsense', left.

"Bloody useless man," Vicki said when Rush had gone. "He was like something from an Agatha Christie novel."

"Certainly quite a character," Ginny replied.

"And so damned pedantic. 'I've been here for twenty-eight minutes and thirty-two seconds'. Why couldn't he just say 'for half-an-hour'?"

"Well, let's hope his attention to detail means he's

just as focused on finding Jack."

Vicki huffed, went to the window and glared out.

"What the hell is he doing now?" she asked the curtain.

"What *is* he doing?" Ginny asked, starting to clear away the mugs.

"He's just standing there, staring at Jack's car."

"Maybe he's a classic car fan," Ginny said.

Vicki moved out of the way for Ginny.

"Come and look! He's just staring at it."

Ginny craned her neck up and down The Green.

"There's no-one there," she said.

"Well, he was there a second ago."

Vicki glared out of the window.

"He's certainly quicker on his feet than in the brain department, that's for sure."

She stared again and shook her head.

"What an infuriating man."

"Well, I admit he was rather strange," Ginny replied, going through the hall into the kitchen, "and yet I found him oddly comforting."

She put the mugs in the sink and took an already-opened bottle of Chardonnay out of the fridge. Pouring out two glasses, she sat down at the small kitchen table by the back door.

"I mean, to most people it *would* probably look like I'd done him in. The wife or the husband is always the first suspect. But he seemed so sure I hadn't."

"No-one who knew the two of you could ever think that, Ginny," Vicki said, joining her at the table and knocking back a large slug of wine.

"But he *didn't* know us, did he? And yet he seemed to know things I'm sure I hadn't told him – about my career, and certainly not about Jack's commission. I'm sure I never mentioned that to him or to the desk sergeant when I rang the station."

"Oh, they have their ways, darling," Vicki said, taking another slurp of her wine. "Big Brother and all that. And quite honestly, the more they know, the better. The police should be out there now, checking CCTV, the Underground, the railway stations, bus termini. They should be calling your friends and relatives to ask if they've seen him. You haven't called anyone have you?"

"Well, the very nice desk sergeant called all the local hospitals for me, but Jack hadn't been admitted to any of them. I rang Jack's mum last night, and you this morning... which reminds me, I must call Nancy and give her an update."

Vicki reached across the table and squeezed Ginny's hand.

"You must be going through hell, my darling," she said. "I wish I could do more to help."

"If only Jack had let me buy him a mobile," Ginny said. "At least I'd be able to call him, leave a message... even hearing his voice on the answerphone..."

She suddenly burst into tears.

"Oh Vicki, where is he? Where is my beautiful man?"

Chapter Five

'A few minutes after D.I. Rush had left, while Vicki and I were in the kitchen and I was blubbing my eyes out, there was a knock at the door. I wiped my face with a piece of kitchen towel, checked myself in the hall mirror and went to answer it. A young, uniformed policeman was standing there looking at me expectantly.

"Mrs Marlowe?" he asked, showing me his identification card (which Rush hadn't).

"Ye-es," I said, thinking he may have news – bad news – already.

"My name is Detective Constable Boddington, I'm here regarding your - er – missing husband?"

Vicki was standing in the hall behind me and dashed to the door when she heard his voice.

"What's happened?" she said, putting her hands on my shoulders.

D.C. Boddington looked rather non-plussed and asked to come in.

"Nothing, as far as we know," he said, stepping into the hall. "I'm just answering your call about your husband, Mrs. Marlowe."

"But we've already had a visit from one of your Detective Inspectors," I told him. "Rush, I think it was?"

Vicki made a 'Tssshhh' sound as Boddington looked puzzled and shrugged his shoulders.

"Sorry, don't know him but I'm new. I only started at Chiswick a couple of days ago, so I don't know everyone there yet. But, if you've already spoken to one of my superiors then I probably don't need to trouble you. Rest assured we will do all we can to find Mr. Marlowe, wherever he is, and I will make sure a report has been filed when I get back to the station."

He nodded at me then at Vicki, like a boy asking for permission to leave. I thanked him for coming out and apologised for him wasting his time, which he was very sweet about. As he was on his way out, he said, "D.I. Rush, you say?"

"Yes," I replied, "he was very kind."

"Okay, thank you, Mrs. Marlowe, we'll be in touch if we hear anything at all. Good day."

Needless to say Vicki was not at all impressed.

"Useless!" she shouted at the closed door. "These people are bloody useless. Can't even synchronise their appointments. God knows how they're going to organise a proper search."

A couple of days later, when I'd heard nothing more, I called the police station and asked for D.I. Rush. After waiting a few minutes, a lady came on the phone and told me that no-one at the station had heard of him. She asked me if I'd maybe got his name wrong, but I knew I hadn't as I remembered how it had made me smile, he was so laid-back, not in a 'rush' at all. But I gave her my number and asked her to call me if she had any news.

She did call a few hours later, saying she still had no news about Jack, but had found something interesting about D.I. Rush.

"After a little bit of research through our files, and a visit to the Microfiche library, I discovered there *was* a detective with that name who worked here, but he died in 1907."

She chuckled and sounded a little embarrassed.

"Apparently, he was shot in a brothel in Bethnal Green, but the case was never solved. The only information here is that a friend of his by the name of Lockton, who was with Rush that night, gave a statement to the police and then disappeared. Are you sure the officer who came to see you was called Rush?"

I told her I thought it was, though he hadn't left a card.

"I have a record of your call reporting Mr. Marlowe missing," she told me, "and we sent D.C. Boddington out to see you…"

"Yes," I told her, "he came just a few minutes after Rush had left, which seemed a little odd. Poor man, he'd made a bit of a wasted journey."

"Well I have his report here," she said, "and we will continue our enquiries."

I thanked her for calling me back, replaced the receiver and decided I needed a cup of tea. Making my way to the kitchen, the name Lockton kept hovering in my mind. Then it came to me. Lockton Manor, the house which used to stand here before the bungalows were built. I smiled at how D.I. Rush had looked almost comically Edwardian. Then my mobile rang. It was Vicki inviting me to lunch, and the strange coincidence went out of my mind.

***

The days, the weeks, the months crawled by. Being without Jack became, much to my surprise, the new normal. It's amazing how quickly we can heal from terrible trauma, as though the body and mind goes into overdrive to get you back on an even keel. A kind of self-preservation kicks in.

I finally started to wake up each morning without that horrible sinking feeling in my stomach, though I never stopped missing Jack. Some days the ache of loss was unbearable, but in the end I simply had to get on with my life. Even with that nagging question burning into me – 'why, *why* would he leave me?'.

Although Vicki constantly told me that I needed to go home and rest, I found that being at work was my saviour, my sanctuary. I began immersing myself in the things about my job I loved the most, talking to excited young songwriters we'd just signed. It gave me something other than myself, and the gaping hole in my life, to think about.

Of course, I'd still come home and half-expect Jack to be there, apologising to me profusely, explaining everything logically. And that was when the house felt at its emptiest, when I opened the front door and stepped into him not being there anymore.

It took me months to do it, but I finally plucked up the courage to get in Jack's MG and drive it into the West End. I pulled the top down and felt the air blasting the cobwebs away. It was truly exhilarating. As I parked it in the Poland Street multi-storey, I patted it like a beautiful horse which had dashed me across the meadows to my destination.

"She's in safe hands, Jack," I murmured, stroking the boot as I strode towards the steps leading up to Oxford Street, joining the stream of anonymous crowds rushing by.

As I reached the office in Soho Square, I did feel strangely happier, lighter. It was as though I'd shared something of Jack's which he'd loved. It was all I had left of him, apart from his paintings of course. For the time being, they would remain in my mental pending tray until I was ready to deal with them.

Vicki of course was always there for me, day or night. Each evening, I'd pop my head into her office and, unless she was on an important call, she'd ask me if I fancied a nightcap and, of course, I always did. It meant I could distract myself with chats about our day. There was always something we could discuss, get excited about or even have a giggle over.

The feeling of being alone, abandoned, is lessened by the way friends and family rally round, purposely talking about the future, about work plans, about upcoming get-togethers.

"There's still so much to look forward to, Ginny," my mum told me when I was visiting my parents for lunch one Sunday. "You have a wonderful future ahead of you, try to think about that as much as you can."

I nodded and smiled as she enthused about their recent holiday in Barbados, while Dad, bless him, poured me a large glass of wine and put his hand on my shoulder as if to say, 'she's only trying to help, darling.'

Of course the conversation, as always, came round to Vicki. I loved hearing Mum reminiscing about 'the old days', and joshed her about how much Adam Faith had fancied her.

"I'd have knocked his block off if he'd come anywhere near my Trudi," Dad said, winking at Mum as she went pink, clearly thrilled that her Andrew was still her knight in shining armour.

Their shared memories cheered me up, coming from a time I hadn't known, when things did seem to have the sheen of naïve innocence, all sunshine, ice cream and pink milk shakes.

But there were also times when I just wanted to be on my own. To sit curled up on the sofa with a bottle of wine and one of Jack's sweaters wrapped round me, listening to Springsteen's *Born In The USA*, Jack's favourite album. Singing my heart out to 'Dancing In The Dark' somehow brought him close again, allowed me to pretend for those few minutes that he was here, singing it with me, like we used to.

One time, going home on the tube after a boozy night out with friends, I thought I'd actually seen him striding along the platform as my train pulled out of the station. I almost got up and ran down the carriage to keep him in sight, but it pulled into a tunnel as soon as we'd set off.

Another time, I was sure I saw him at a George Michael concert Vicki had invited me to. Both Jack and I were huge fans of his and he'd have loved the show, but the crowd was too large to get through before he was gone, whoever it was.

When George sang 'A Different Corner' and tears were streaming down my face, Vicki put her arm round me as candles were lifted and the crowd swayed along. Happily, George followed it with 'Wake Me Up Before You Go-Go', and by the first chorus the two of us, and thousands more, were throwing ourselves around like idiots, screaming, 'Take me dancing tonight' at the tops of our voices. The release of all that grief into roars of unbridled joy was one of the most cathartic moments I'd ever experienced. God bless George Michael.

***

On New Year's Eve 1999, I joined Vicki and the rest

of the Original staff at her Kensington house for a New Millennium party. On the stroke of midnight, we were all gathered in her back garden with glasses of champagne to watch the fireworks explode across the sky. I glanced at the smiling faces turned upwards and 'woo'ing' at the colours rainbowing above us, longing to see Jack standing next to me, both of us wondering what the new century would bring us.

I stayed the night, having had a few too many Tequilas to drive home, and when I woke the following morning to a large mug of very sweet coffee, I asked Vicki if she'd come with me to Jack's Covent Garden studio. It felt like the right time, the beginning of a new century, to face a part of my past I'd once loved, but which had become something I'd dreaded seeing again for too long.

When I slid open the large wooden door, which had stayed locked for more than two years, and stood there looking at a roomful of enormous, brilliant works of art, I automatically grabbed Vicki's hand. We remained in the doorway for a few moments, staring at these massive, beautiful canvases like two awestruck little girls on the edge of a wonderland.

As we wandered in and walked around, Vicki said that I should organise an exhibition of Jack's work.

"These have been hidden away for too long," she said, "you need to show the world just how amazing he is."

I loved her use of the present tense, something she always did when speaking about Jack. We began discussing how to arrange it, Vicki saying she'd ring a friend of hers at The Tate, and me imagining the invites, the setting, and feeling the excitement at finally shining a light on the work of my brilliant husband.

"It will show off the genius that Diana recognised," Vicki said, her eyes welling up at the thought of it.

A few months later, on the eve of the press preview night, with a chilled glass of champagne in my hand, I wandered around three huge rooms full of Jack's work. Once again, I marvelled at his talent and told myself there was no way he could have ever left all this behind voluntarily.

The exhibition was a big success, the paintings all selling very quickly, mainly to American and Japanese collectors, The National Portrait Gallery, The Royal Academy and The Tate.

Whenever I felt that Jack was becoming more a memory than a present reality, I'd visit one of the galleries and remember when he'd showed them to me for the first time. I always felt stronger, knowing I had loved and known this amazing man who had created these great pieces of art.

To preserve his legacy, I decided, with Vicki's and my dad's help, to set up The Marlowe Trust. The money I'd made from the sale of the paintings gave us a sizeable down-payment to convert the studio into an exhibition space. We hung the paintings we hadn't shown at The Tate – mainly due to a lack of space - as well as a few works of up and coming artists who were fans and followers of Jack. He would have approved of that. One of them even designed the logo for the Trust.

We established a fund to pay for art students at The Slade, where Jack had studied and taught, who were struggling with the fees. We quickly began to attract fans of Jack's work as donors, who simply wanted to help in any way they could to spread the word about 'the great, lost genius', as one reviewer of the recent exhibition had written.

The ironic thing was that, setting up the Trust and watching it grow, turned Jack, the man, my husband, the life we'd had together, into an enigma. As much as I tried to hold onto the sound of his voice or his adorable dirty laugh, those memories became increasingly tenuous. I had to accept that I was now officially a widow. Original Songs and the Trust became my life, my reason for getting up in the morning. Expecting a miracle was no longer an option.´

Chapter Six

'By the early 2000s, Reality TV talent shows were discovering and creating new stars, young, ambitious singers who craved fame and, importantly for me, needed songs. The likes of Simon Cowell and Louis Walsh were crying out for hits for their 'new Whitney' or 'the latest Take That'.

At the time there was a young transgender artist called Candy, who'd made a big impression on the talent show *Pop Stars*. Candy had been the vocalist Andy Mitchell in the almost-famous boy-band Bad in the late '90s, but really cut through into media headlines when she transitioned and developed a fabulous new image, an amazing charisma and a talent for self-promotion. She clearly now felt a new freedom to express herself properly, and basked in the spotlight that appearing on the nation's most successful talent show had given her.

Candy also had a great voice, but she needed a hit song. And that's where my future second husband, Simon Terence Baker, came in. In 2002, he brought a song to Darren, one of my A & R guys, which he'd written with Westlife in mind. As soon as Darren played me Simon's demo of 'I Can Wait Forever' I knew it had the potential to be a massive hit.

There was something eerily familiar and yet excitingly brand new about the demo and I wanted to meet this young man, so I rang him and invited him to lunch.

As he nattered away on our far corner table at The Ivy, which always gave me a great view of everyone who came in and out of the restaurant, he told me about the kind of music he liked and how he saw his future developing. I smiled to myself at the thought that Simon was born the year I'd joined Original.

"I'm a huge '60s fan," he told me, "that's when songs had great melodies and made people feel good. Those are the sort of songs I want to write."

He had this knack of sounding incredibly old-fashioned and yet right on point. He wasn't particularly attractive physically, rather large and ungainly in fact, 'blubbery' as my mum used to say, but there was a child-like charm about him which grabbed your attention when he was speaking.

I included him in a meeting with my whole team at Original, and without coming across as bombastic or crass, he managed to make his point about songwriting and the importance of great tunes in a way that clearly impressed everyone.

Every time I played Simon's demo, usually in the car driving home, my favourite place and time to listen to new submissions, I could hear Candy singing the song, and invited her manager, Laurie, to the office. As soon as she heard 'I Can Wait Forever' she virtually ordered me not to play it to anyone else.

Candy, with her studio band I-Candy, recorded a fabulous version, was signed up by Sony Music as soon as they heard the track and had a huge hit with it internationally. The record even breached the American Top Forty. She looked set for long-term stardom, performing the song on pop shows across Europe, fans queuing round the block wherever she appeared.

Simon, of course, was suddenly earning enormous royalties. I extended his one-song deal to a long-term contract with Original before anyone else nabbed him. We paid him a massive advance, so sure were we that he could write at least an album's worth of songs for Candy and keep the royalties flooding in.

When 'I Can Wait Forever' hit one-million sales, we hosted a party for I-Candy at The Dorchester. Vicki, then in her mid-sixties, was guest of honour, and she presented Candy with a Platinum disc. As the two of them posed together for photos, which would be on the following day's national front pages and in all the music magazines, I was struck once again by how amazing Vicki looked, still skinny as a rake and able to wear her now vintage clothes with astonishing aplomb.

Sitting down later, I told her how much I admired her cute print dress, an Ossie Clark concoction of abstract summer flowers against a background of radiant blue, and she giggled in that embarrassed little girl way which had become her trademark deception; it had fooled many cigar-toting record execs who'd thought she was just another 'pushover chick with great legs'.

"Twigs gave me this dress in 1966," she told me, as we watched the paparazzi circling our table. "It was a birthday present from her and Justin."

"Well, you look fantastic," I said, pausing to pose with her for The Daily Mail's 'Entertainment Catch-Up' columnist.

"Yes, I still do, don't I?" she replied, winked at me and tapped her nose. "You never lose who you were if you never lose the love of who you were."

She squeezed my arm.

"That's what got you through the loss of Jack, darling. It's why you're sitting here tonight. It's why you're a winner."

Out of the corner of my eye, I could see Simon hovering, dying to be introduced, and waved him over, excited for Vicki to meet the man behind our most successful song that year. She'd always been chatty and gracious with anyone she met at functions, especially young songwriters, but for some reason she became fidgety and uncomfortable as soon as he extended his hand and said, "I've heard so much about you. It's great to finally meet you."

"Er – thank you," she said, staring at him and shaking his hand as though there was something unpleasant on his fingers.

As Simon towered above her, grinning away, she stood up, clearly avoiding any further eye contact with him, and said, "Congratulations on writing such a fabulous song, but I'm afraid I have a migraine coming on and I must go home."

She looked at me pleadingly and asked me to get her a cab.

"Well, it was very nice to meet you, Vicki," Simon said, "I hope we –"

"*Miss Palmer!*" she said angrily. "It's Miss Palmer."

Simon looked a bit shocked, went red and made a stuttered apology, jumping out of her way as she swept past him towards the exit. Embarrassed for Simon, but more concerned to see if Vicki was okay, I caught her up as she was striding out into Park Lane, where a line of taxis were parked. As carefully as I could, I asked her why she'd been so phased by Simon.

"I don't know what it was, Ginny," she told me, busying in her Gucci handbag for a hanky, "but he made me feel – oh, I don't know - for a moment, he sounded exactly like my ex-husband and it really spooked me."

She dabbed her nose delicately and chattered on.

"I mean, Terry would be in his seventies now, if he'd lived, and –"

She stopped and stared ahead.

"I wonder if he's related?"

She turned to look at me.

"Do you know anything about him? His family? Where he's from?"

"He told me he grew up in children's homes, and when he reached sixteen he went out gigging with various bands. Amazingly, 'I Can Wait Forever' is the first song he's written."

Vicki sighed heavily.

"Well, all I can say is he gave me a really weird sense of déjà-vu, and a very nervy tingle down my spine – and not a nice one either."

She widened her eyes naughtily, and we both chuckled. But I still felt I needed to speak up for the poor boy.

"If you don't mind me saying, darling," I said, "I think you were a little unkind to him. He's a good guy and an extremely talented writer. His song has made Original a lot of money this year."

Vicki stopped, put her hanky back in her bag and rested her hand on my shoulder.

"I'm sorry, darling, I probably was a bit sharp with him. But, my advice, my dear Ginny…"

She paused and made me look at her, her eyes burning into me.

"… is to *watch* him. There's something about him, I don't know what it is, but he had the same vibe as Terry, that jolly, boyish bonhomie, which in Terry's case was hiding a very screwed-up guy. You of all people do not need, nor deserve, anymore sadness in your life."

She kissed me on the cheek, a gorgeous wave of Chanel floating between us, stroked my face and got in her cab. As it sped off towards Marble Arch, I walked back inside, thinking about what she'd said.

Vicki had rarely spoken about her ex-husband, always batting away enquiries anyone made about him. I knew he'd been a songwriter in the mid-'60s, one who'd made a lot of money for Original back then. I'd heard from a music business friend that they'd split up in the '70s and he'd moved to L.A. where he later died.

"From what I've heard," my friend had told me, "he was a real piece of work."

I made my way back towards the strains of I-Candy performing their hit on stage and, spotting Simon at the back of the crowd, I went to join him.

"What was *her* problem?" he asked me, jigging up and down.

"She wasn't feeling too well," I replied, raising my voice over the music. "It isn't like her to be so –"

"So bloody *rude!*" he yelled.

Along with the rest of the room, as the song reached its final climactic chorus he threw his arms in the air and, smiling delightedly at me, sang along at the top of his voice. I tried to imagine what it must feel like seeing your song being adored by a roomful of people, confirming for me once again how much I loved being part of someone's dream come true.

***

As it turned out, our plans for Simon writing the songs for Candy's debut album didn't materialise. She had a different agenda entirely, declaring over a very expensive lunch - on me - that she wanted to record all her own songs in future, not even allowing 'I Can Wait Forever' on the album. She was happy to let me have the publishing on her songs, but insisted 'creepy Simon' didn't come anywhere near her. I pointed out to her that he had just written her first million-selling song and tried to argue his case, but to no avail.

"He's written one good song, Ginny," she told me, "it doesn't make him indispensable."

Of course, her record company didn't want to upset their newest, hottest star, and let her do her thing. But it transpired that Candy was a terrible songwriter. Her album bombed and she never had another hit.

Simon took the news of Candy's rejection badly, going into a crazy spin and spending his money on 'things to cheer me up'. He rented an enormous luxury apartment on the South Bank, employed a 'lifestyle designer' to furnish it and bought a gold Porsche. After clubbing all night, he'd get home around noon and then collapse in bed for the rest of the day.

Then, one morning he declared he'd had 'enough of over-indulgence!' and joined an exclusive fitness club. Over the next few months he lost almost four stone, gaining an impressive new physique and had laser surgery on his eyes, dispensing with his thick-framed, Eric Morecambe glasses.

Lastly, his long, lank locks, which had previously wafted around his shoulders, were chopped off and replaced by a rigid flat-top. With the physical changes and the new hard-edged image, he was totally transformed.

While I fully approved of his new healthy lifestyle, thinking it would give him back his muse, very soon he was asking me for another advance.

The problem was that calls from artist managers for 'another Simon Baker song', which had been coming in constantly after I-Candy's hit, had now petered out completely. Twelve months is a very long time in the music business, and people forget about yesterday's successes as newer hit-makers arrive on the scene.

I was also beginning to wonder if he wasn't, as one colleague had suggested, a one-hit-song-wonder after all. The deal I'd signed him to was beginning to feel a little hasty. The hits compilations featuring I-Candy's single had been and gone and, unless a movie came along which needed Simon's song in the soundtrack, there was little chance of getting the rest of the advance back. I just hoped that 'I Can Wait Forever' lived up to its title and 'forever' arrived at some point.

***

Foolishly, I began taking on the responsibility of paying Simon's bills – from my personal bank account – and gave him a small monthly allowance so he could keep himself from sinking into a financial pit.

I knew it was a stupid thing to do but the more dependent on my support he became, the deeper my feelings for him grew. I think on reflection it was a mixture of pity and the sight of that now gorgeous hunk staring at me across the room. It brought out maternal instincts I'd never had before, and a sexual connectivity I hadn't entertained since Jack.

Unfortunately, none of my friends or colleagues approved of this developing relationship, especially when, to everyone's surprise including mine, I accepted Simon's rather endearingly old-fashioned proposal while holidaying in Monaco. We were having dinner in a small, intimate restaurant we´d discovered on our first night, when he suddenly got up from his seat and went down on one knee.

Presenting me with a beautiful ring I'd unknowingly paid for, he asked me to be his wife. The whole place burst into applause and the head waiter brought us a bottle of champagne on the house.

It was only when we got back to the hotel that, as Simon slept like a baby, I lay in the dark apologising to Jack for my 'betrayal'. Even though he'd been gone for over ten years, officially 'Missing Presumed Dead', I could never rid myself of the feeling that he was out there somewhere. After hours of self-recrimination, I finally dropped off about five o'clock in the morning, telling myself that Jack would want me to be happy.

Simon and I were married on a beautiful summer´s day in St. Peter´s Church in Hammersmith. Looking back, amidst all the smiles from friends and family who were there, throwing confetti over us as we emerged into the scent of the cherry blossom trees in full bloom, I felt that the only people truly happy at our wedding were Simon and me.

Although she didn't come to the wedding, citing 'a gippy tummy' as her excuse, Vicki had given me one of her vintage Givenchy dresses to wear on the day. The '60s theme was continued with Simon looking great in a Pierre Cardin suit my dad had worn when he'd married my mum in 1965.

"Your father has finally accepted he'll never get into it again," Mum told me when she'd dropped it into the bungalow a few weeks earlier.

During the reception at the Hard Rock Café in Piccadilly, I slipped out to the loo, boogying along to Bon Jovi's 'It's My Life', which summed up how I felt that day. To my horror, I heard someone at the bar shouting rather drunkenly,

"She's got a new toyboy then. It'll never last."

I didn´t want to check who´d said it, but the comments stayed with me for the rest of the day. Of course, it made me even more determined to prove them, and everyone else who congratulated us rather half-heartedly that day, utterly wrong.'

Chapter Seven

'Although Simon had accepted the idea of us living in Butterfly Cottage once we were married, within days of us returning from our honeymoon in Barbados, he began criticising the bungalow; it was 'too small, with not enough space for us both'. He said he needed his own music room and when I suggested the spare bedroom Simon looked at me as though I'd told him to use the shed.

His announcement that he wanted 'to make a few improvements' to the house actually pleased me, the fact he'd found the motivation to do something constructive. But, as he hired a team of architects to help him 'redesign and reconfigure' the bungalow, I felt my enthusiasm turning to a flutter of concern.

Why I didn't nip it in the bud there and then, I'll never know, but my mind was elsewhere. I was making regular trips to publishing partners in New York, Paris and Berlin, and also negotiating several new deals with some of our most successful writers.

It only dawned on me what a huge mistake I'd made when I arrived back from a long, tiring trip to the States, feeling extremely jet-lagged and dying to simply soak in a bath with a strong G & T and a good book.

Donning a rather fetching hard hat and supervising a team of builders who were in the midst of knocking down one of the walls, he welcomed me home by announcing that 'the guys are creating a whole new upper floor'.

As I watched my lovely little home being decimated before my eyes, it felt like my heart had been wrenched out of my chest. To avoid having a major row with Simon in front of his team, I got back in the car, telling my bemused husband that I needed sleep, and drove to the Mayfair Hotel, checking in 'for an indefinite period'.

For the next few weeks, I stayed permanently busy at work, travelling all over the world for meetings and only half-listening when Simon rang to give me excited updates on how 'the project' was going.

Finally, the moment I'd dreaded arrived. I was coming out of the boardroom from a meeting and saw a message from my secretary: 'Simon rang to say the house is finished'. It sounded more like a death sentence. I closed my office door, poured myself a stiff whisky and called him back.

"You have to come and see it, Ginny," he shouted down the phone. "It's magnificent!"

***

When I turned into The Green I actually gasped. My beautiful bungalow had been turned into a Grand Designs monstrosity. Its white concrete exterior towered above me, the enormous windows were like vast eyes daring me not to love them. There wasn't an inch of Butterfly Cottage left standing. It had been completely subsumed by Simon's dream of creating a rock star's mansion.

As I got out of the car, Simon appeared holding two glasses of champagne.

"To our new home," he declared.

Handing me a glass and clinking it with his, he stared at the house like a king before his fortress, while I inwardly apologised to the bungalow for being party to such a betrayal.

Like a professional tour guide, Simon led me through the gate, extolling the virtues of the flint and stone-paved front garden and an enormous baronial front door, 'specially made by one of Germany's top manufacturers'.

"Where's the original front door?" I asked him, praying that the gorgeous stained-glass wasn't lying in a skip somewhere.

"Ah!" Simon said, beaming at me. "That, my darling, is a surprise for later."

He opened the door, said 'prepare to be amazed' and waved me into a vast open-plan space. The new kitchen was one of those gleaming landscapes which stretched out to infinity, with an enormous granite-top island surrounded by work surfaces and cupboards that would never be filled. As he led me across the shiny slate flooring, my one thought was that it would probably need a 'Caution Wet Floor' sign every time you got the mop out.

The vastness continued with the sitting-room area, with enough white leather settees for three families and a huge wood burner standing on a mottled cream tiled floor covered by several enormous rugs.

To the left was a satinwood and steel spiral staircase, which I presumed led up to the new first floor and I was preparing to clamber up it when Simon strode towards the 'specially misted' bi-folding doors and pressed something on a remote on the wall. As they demisted like a magician's reveal, my heart actually broke.

My haven of wildflowers was now a Japanese-style sprawl of water features, stepped levels and various grasses wafting wanly by a false wooden bridge.

"It was designed by New York's top landscape gardeners," Simon said, coming over and taking my hand.

He led me out along a winding path through his Disney Fairyland of bad taste, pointing out various features he was especially proud of, like the rock pool 'which will soon have shubunkin goldfish in it' and extolling how their calico colouring 'will match the stones at the bottom'. All I could think was, 'then how will you spot one?'.

We finally reached a clearing and I involuntarily gasped. There, like an old friend, was the summerhouse, still intact. I nearly hugged Simon but thought, 'Why should I? He's ruined my home.' I wanted to run onto the veranda and stay there, but he was already striding back towards the house, announcing over his shoulder, 'I have so much more to show you'.

I followed him back into the sitting-room and up the spiral staircase onto a room-size landing which led to the vast master bedroom. The ensuite, which was bigger than the first flat I'd rented, had that oddly unsettling lighting under the units, which went from Mediterranean blue to a kind of glowing amber.

"Very calming when you're on the loo," Simon told me, looking quite offended when I laughed my head off.

But there was more. The house had actually grown *two* storeys. You accessed the top floor up another spiral staircase which led to a fully fitted out music room. Fleetwood Mac would have felt overwhelmed by its size.

"This is where the magic will happen," Simon dreamily told me. "Where I will create my masterpiece."

"But who's going to dust it all, Simon?" I asked him, his face falling at my lack of vision.

Back on the ground floor, Simon promised me

'another nice surprise'. He led me down a narrow hallway where the old front door, with the sunburst and butterfly stained-glass window, opened into Jack's old painting room. It looked as it always had, his easel standing by the old settee Jack's parents had given him when he left home.

Needless to say, it and the summerhouse became the places I'd escape to when I needed to immerse myself in memories - of when I was in control of my life, and sharing it with a man who would be horrified at the destruction of our dream.'

Chapter Eight

'Over the next five years, Original Songs grew in size at about the same rate Simon did. He installed a gym in his music room, hired a personal trainer and a 'health guru', honing his body into an ever more powerful machine.

He gained the four stone he'd lost, but this time entirely in muscle. His strict new vegan diet and regular sessions at the tanning parlour turned him into an extraordinary-looking man, with not an ounce of superfluous fat anywhere and muscles which were like polished steel – his biceps actually shone, the skin so tightly stretched around them.

He then had his nose reshaped, which was so radical it changed his face completely. Then came a course of Botox injections, destroying his rather endearing sideways smile and basically removing any expression from his features.

The final bit of surgery he put himself through was on his ears. He'd always hated the way they stuck out a little, and so had them virtually pinned to his skull. By the time he'd finished the latest make-over, he'd become unrecognisable from the man I'd met ten years earlier. Even friends who'd only known him since the wedding did a double-take when they saw the transformation.

With the succour of success long gone, he instead fed his infinite hunger for achievement on making himself physically astonishing. He basked in the eyes which followed him around any room he entered. The physical strength he'd built up was almost tangible, the air seemed to move out of his way. At music functions, I could almost hear him purring at the admiring glances he got from women and men alike.

One morning, I was sitting at the kitchen island, recovering from yet another row with Simon. We'd been due to go out for lunch to celebrate our fifth wedding anniversary, but our conversation over coffee had resulted in him ruining any anticipation of a good day together – and there were increasingly less of those.

As he'd sipped his latte and I knocked back a very strong espresso, he blithely told me that he wanted to bulldoze the Japanese garden away and fill the space with a state-of-the-art recording studio.

"I want a big enough area to hire an orchestra," he announced, "so I can finally create the symphony I've been working on."

I'd heard bits of it, as he'd plonked away on his numerous keyboards in the music room at the top of the house. To me it sounded like an amalgam of Beethoven, Mozart, McCartney and Burt Bacharach. I told him definitely not, I simply wouldn't tolerate him creating havoc in my home again on yet another whim.

As I watched my outright 'No' sink in, I saw something new in his eyes which chilled me. He launched into a vicious verbal assault, getting unnervingly close as he yelled into my face. Suddenly, a rage I'd never seen before engulfed him, and he began throwing things around the room.

At one point, he narrowly missed my head when he tossed the Music Publishers Association award Original had won for 'I Can Wait Forever'. It crashed against the wall and tore into the painting Jack had done of me. I cherished that portrait, loving the happiness in my eyes he'd captured. It reminded me of how in love I'd been that day, looking forward to our life together.

As the award hit my painting, slashing it down the

middle, I saw red. We were suddenly screaming like banshees at each other, accusations flying round the room. Till that moment, I'd had no idea of how much I resented him, nor of how deeply he hated me. The venom being hurled by us both was a massive emotional release and yet completely debilitating.

As the insults finally ran out of steam, we stared at each other like boxers at the end of a round. I was shaking as I watched Simon deciding what to do next but, to my surprise, he simply grabbed his Gucci leather jacket from off the back of a chair and stormed out.

The silence which descended on the room was actually physical and totally blissful. The lack of Simon's presence, which could be overwhelming, was such a welcome relief. I felt all the stress and tension draining away as I picked up the things he'd thrown and gently put them back where they'd been. I took Jack's torn painting off the wall and, stroking it like a wounded child, popped it safely into a cupboard, making a mental note to get it restored as quickly as possible. Then, pouring myself a large glass of Cabernet Sauvignon, I sat down at the granite island and burst into tears.

And that was when it happened. I heard a strangely loud tinkling sound which filled the room, along with a strong scent of freesias. From behind me, a voice I instantly recognised shouted, 'What the *fuck*?!'. I turned around and there was Jack, standing by the utility room door, looking exactly as he had on the morning he'd disappeared. As we stared at each other, he said, 'Ginny?' and passed out.'

Chapter Nine

'My name's Jack Marlowe and what I want to say straight away is, if I had been given a choice, I would never have left my fantastic life with my incredible wife for a second – let alone for fifteen years.

Ginny and I met during a Bruce Springsteen concert at Wembley in 1985, when I spotted her in the interval, struggling behind me through a crowd of wannabee drinkers in the chaotically overcrowded bar. I bought two bottles of beer, walked up to her and handed her one. She told me later that she fell in love with me at that moment, more because of my shoulder-length blonde curls, which reminded her of her teen hero Robert Plant, than any knight-in-shining-armour deed for which I was patting myself on the back.

I adored her short dark bob, the high cheekbones and her slim frame which modelled perfectly the simply-coutoured blue cotton dress. She looked like an '80s version of Audrey Hepburn, my favourite film actress. It was as though fate had meant us to meet.

As we found a space at the back of the bar, she told me that she worked for a music publisher's run by a fantastic-sounding woman, Vicki Palmer, who had, Ginny told me, 'rewritten the music biz rulebook single-handedly'.

"And she seems to like me," Ginny said, "so hopefully that'll help."

"You won't need any help, I'm sure," I replied, realising immediately how lame that sounded.

Her smile told me I was right, but thankfully I hadn't completely blown it as she asked me what I did, always a good sign. I told her I was an artist who currently had several portraits of friends lined up against the walls of my top-floor studio flat in Streatham. Her adorable laugh was a sound I wanted to hear for the rest of my life. I had fallen head over heels in love.

"I'd really like to see them," she said, adding not a little flirtatiously, "your paintings."

"Unfortunately," I said, moving in a little closer, "I don't have any etchings."

And there was that laugh again.

I woke the next morning to the gorgeous sight of her dressed in my white painting shirt, standing by the window holding one of my sketches up to the light.

"I *love* this one," she said.

It was a pastel study of one of my students at The Slade, Harry Mainstay. His parents, Jim and Esther, had commissioned me to paint his portrait and I was planning to show them the preparation sketch in a few days' time, when they'd invited me to spend the weekend at their house in Oxfordshire. On a whim I asked Ginny if she'd accompany me, knowing they'd fall in love with her.

***

I was ten years old when my parents took me to my first Impressionist exhibition at the Tate, and my future was decided. As I wandered around holding my mother's hand, staring up at these visual delights shimmering with light and colour, I knew that this was what I wanted to do. The ambition to create something as visually intoxicating, and to thrill the viewer as I had been thrilled, began a fire within me which never went out.

Although my style changed as I got older, and I began

preferring a more 'super-realism' approach, I never lost the love of the use of light and the effervescent colours which the Impressionists created. In fact, I coined a new phrase for my style of portraiture – 'Impressionist Realism'.

My mother Nancy (née Cairnforth) had also studied art and design at The Slade in the 1950s, becoming a close friend of the stage designer Yolanda Sonnabend, who used to occasionally come to dinner at my parents' home in Epping in the '60s.

One particular visit stuck in my mind. I was about eleven or twelve, and as Yolanda was chatting to Mum and Dad about a ballet she was designing for Kenneth MacMillan, she looked at a drawing I'd done of my dad, which Mum had stuck on the fridge.

"Oh my!" she said. "Who did that?"

"Jack did it," Mum replied proudly. "I really love it."

"So do I," Yolanda said, getting up to have a closer look. "This is so much like a collection of pastel sketches I used to have. Your sense of colour, Jack, is very reminiscent of them."

She smiled at me and shook her head in a kind of wonder.

"You have a great talent, young man," she said. "I wish I could show you those sketches but, sadly, I no longer have them. Do you remember Nancy? They were left for me at The Slade when we were studying there."

"I remember you telling me about them," Mum replied. "Did you ever find out who left them for you?"

"I never did," Yolanda replied. "Tessa, the receptionist, just said a very elderly gentleman, who wouldn't give his name, had left a parcel for me. She was all aquiver about a sketch of her the chap had dashed off and given her before he left. By the time she realised it was unsigned, he'd gone."

"I *found* her 'all aquiver'," Mum said, laughing. "Just after he'd gone. She showed me the sketch and it was rather beautiful. Tessa couldn't wait to show it to her mum."

Mum and Yolanda laughed at the memory.

"I hope you'll encourage Jack's talent," Yolanda said, smiling again at me.

"He's a bit young to start planning his future," my dad said, pouring more wine into Yolanda's glass, "but if he wants to take up painting professionally, I would be more than happy."

Rather than let them begin talking about me, which no kid enjoys, I wanted to hear more of Yolanda's story.

"So, these sketches, they were in the parcel this chap left for you?" I asked her.

"Yes, Jack, they were," Yolanda replied. "There was a short note inside which said, 'From a long-time friend' but no name. The sketches weren't signed, but oh my, they were fabulous."

"And you never found out who'd done them?" I asked her wide-eyed.

"No. I kept them at my apartment for several years, looking at them from time to time, wishing I knew who'd drawn them. But, you know, in a strange kind of way, I rather enjoyed not knowing. They were my little secret, meant for me. Then a couple of years ago, the Summer of 1972 I think it was, I showed them to a friend who'd come round to the flat to discuss a theatre set I was designing. She suggested I take them to a Modern Art forum I was lecturing at in New York, where I might meet someone who would recognise the artist."

"And did you take them?" I asked her, as Mum checked the joint of lamb she was cooking for us, the delicious smell of rosemary and garlic wafting from the oven.

"Yes. I did and it created an interesting discussion, that's for sure. One or two suggested Cézanne, another Matisse, one Impressionists expert thought they may be drafts for a painting by someone like Sisley. But none of their suggestions really convinced me. Why would a perfect stranger leave me a set of sketches by one of the Impressionist masters? Surely, he'd try and sell them? And anyway, I always assumed that the old man had done the sketches himself. Then, on my last night there, a very odd-looking chap approached me in the hotel bar and asked to see the drawings."

"Odd-looking how?" Dad asked Yolanda.

"Kind of an old-fashioned dandy, dressed like a Conan Doyle character, even the way he spoke sounded like something from a Victorian novel. But he was quite insistent that he wanted to see them, so I went to my room to get them and when I returned he'd already got his magnifying glass ready. He studied them intrinsically, becoming increasingly excited with each one."

"How did he know you had them?" Mum asked her.

"He wouldn't say, but I assumed he must have known someone at the forum who I'd shown them to. Anyway, he offered me a lot of money for them, a *lot* of money, which I simply couldn't turn down."

"Did he say who the artist was?" Dad asked Yolanda.

"No. He told me he wanted to do more research before he could be sure, and quite honestly I didn't want to press him on it. I had quite a few debts I needed to pay at the time so…"

"Did you ever see him again?" I asked Yolanda.

"No, I didn't. He told me to check with my bank the next morning, which I did, and sure enough, they told me the money had been deposited. All of it."

"Under what name?" Dad asked.

"A company name, can't recall it now. Anyway, I did as he'd instructed and delivered them to a gallery on Fifth Avenue, marking the parcel 'From Yolanda', then got a cab to the airport and that was that."

"And you never found out who the artist was?" Mum asked her.

"No. For a couple of years, I'd check the papers to see if there was anything about the sketches or the artist, but there was absolutely nothing. All very mysterious."

She glanced again at my drawing.

"Anyway, Jack, I do hope you follow in your mum's footsteps, and study art at a good college."

When I got into The Slade, I was hoping Yolanda would be one of my tutors, but she'd left shortly before I started there. However, I enjoyed bragging to my fellow students that my mum was a great friend of hers, and how she'd admired a childhood sketch of mine.

***

The weekend at Jim and Esther's was great fun and as I anticipated, they loved Ginny. During lunch on our first day there, Ginny was nattering away about my paintings when the doorbell rang.

"That'll be Albert," Esther said, jumping up to get the door.

"Albert Rothwell," Jim explained. "He's a good friend of ours, has been for quite some years. He's from

New York and whenever he's in the UK he pops in to see us. Quite a character."

At that, Esther came bundling in on the arm of a formidable-looking man in his fifties. Not overweight, just enormously built, 'a moving mountain' as my mum used to call beefy attractive men. Jim got up to greet him with an American-style bear hug and Esther introduced us.

"Two of our good friends, Jack Marlowe and Ginny…?"

"…Taylor," Ginny said, shaking the massive, meaty hand which was enthusiastically proffered.

"We only met Ginny today," Esther explained. "She is Jack's delightful young lady."

"Delightful indeed," Albert purred, glancing at me approvingly.

Jim got an extra chair for Albert who apologised for bursting in on our lunch, while Esther brought over a plate, some cutlery and a glass.

"Oh, not a problem Albert," she said, pouring the Merlot into his glass. "There's more than enough to go around… if you're hungry, that is?"

Albert clapped his hands.

"Always ready for good food, Esther."

As she filled his plate and passed him the gravy, Esther said, "Albert's dating a very famous actress, but he simply refuses to tell us who."

"Esther's been guessing who she is for ages," Jim laughed, "but he won't budge."

"I think that's laudable, really," Ginny said, "not boasting about who you're dating."

"Thank you, Ginny," Albert said, tucking in. "She is very keen to protect her privacy."

"Are you in the film industry?" Ginny asked him.

"Used to be, on the finance side, but I'm retired now."

He beamed around the table.

"Now, folks, no doubt I interrupted a conversation when I arrived, so please, continue - whoever was talking as I burst in."

"It was you, Ginny," Jim said, "you were talking about Jack's work."

"Which is?" Albert enquired, taking a sip of his wine.

"Jack is a wonderful artist," Esther said. "He is definitely going places."

"You were telling us about a painter Jack admired, Ginny," Jim said, gently pushing the conversation back to her.

With a slightly embarrassed cough, Ginny said, "Yes, Sergius Pauser. He was a Viennese portraitist whose paintings Hitler had labelled degenerate and threw him in a concentration camp."

"How dreadful," Esther said.

"Happily, Pauser survived and continued to paint and became one of Austria's foremost painters of the Twentieth Century."

I took up the story.

"I'd not heard of him until, a few years ago, when I was still a student, I saw this book on his paintings in a shop in Charing Cross Road, loved the cover, bought the book and spent hours poring over it."

"Fascinating," Albert said. "I must look him out. And, Jack, I'd love to see your work sometime."

"Yes, do," Esther enthused, glancing over at me as if to say 'he could be good for you, Jack'.

About a week later, Jim rang.

"Are you in for a few hours?" he asked me.

"Yes," I replied. "Ginny's here too. Are you coming over?"

"No, but something should be arriving for you in the next couple of hours or so. You'll have to sign for it. Okay?"

Intrigued, I tried to get more details out of him, but he was amusingly secretive.

"Just be patient, lad," he told me. "I hope you'll be pleased."

The doorbell rang about noon, and I skipped downstairs to get the package from the courier. When I opened it, I was completely unprepared for what it contained. It was Pauser's *Portrait of A Lady*.

The note inside said:

Albert saw this yesterday in a Christie's catalogue and rang to tell us about it. Ironically, we were just on our way out to our six-monthly visit to one of their auctions. Can't believe the timing! We thought you'd like it. Esther and I send you and Ginny our love, Jim.

"That is *so* beautiful," Ginny said as we both stared at the painting. "Esther and Jim clearly love you very much."

"And I them," I replied, wondering where to hang it.

"Every visitor should see it as soon they enter this room, and you should see it every morning when you wake up," Ginny said. "So hang it there, on the wall opposite the door."

Later that evening, lying in bed and looking at the painting, I said to Ginny, "Your portrait will hang next to Pauser's."

"You've done a portrait of me?"

"Not yet, but I'm going start on my own Portrait of A

Lady very soon."

"Why me?"

"Because you are my inspiration; because you should have your portrait painted, and because the world should see it – and one day it will."

***

Within a few weeks, Ginny had moved in with me and I began drawing sketches of her in preparation for the portrait. She used to looked delightfully embarrassed whenever we were sitting in a café or a pub, or just relaxing on the dilapidated sofa my parents had given me, as I'd be working on yet another pencil or pastel study of her.

I completed the painting in my work area at The Slade, took it home and hung it next to the Pauser. When she arrived back from work and saw it Ginny literally gasped. She threw her hands up to her face, her eyes welling up, and stared transfixed at the painting.

"Two stunning ladies side by side," I said.

"I love it, Jack," she said. "I'm going to love it forever."

Ginny and I were married two years later. Harry was my best man and Vicki was Ginny's maid-of-honour. It was a simple registry office wedding with just a few close friends and family attending. Neither of us really went for the full-on church and big reception extravaganza, which was becoming the new thing. We'd seen it overwhelm friends who'd chosen that route and decided it simply wasn't for us. Both our mothers were disappointed, of course, Ginny's especially, but they stood together on the day, looking magnificent and beaming at us proudly.

I felt like the luckiest man alive.

We decided to continue living in my Streatham flat. We were happy there and were both too busy to start looking for something bigger. But then, just a few weeks later, my father rang to say a friend of his was taking a job in Brussels, and needed tenants to look after his flat while he was gone.

"It's twice the size of your Streatham place," Dad told me, "and it looks like Sean won't be back for quite some time, if at all, so…"

It was a ninth floor apartment in King's Court in Hammersmith, which both Ginny and I were immediately taken with. The fact that the rent was half what we were currently paying made it, as they say, 'a no-brainer'. On a lovely morning in the Autumn of 1987, we moved into the apartment and began our new life together.

King's Court was a 1930s block which, so one of the tenants told us, had once boasted a sweeping art deco reception with a uniformed commissionaire. By the time we moved in, it was just a large, empty space with a couple of bikes leaning against the wall. But I liked to imagine it with a flurry of beautifully-dressed residents coming and going, collecting their mail from a smiling receptionist and bidding the commissionaire – or George, as I'd named him in my mind - a friendly 'good morning' as he went out to hail them a cab.

Ginny became very friendly with our next-door neighbour, Suze, who had a florist's just across the road and had lived in King's Court for about twenty years. Ginny loved popping in to have a coffee and a chat with her, someone she could confide in 'woman-to-woman' who wasn't involved in the music business or a family member. Some days I'd be working on a new sketch and could hear the two of them suddenly bursting out laughing at one of Suze's no doubt very dirty jokes.

Sadly, our stay at King's Court didn't last as long as we'd hoped. In 1992 my father's friend wrote to say he had to return 'for family reasons' and needed his apartment back. Fortunately, Ginny was doing very well at Original by then, and my portrait commissions were beginning to add a substantial slice of income to what I was earning at The Slade, so we decided the time was right to buy somewhere.

We loved Butterfly Cottage as soon as we saw it.

"It's perfect!" Ginny almost shouted at the agent, who looked at us like we were a couple of tripped-out hippies.

Ginny would return home each evening happily exhausted and ready for a G & T, which I'd get for her while telling her how my latest painting was going. On warm summer evenings, we'd sit on the summerhouse veranda looking out at the fantastic wildflower garden Ginny was creating. One doesn't often feel like you need nothing more than this moment, but that's how we felt.

***

On that August Bank Holiday morning of 1997, my wife and I were in a very good place. She was now A & R Director at Original and I was about to start on my portrait of The Princess of Wales. I'd been asked to arrive at Kensington Palace at eleven o'clock 'prompt' and begin what would be a huge leap forward in my career. The world's most adored woman sitting for me.

Apparently, Diana had expressed an interest in commissioning me after she and a friend visited an exhibition of mine in Bond Street. Her friend knew the owner of the gallery who told my agent.

Of course, I was nervous as hell about painting Diana but really excited too. I began creating imaginary scenarios for our conversations as I drove to my studio each morning. I briefly considered asking her about her much-publicised romance with Fayed's son Dodi, and then decided to keep it to chatting about the sons she clearly adored, finally to just getting on with the job and letting Diana do the talking should she wish to.

I kissed Ginny goodbye with a 'good luck' for the *Titanic* screening, had a quick shower and then made for the bedroom, laying out the outfit Ginny had advised the night before - black open-necked shirt, black jeans and her favourite dark blue jacket, finished off with well-polished brogues.

Deciding I was happy with it, I put on my 'chill-out gear', tracksuit and canvas shoes and lay on the bed, contemplating whether to put my art materials in the MG and drive there or, thinking that may be too poncy, order a cab. As I was happily mulling over my morning, I heard the phone ringing in the hall and got up to answer it. And that was when my world turned upside down.

I walked out of the bedroom to the sound of very loud wind chimes, and found myself in a kitchen that went on forever. A middle-aged lady was sitting with her back to me at an enormous granite-covered breakfast bar and, wondering what the hell was happening, I swore, rather loudly. It made her turn round and she stared at me as though she'd seen a ghost. Just as I realised who it was, everything went black.'

Chapter Ten

Jack slowly opened his eyes, sure he was waking from a bad dream. He was lying on the floor and a bright overhead light was making his head hurt. A woman in her mid-to-late forties was peering down at him. She wore a pair of large, red spectacles from which hung a gold chain and her hair was pulled back into a loose bun, tied with a black and white silk scarf which draped around her neck. As his vision cleared, the realisation which had struck him just before he´d passed out was confirmed. It *was* Ginny, but looking unnervingly like her mother.

"What have you done?" he asked her. "Where is this?"

He looked over at the door he´d come out of.

"What just happened?"

She smiled and he saw that her eyes had lost the happy sparkle he'd always loved. The woman looking down at him was definitely Ginny, but an older version. He turned his head towards the floor-length mirror on the far wall and could see that he was still the same young man, not a day older than when he'd been thrust into… what? It was like being in some science fiction novel. Panic began to engulf him.

"This has to be a nightmare, Ginny," he said, shaking his head. "I fainted and I'm still unconscious. I must have fallen and hit my head when I went to answer the phone. I need to wake up, Ginny, wake me up. *Please*!"

Ginny looked at the door from where Jack had appeared.

"It can't be…" she murmured.

"What? What can't it be?"

"Okay," she said, "you need to calm down and listen to me. This is going to sound completely insane but you have to believe me. It's not a dream. This is real. Okay?"

Jack nodded like a child.

"Otherwise, how can you still look like that…"

She pointed at his reflection.

"And I now look like this?"

"Because this *is* a dream, Ginny, it's a terrible dream."

"No, it's not, Jack. I know it's not, because here I am, holding you, *fifteen years after you disappeared*."

Jack seemed to sag in her arms, staring at her like a confused, frightened animal. She could see the awful realisation of what had happened to him finally sinking in. Stroking the golden curls she thought she'd never see or feel again, she began explaining how, all those years ago, her world had collapsed into a million pieces when she thought he'd left her, and about everything which had happened since.

Chapter Eleven

The two of them sat on the floor together in silence, Jack trying to take in everything Ginny had told him. It was a lot. He'd need time to digest it, the enormity of it all, the unbelievable, catastrophic result of him disappearing from her life, a life she'd had to rebuild with someone else, someone who had made her so unhappy.

As he watched her stroking his arm and trying to be supportive, he felt guilty. And angry. And, even more infuriating, helpless. For the first time since they'd met, he couldn't make things better for Ginny, he couldn't undo the loss and the pain he had unknowingly caused her. And then the ramifications of it all hit him. What were they going to do? How could they simply just get on with life now?

"You know," Ginny said, "when you disappeared, some people thought you'd had a kind of nervous breakdown. The shock of Diana dying on the day you were about to start her portrait, the day that was going to change your life, your career, the sudden loss of all that, some people suggested it sent you over the edge."

"A bit dramatic."

"I know. It didn't make sense and anyway, that's just not you."

She stroked his hair, wondering if she should say what was on her mind.

"What all this means is…" she began cautiously, "it means… you were somehow… taken."

He raised his eyebrows and sang *The Twilight Zone* theme tune.

"You mean… by *aliens*?"

"Well, why not? It's one way of making sense of all

this. Look, let's go and sit down and you tell me your side… what actually happened to you that day, and maybe we can put it all together."

***

When Jack had come to the end of his tale, to the point where he´d walked into an unrecognisable kitchen and, for a moment, saw a woman he didn´t know, she said, "That phone call you heard? That was me ringing to tell you about Diana. I'd just heard about the crash on the car radio."

"Bloody hell."

"And you know what infuriated me? That you'd refused to have a mobile. That I could only contact you on the home phone."

She smiled wryly at him.

"Of course, I know now it would've made no difference."

"I told you I didn't need one."

She squeezed his arm playfully, loving its firmness, its innate strength.

"Sorry," he said, "but I suddenly need to use the bathroom. This time-travelling lark is clearly not good for the bladder."

"It´s through the door on the left, across the hall, first door on the right."

Jack nodded and got up, then turned to her and said, "Our lovely bungalow, eh?"

"I know, I'm so sorry."

He pointed at the bi-folding doors.

"And what's with the misted glass wall?"

Ginny's heart sank.

"Oh, that leads out to the garden."

"Well, when I get back, we can have a walk through it. At least that's still there."

Ginny felt suddenly nauseous, the garden was the one thing she'd forgotten to tell him about. As Jack smiled the smile which had always made her feel that everything was alright, she knew it would never be alright again.

Chapter Twelve

'Trying to find my way back to the kitchen, I got hopelessly lost and wandered along corridors past a labyrinth of rooms, shaking my head at the excess and knowing how much Ginny must have hated it. The more I wandered, the more lost I became, until I finally came to a door I recognised. It was our old front door with the lovely stained-glass window.

"What the fuck is going on here?" I asked myself, beginning to feel like a character out of a Kafka novel.

I opened the door and found myself in my old painting room, and there they were again, those deafening wind chimes and that sweet scent wafting around me. Then darkness.

When I came round, someone was helping me onto the sofa and then sat next to me. When I turned to thank them I got the shock of my life.

"Grandad?" I said. "What are you doing here?"

But when he spoke, he had my voice.

"Hello, Jack," he said, smiling my smile. "I´m afraid you've time-slipped again."

"So, where am I this time? And who the fuck are you?"

"I'm you, Jack. Fifty years into your future. This is your old house, Butterfly Cottage, but not in your time."

He watched me taking it in, took a deep breath and asked me not to interrupt him, to just listen.

"Imagine several almost identical pieces of stained glass, lying one on top of the other, where the panels tell a story. The same story, but which gradually, in each one, begins to unfold differently. Although they feature the same person, often the same people, the pictures evolve in a different way, the stories begin to diverge along disparate paths which continue completely independently. They're called time-spaces. They exist side by side, usually not colliding… until they do. You're a time-traveller, Jack. *We* are time-travellers, and what has happened to you should not have occurred."

"Well, great, that's a big help!"

He put his hand on my shoulder.

"I will help you, Jack, I'll get you back to the morning in 1997 when it all went belly-up for you. But you must do as I ask. Once you're back, you'll be completely unaware that any of this happened - seeing Ginny again, meeting me here, it will vanish from your memory. Novices like you, once back in their own time, remember nothing of the trip they've just taken."

"That suits me fine, I've had enough of all this."

"Okay, Jack. Come with me. We're going back to your old bedroom. I want you to open the door and walk in, where everything will be just as you left it."

Older Jack put his hand on my shoulder.

"And this is important, Jack, when you hear the phone ring, do *not* go and answer it, let the answering machine take it."

A thought struck me.

"Hold on, if I don't remember any of this, how will I know not to answer the phone?"

"Good question, all I will say is, trust me, you will know."

As we stood up, I noticed behind the settee my old easel leaning against the wall. It had a pastel sketch on it and I went closer to get a better look. It was of a couple, the lady sitting and the man standing behind her, his hand on her shoulder. At the top were the words *William & Kate*.

"This is very nice," I said. "I vaguely recognise him but who is she?"

"It's just a preliminary sketch for a commission I'm doing," Older Jack replied a little impatiently. "But we really should get going, time, pardon the pun, is running out.'"

Chapter Thirteen

Ginny woke up on the sofa in a panic. She looked at her watch and cursed herself for dropping off into such a deep slumber. It had been an hour since Jack had gone off in search of the loo, and she wondered if he'd collapsed somewhere.

She went through the house from top to bottom, the rising panic she'd felt fifteen years earlier when she couldn't find Jack in the bungalow beginning to overwhelm her once more.

She knew he couldn't have gone into the garden as the bi-folding doors were still locked shut. Finally, her heart thudding in her chest, she had to accept that, once more, he'd disappeared.

'Poor man,' she thought, 'what must he be going through now?'.

Feeling beaten and exhausted, she saw her reflection in the mirror, studying what Jack had seen when he'd suddenly appeared out of nowhere in the kitchen. The optimistic joy in her eyes, the smile which used to come so naturally to her, the openness of that young, fresh face Jack had fallen for, had gone. It had all been lost in the constant uncertainty, the daily stress of living and coping with Simon, and in the years which had passed without Jack.

She touched the crow's feet around her eyes and tried to stretch them away; she pulled back the lines around her mouth with her thumb and forefinger; she unpinned her bun and let her hair fall naturally over her shoulders, trying to ignore the streaks of grey which were beginning to swamp the youthful glints of auburn and copper.

Lost in memories of how she'd looked when she first

met Jack, the sound of Simon's Porsche roaring into the street and pulling up outside was like a slap in the face. As she heard his key in the front door, she braced herself for another almighty row.

Simon strode in, threw his keys onto the granite worktop and, without looking at Ginny, walked over to the coffee machine and poured himself a mug.

"I had a few drinks in the bar," he said, as though she'd asked him where he'd been.

He got milk from the fridge, poured some into his coffee and noisily stirred it.

"I had a great talk with one of my musician friends," he continued, still not looking at her. "He has an incredible studio in his back garden. He agreed with me, I should definitely build one in ours."

Ginny stayed calm and in a tone of voice which was quiet and yet firm, she said,

"May I remind you that your musician friend is *not* your wife, nor the one who has paid for *everything* you've done to this house, and to yourself, and who has basically kept you alive these last five years. Please get this into your thick, arrogant head, Simon, I have no intention of paying another penny for any more of your self-indulgent whims."

Simon was now looking at Ginny and watched in a stunned silence as she got her handbag off the coffee table and marched towards the front door.

"Make sure you've packed your bags and gone by the time I get back," she said and left.

Staring into space and feeling suddenly vulnerable, Simon listened to the emptiness. He went to the drinks cabinet, poured himself a large whisky and stood, imagining a future he'd never contemplated.

A gentle tapping sound at the front door slowly broke through his thoughts. He gulped the whisky back, went down the hall and looked through the spyhole. An elderly chap was standing on the path, smiling pleasantly around him.

Simon opened the door.

"Can I help you?" he said, thinking this old guy looked oddly familiar.

"It's more how I can help you, actually," the stranger replied, extending his hand. "You must be Simon. My name's Jack Marlowe. Can I come in?"

Chapter Fourteen

'After walking out of the house, I drove down Chiswick High Road, letting thoughts simply float around my head. Passing King's Court, I looked up and saw the window of the flat where our old next-door neighbour, Suze, lived.

We'd stayed in touch after Jack and I had moved into Butterfly Cottage, getting together for lunch or a coffee and always enjoying catching up. Shortly after Jack's disappearance, she'd taken me out to dinner at the Greek restaurant across the road from the flats, where we'd always go when we needed a lengthy girl-chat. She let me pour my heart out, never once interrupting, just listening as I fell to pieces, rallied, and then fell to pieces again.

She'd poured me copious amounts of Retsina as I rabbited on, finally walking me across the road, into the lift at King's Court and settling me on her deliciously comfy settee. I'd fallen asleep and dreamt of Jack painting me lying there, and woken up to hot croissants, steaming coffee and a hand to hold.

Over the next few years, Suze was a real rock, but things changed when I became involved with Simon. I'd hoped she'd approve and maybe even like him, but I could tell immediately that she wasn't impressed. We became more distant, only seeing each other occasionally for a quick coffee en route to somewhere else. Although we did our best to ignore the elephant in the room whenever we met up, our paths began to do their best not to cross, until we finally lost touch.

Now, on a whim, I turned left into a side street and

parked the car. I called Suze's number, wondering what reception I'd get, so when she answered with a pleasantly surprised 'Ginny!' I felt a surge of emotion.

"Suze," I said, trying to stop my voice wobbling. "I-I know it's been a while but… are you up for a coffee and a chat?"

"Of course," she said. "How incredible to hear from you."

"It's not been *that* long," I replied.

"Well, it has been quite a while actually," she said. "But, believe it or not, I was just about to call *you*."

"Really?"

"Yes. Where are you?"

"I'm parked outside."

"Then come up!"

King's Court had changed somewhat since I'd last visited Suze. The empty old foyer had been transformed into a gleaming tiled and slate-floor marvel. It had three lifts, with shiny maroon doors, swish burgundy leather seating by the revolving doors and a whole wall on the left had been turned into a post collection area. There was a brand new smart reception which resembled a New York hotel lobby, and, while impressive, I did regret the loss of the decayed grandeur I so fondly remembered.

A smart young receptionist, whose laminated badge informed me her name was Tammy, beamed at me and politely asked me what I wanted. When I told her who I was visiting, she checked her pc screen, pressed her Kate Bush style earpiece and, after a couple of moments, said, "Good morning, Miss Harper, I have a…"

She glanced a query at me.

"Ginny," I replied to her unspoken question.

"A Miss Ginny to see you. Shall I send her up?"

She nodded briskly, pointed her pen at the lifts and said, "Ninth floor. Number 182."

I was tempted to tell her that I knew where Suze was, thank you, but she'd already dropped her eyes to whatever she'd been doing when I arrived. I got into one of the lifts, checked myself in the spotless tinted mirror and pressed '9'. Up it swished, without any of the clanging chains and occasional juddering I remembered from my time there.

When I stepped out into the corridor, the smart hotel theme continued. Gone were the dirty fluorescent tubes in the ceiling which had sporadically lit the way along a yellowing tiled floor. Smoky brown shaded lights on each side now cast a classy warmth over the cream and chocolate brown carpet.

Walking past the bottle green doors which had replaced the old grey hardboard ones, I reached Suze's flat and rang the bell. I could hear Frank Sinatra's *Songs For Swinging Lovers*, her favourite album, playing and unconsciously adopted an upright pose and the confident expression of 'good old friend dropping in'.

When the door opened, we just stared at each other, unable to hide the shocked realisation that we'd both aged more than a little.

"Ginny, darling," she said, "come in."

We hugged one another, both declaring how well we looked, and I wandered into the room I used to love visiting. To my surprise and mild disappointment, it had also had something of a makeover. While it was fabulous and open-plan, like a tiny version of what Simon had done to the bungalow, I instantly mourned the comfy, ramshackle feel I'd loved so much.

"The place has changed a lot," I said, with entirely insincere conviction.

"Yeah," Suze replied, looking round her sitting-room. "The new management offered to contribute a large slice of the cost if the residents agreed to have the flats' interiors smartened up. Most of us did. One or two objected but, I thought, 'Why not?' it was about time. The old place was starting to look a bit sad, to be honest."

She smiled at me and said, "Anyway, come and sit down. G & T?"

"Lovely."

She fixed the drinks and joined me on the sofa, clinking my glass.

"The thing is," she began, "and this is why I was about to call you… Jack was here."

"Jack?"

"Yes, Jack! And, this is where it gets really weird… he, well, he –"

"Yes?"

My heart was about to beat out of my chest.

"He was so *old*, Ginny."

That wasn't what I'd been expecting.

"What do you mean – old?"

"Old. Too old. How old would he be now?"

"He was born in 1962 so… he'd be fifty."

Suze shook her head.

"No. He looked much older than that, he looked like a man in his eighties."

She seemed to be expecting an explanation and, while I was dying to tell her what had happened to me, I decided to keep schtum and find out more.

"Well, that makes no sense," I said, as casually as I

could muster. "When was he here?"

"About an hour ago. I was reading the new James Runcie novel, about a vicar living in Grantchester who solves crimes, and I was just about to find out who murdered the solicitor."

I smiled to myself. My friend was still delightfully scatty and constantly deflected during conversation.

"And?"

"And there was a knock at the door. That in itself was unusual, all callers, as you've discovered, have to go through Tammy now. She won't let anyone she doesn't know get anywhere near the lifts until she's given them the third degree, and if she has a problem, there's Beefy Bob."

"Beefy Bob?"

"The security guard, and you wouldn't want to mess with him. He's built like a brick shithouse."

She giggled and took a swig of her drink.

"Anyway, I peered through the spyhole and saw this very old man. I didn't recognise him and called through the door, asking who it was. When he said, 'an old friend', I knew immediately. I opened the door and there he was. I couldn't believe it. After all these years."

Trying to keep my voice steady, I said, "Did you let him in?"

"Yes. Of course I did. It was Jack."

"What did he say?"

"Well, as you can imagine, it was all rather awkward. I couldn't truthfully tell him he looked great when he looked so ancient. He looked around and said he liked the changes I'd made… though he clearly didn't."

She glanced at me then went on.

"I offered him a drink which he refused and then he

asked if I'd seen you. I told him I hadn't for a while and he said, 'You will see her soon, and when you do, send her my love.'"

I suddenly realised tears were pouring down my face. She handed me a tissue from a box on the coffee table, dabbing her eyes with another one.

"Oh Ginny," she said, grabbing my hand, "my poor girl. What you've been through."

"Why did he come to see *you*?" I asked her, immediately aware it sounded on the verge of rude.

"I have no idea," Suze replied, more puzzled than offended. "I'm afraid I rather lost it, Ginny, and I yelled at him. I told him he was a swine to leave you and how devastated you'd been when he disappeared. I felt so angry with him."

I squeezed my friend's hand.

"And what did he say?"

"Nothing. He just smiled at me, in a sad kind of way. I was about to accuse him of having another woman, but, to be quite honest, he didn't look capable and, well, that smile... you know what I mean... it just melted me."

"How long did he stay?"

"Not long. Ten minutes at most. I did ask him where the fuck he'd been and he said, 'I've been looking after Ginny.' And before I could do or say anything else, he kissed me on the cheek – he still smells glorious by the way – and said, 'when you see Ginny, please tell her not to worry. All will be as it should be.'"

As I wiped my eyes again, she said,

"I had no idea what he was talking about, but I found myself nodding like an idiot. I even think I said, 'Okay,' or something equally inane. Then he opened the door and walked down the hall. But – and this was very weird

- instead of taking the lift, he went out by the emergency stairs."

She looked at me, waiting for a reaction, but my face must have been as blank as a new blackboard.

"First of all," she explained, undaunted by my dimness, "going that way he'd come up against Bob the Brute. His office is right by the emergency exit on the ground floor. But here's the really bizarre thing, the stairwell's like an echo chamber, it sounds like a herd of animals if anyone goes down there. But there wasn't a sound. I thought, being so decrepit, he may have collapsed against the wall or something, so I went and checked the landing. But there was no-one there. I even looked over the banister just to make sure he hadn´t, you know… although I would have heard the crash… but it was like he'd vanished into thin air. Fair gave me the shivers, I can tell you."

She heaved a sigh, stood up and went into the kitchen.

"Sorry, I've got a casserole slow-cooking, I just want to…"

She looked in the oven, banged a couple of pans about, came back into the sitting-room and sat down.

"I thought about calling you, but what was I going to say? I to'd and fro'd for about half an hour wondering what to do, then finally I picked up the phone and - "

She cheered me with her glass.

"- you beat me to it! Another one?"

"No, I must get back."

My head spinning with Suze's news, I got up and noticed a collection of small sculptures on a shelf unit by the door.

"These are lovely," I said going towards them. "Who did them?"

Suze's face brightened as she picked one up and held it tightly in her hand.

"Aren't they great, "she said. "Jack noticed them and admired them as well. They were all done by Tee."

"Tee?"

"God, has it been *that* long?"

She looked fondly at the sculpture and handed it to me. It was of a lady jumping for joy, with a brass plaque on the base which read *Suze by Verity Braintree*.

"I love your name for her, 'Tee'."

"All her art world friends call her that. She always hated 'Verity', said it made her sound angelic – and angelic is not a word I'd use to describe her."

We both laughed and it felt good.

"We met a few months ago and I adore her, Ginny. She's great."

"And a great sculptor too," I said.

"She's a genius. She exhibits all over the world now. Her mother used to live in Butterfly Cottage."

Then it hit me.

"Braintree! Yes, that was the name of the family who Jack and I bought the bungalow off. It was Alistair Braintree, I think, who we, or rather our solicitor, dealt with."

"Yes, Tee's brother. She never really got on with him."

"I must meet Tee," I said, "and ask her about her mother. I knew there'd been an old lady living in the bungalow before we bought it, but that's all."

Suze grabbed my arm and slapped her forehead.

"Oh God, where is my brain today? That's what I meant to tell you."

"What?"

"I told Tee about Jack disappearing from the bungalow, and, guess what? Her mum did the same. Went into the kitchen one morning and - puff! – gone."

My heart involuntarily fluttered.

"Did they find her?"

"No. They did a big search for her, but in the end they declared her Missing Presumed Dead – just like Jack."

Her eyes widened.

"Oh Ginny," she said, "I wonder?"

"Wonder what?" I asked warily.

"About Jack and Tee's mum. I mean, do you think the house is – well, before Simon ruined it of course –"

She grabbed my arm again.

"Oh God, I didn't mean to say that, I'm really sorry, Ginny, I –"

"We're separating," I said. "Simon and me. It's over."

Suze tried to feign sadness but failed miserably.

"Since when?"

"Since about half an hour ago. I've kicked him out."

"Oh darling, I am so sorry."

"I'm not. I'm relieved. It's why I came to see you, I wanted you to know."

She gave me a big hug.

"Oh, thank you, Ginny. That means a lot."

"I'm really pleased to see you looking so happy, Suze."

"I am, Ginny," she replied.

After we'd bid our goodbyes, promising to see each other soon, I walked down the hall towards the elevator feeling oddly uplifted. The very fact that Jack was out there somewhere, meant that maybe, just maybe, I hadn't lost him.'

Chapter Fifteen

'I drove back home imagining Simon gone, but as I approached the house and saw his car still there, I swore loudly, expecting another row. I opened the door, my heart banging in my ears, but walking in, I knew immediately that the house was empty. Buildings transmit the lack of a sentient being within their walls as soon as you enter, as they do the sense of life when someone's there. When Jack had reappeared from the past, even before I'd heard his profanity and turned round, I knew I wasn't alone. Life exudes a vibration.

I couldn't understand why Simon hadn't taken his beloved Porsche. Had he gone for a long walk and was about to return? And, more importantly, did I care? Standing alone in the middle of a house I no longer thought of as home, I made a decision. I was going to sell the place. It was time to move on.

Original Songs was opening an office in Sydney, and the board of directors had been trying to persuade me for weeks to relocate and become Managing Director there. I'd pushed back on it, feeling my place was here, running the company Vicki had left to my care. But, in truth, it was running itself now. It had become such an established part of the music business, it followed its own momentum. Success breeds success, as they say.

I went upstairs and took a shower, my head suddenly full of plans. As the warm water cascaded around me, I wondered what price I should put the house on for and which estate agents to choose.

Still mulling everything over, I dried off and wandered over to the bed to comb my hair. I was thinking it was probably time I got a new hairstyle for my new adventure, when I saw a note propped by the lamp on Simon's bedside table.

'To Ginny', it said, in his rather scratchy scrawl. I leaned over, folded it open, and read it.

Dear Ginny,

Neither of us are happy with each other anymore. I've been offered a new start by... let's just say a mutual friend. I can't tell you anything more except to say our paths are unlikely to cross, but our times might!

Take care, be successful, of course you will be.

Goodbye. And in spite of everything, I love you.

Simon x

As I was taking that in, I went to the dresser to get some clean underwear out of the drawer, and there, lying on the top of my clothes, was an envelope. 'For my darling Ginny', it said, and I immediately recognised the handwriting.

I held the envelope to my mouth, kissed it, and tore it open. But just as I was about to read the note inside, my mobile rang. It was Mum.

Cursing her for her appalling timing, I picked it up and answered rather tetchily.

"Hello, Ginny," Mum said. "Are you alright?"

"Er – yeah, I'm fine, but I can't really talk right now. I -"

"Well, darling, I'm sorry, but this won't wait. I've just had some rather bad news. Vicki passed away this morning.'"

Chapter Sixteen

"Okay," Terry Simon was saying on the phone, "I'll see you at the session at eleven."

He bade his publisher farewell, replaced the receiver and walked past several gold discs on the wall of his study, one of which had been turned into a clock which displayed the date as well as the time – '9 a.m. May 13th 1966' in a large geometric typeface. It had been given to him by Pye Records when Terry had written his first Number One hit for them.

He went up the stairs of his Mews house in Mayfair and into his bedroom which boasted the four-poster he'd recently bought from Keith Moon. Putting on his red and green paisley shirt, mauve corduroy hipsters and knee-length yellow boots, he studied himself in the mirror.

Yes, he thought, at nearly thirty he was quite old to be mixing with these young groovy artists, but he was younger than George Martin and looked a damned sight more hip than he did. Anyway, success – and the millions his songs brought in - meant he could get away with looking like mutton dressed as lamb.

Going back downstairs, he donned his pair of Dylan shades, got the purple fedora he'd picked up at Granny Takes A Trip from off the hat stand, checked himself in the hall mirror one last time and swanned out of the house into his chauffeured limousine like he owned the '60s. And in many ways, he did.

As the limo sped through the West End, full of trendy boutiques and 'beautiful people' in kaftans, beads and spaced-out smiles, he reflected on how his life had changed since he'd moved to London and met Vicki

Palmer at the 100 Club.

Georgie Fame had been performing his chart-topper 'Yeh Yeh' in front of a packed crowd, and, as Terry mulled over an idea for a song he thought might suit Georgie, he'd noticed the attractive, skinny lady bopping away by the stage. He waited for her to make for the bar and, neatly bumping into her, introduced himself.

Ordering them both Scotch and Cokes, they easily fell into conversation, chatting about the pop scene and their favourite hits of the moment. But her obvious interest had turned to genuine excitement when he mentioned he was a songwriter. She gave him her card and asked him to drop by her office in Denmark Street.

"I'd love to find out what you have to offer," she'd said, her eyes glinting at him.

A few days later, he was sitting at the upright piano in the corner of Vicki's office.

"Go on, then," Vicki said, "amaze me."

As he played the opening chords, he had the oddest feeling. He knew that he'd written this song, he was sure it was his, but he couldn't remember when or where he'd come up with it. As the tune floated around the room, he had no recollection of composing it.

"That's fantastic!" Vicki shouted when he'd finished. "And you're definitely not signed to anyone?"

"Not yet," he'd replied, leaning forward in his chair.

"Then consider yourself an Original Songs writer. I'll ask my secretary to draw up a contract for you to sign. Now, let's hear some more."

The following day, Vicki booked Terry into Regent Sound Studios a few doors down from her office, where The Stones had recorded their first hits. Seeing her face when he'd played the demos to Vicki that evening, he was convinced he'd found the person who would make the songs hits.

Now, all these months later, as his car coasted along, he smiled to himself remembering how she'd gently broached the subject of his age, explaining that while he looked terrific for twenty-nine, he was a little too old to become a recording artist.

"Oh, I don't want to sing my songs," he'd replied, "I just want to write hits."

It was a truthful reply. He'd liked the sense that he could become the pop Svengali who gave million sellers to some of the UK's most successful artists. The fruits of his genius – the gold discs, the money, the respect from everyone in the music business – were enough for him. Being 'the driver of the star bus,' as someone at Original had said, rather than a temporary passenger, was the career he craved.

Vicki had taken his demos first of all to Pye, one of the most successful labels at the time. Very soon, The Searchers and Sandie Shaw were recording them as their next singles, which went on to hit the Top Ten within a couple of weeks of release. She then moved onto other labels like Decca and EMI, who were clamouring to hear more of Terry's songs.

He was now writing like a dam of creativity had burst, bringing artists like The Fortunes and The Swinging Blue Jeans back into the upper echelons of the charts. Vicki's phone was ringing off the hook, managers and A & R men almost begging her for a Terry Simon song which could reignite their artists' flagging sales.

With his whirlwind success, speedy even in these fast-moving times, Terry made a new stipulation – he wanted to produce the records as well as write the songs. Vicki was dubious at first, saying she preferred to let the big boys like Micki Most and Geoff Stephens create the hits, but she'd given him his head and Terry had come up trumps. He was now writing *and* producing Top Tenners for an increasing number of artists who wanted a sprinkling of the 'T.S. magic'.

"You always manage to record the sound of the future," Les Reed once told him. "It's like you instinctively know what's going to be big, and you then create it."

The Searchers' recording of Terry's 'Tomorrow Won't Stand In My Way' had been one of their biggest ever sellers and they were keen to get started on *A Stitch In Time,* the concept album he'd written for them. It was, Terry told Vicki, going to be a psychedelic epic, equalling The Beach Boys' *Pet Sounds* and The Beatles' *Rubber Soul,* 'moving pop music up a gear to a new plateau'.

His name might have been everywhere in pop circles, but rarely did anyone get near him for a quote or a photo. It gave him the sense that he was some kind of mysterious magical maestro.

"If you don't want to be seen," Eric Burdon once asked him when they chatting over a drink at The Marquee, "why do you dress like a peacock?"

"*This,*" Terry replied, running his hand over his latest dandy outfit, "is not for the public, it's for my artists. They need to see me as flamboyantly successful, as the one who has his finger on the pulse of fashion *and* pop."

Something else nobody ever saw were his occasional panic attacks, when bits of his memory went AWOL. As Terry's car floated towards Marble Arch, he felt an attack coming on, his mind went blank and he couldn't recall anything which came before these last few months. As usual, he blamed the chemicals he'd been regularly ingesting at various night clubs and parties, and gradually the memories began floating back into his brain like birds settling on a lake.

Terry sat back into the polished black leather, the panic over for now, and reflected on how great it was to be at the heart of things, when London was at its grooviest. Clubs like The Scene, The Marquee, The Ad-Lib and the Bag 'O Nails were the go-to joints for The Beatles, Jagger, and Townshend, along with everyone else who was part of the In-Crowd. He could be sitting with a Scotch and Coke putting the world to rights with Graham Nash, or chatting about the latest hot tracks with Andrew Loog Oldham; Terry was now one of the golden circle, the hitmakers, a mover and a shaker on equal terms with the cream of British pop.

He often frequented the 2i's coffee bar in Old Compton Street and always bumped into some really hip people there. Last time he'd dropped in, the place had been thick with the scent of marijuana and patchouli oil. He'd waved at a few people he recognised, stopping to chat to one or two, then found a seat at a table where two pretty guys were sitting opposite, deep in conversation. They smiled as Terry sat down and the one with curly hair, trendy gear and the beautiful grin introduced himself.

"Hi man, I'm Marc, Marc Bolan," he said. "I'm a songwriter. I've just signed with Napier-Bell. He's talking about putting me in The Yardbirds."

Terry shook his hand.

"Terry Simon," he said.

"And this is my friend, David," Marc said, nodding at his skinny companion.

"Terry Simon, the songwriter?" David said, looking a little awed. "The 'one-man Lennon-McCartney'?"

Terry noticed his eyes - one was blue, the other green.

"Yep, that's me," he replied, rather pleased that Vicki's recent quote in Record Retailer had stuck.

David stood up, his cheesecloth flowered shirt and tight-fitting hipsters emphasising his skeletal figure, and bowed rather grandly.

"Far-out, man!" he said, extending his hand across the table. "I'm David Bowie."

He took a drag from his cigarette a la Lauren Bacall and blew out a couple of smoke rings. Then sitting down, crossing his legs as though he was being interviewed he said,

"My band's called The Buzz. I've got a single out on Pye – The Searchers' label, as fate would have it."

He grinned, revealing vampire-like teeth which Terry thought should probably be fixed if he wanted to be a pop star.

"We're going to be famous," Marc said, putting his arm round David's shoulder. "It's just… who's gonna make it first?"

He shook his curls as though preparing for a close-up.

"Of course it'll be me," he said, staring at Terry as though challenging him to disagree. "I'm the prettiest star."

"Hm," David said, "that's a great song title."

He mimed writing on his hand.

"Note to self," he murmured.

"What's your single called?" Terry asked David.

"'Do Anything You Say', I wrote it, Tony Hatch produced it."

"The Pet Clark guy?" Marc said, fluttering his eyes. "I met her at one of Napier-Bell's parties. She's a pretty cool chick… for an old lady."

He burst out laughing and David threw his head back, screeching above the noise of chatter around them.

"Well, boys," Terry said, leaning forward, "I don't want to be unkind but the fact is, she's in the charts right now – and, er, you're not."

Marc pouted at Terry.

"Ooh, get you, old man!" he said, giving him the once-over.

"Well, my friends," David announced, getting up. "I'm off downstairs to show what a future star I am, as well as earn a useful crust! I'll be playing my latest 45, don't you know."

He stared at Terry.

"Coming, dear?"

"No, he always sits like that," Marc said, and the two of them howled like banshees.

Watching David sitting cross-legged on the stage and trilling his song to a largely uninterested smattering of people, Terry thought he certainly had charisma, but his song wasn't up to much.

"What d'you think?" Marc asked him.

"Nice try but no cigar," Terry replied.

"Mm. He's written better songs. But he's playing at The Marquee with Syd Barrett's band tomorrow night."

"The Pink Floyd?"

"Yeah, it'll be a gas. I love Syd's songs, so out-there, and their light show is a mind-blow, man."

To muted applause, David stood up, did his pantomime bow and swished off stage.

"This place is *over*, man," he said petulantly, as he joined Marc and Terry.

Turning towards the sparse audience, he cupped his hands and shouted,

"Look out, you rock 'n' rollers!"

With a huff, he strode up the stairs, leaving Marc and Terry to follow.

"Oh dear," Marc said giggling. "Madame's having a strop."

"With the right song," Terry said, as they climbed the stairs, "Bowie could be huge. Maybe I should write him something?"

Marc stopped, fell against the wall and laughed out loud.

"Honey *chile*," he said, tapping Terry's nose. "Don't even *think* about it. David is first and foremost a songwriter."

"Just not a very successful one," Terry replied.

"Oh, give him time," Marc said, reaching the top of the stairs. "David is going to be stratospheric, man."

Terry's limo had hit a traffic jam on Oxford Street and Chas was leaning his head out to see what the hold-up was, shouting, 'What the fuck's going on?', prompting the recollection of a conversation with Brian Jones at the Bag O'Nails.

"I sometimes wonder what the fuck's going on," he'd told Brian, trying to explain his occasional feelings of detachment and the disturbing blanks in his memories.

Brian's response had been heartening.

"Oh man, that happens to us all, y'know. All the chemicals fuck with the mind. I sometimes find it hard to remember who I am."

He'd grabbed his head in mock horror.

"Hey, man, am I a Stone or a Beatle? Or maybe I'm a Small Face!"

They'd both fallen about laughing, high on some great weed Brian had shared with him in the Gents.

George Harrison, who had been sitting nearby with Neil Aspinall, leaned over and said, "I was told by some guy who's been taking acid for months, that once you've had your first trip you're never the same again."

"Isn't that a little disturbing," Neil had said.

"No, man," Brian had chuckled. "It's a groove. I needed a change anyway so…"

At that he burst into a fit of coughing and loud uncontrollable laughter, just as Donovan was walking past. He came over to join them, asking what had amused Brian so much. Terry told him what they'd been discussing, and Donovan nodded enthusiastically. He told them that during a recent recording trip to the States, he'd met up with a guy called Ulric Neisser, an American psychologist who was researching different aspects of memory.

"This dude was fascinating," Donovan said. "He believes that memory represents an active process of reconstruction, rather than a passive reproduction of the past."

Everyone looked puzzled, George though was especially interested.

"You mean… we create our own versions of what we remember?" he asked.

Donovan smiled appreciatively at him.

"I love you, George," he enthused, "you're always right there, man. Neisser told me that our memories are like editing a movie, just leaving in the bits which we like and altering the narrative."

"Is it a conscious thing?" Terry asked him.

"Not sure, he's still doing research, but I said I'd look Ulric up next time I'm in the States and find out more – could be a great subject for a song."

Neil Aspinall leaned forward and said to Terry, "So, what *do* you remember?"

Terry took a long drag on his cigarette.

"Not much. I have this image of someone, like a misty figure, sitting in this enormous room telling me about my past. But the details come and go and never feel real, you know?"

"Wow, man, maybe you're a spy who's been drugged to forget your real life," Brian said, clearly very stoned by now.

"Brian," George said. "Terry's freaking out enough, don't make it worse."

Brian chuckled and lay his head on the back of the seat, staring into a space only he could see.

Terry smiled indulgently at Brian as George asked Donovan what he'd been up to lately. When he said he'd just been to Paul McCartney's house where they'd been writing a children's song together, George mumbled that he didn't much like the sound of that.

"Here's a taster of a line I came up with," Donovan said

"Did someone mention a line…?", Brian asked through half-closed eyes.

"'*Sky of blue and sea of green*'," Donovan sang

happily, telling them, "It's going to be a song for the kiddies."

"We're a pop group," George grumbled, "not children's fucking entertainers."

"'*In our yellow submarine*'," Donovan trilled, beaming at everyone.

"Fuck me," George said, shaking his head, "fucking Macca."

As the guys continued to chat amongst themselves, Terry's mind wandered to the cold January morning when he'd woken up on a bench in Soho Square looking up at a smiling Phil May. It was his clearest recollection, the first one which felt like it had really happened to him, rather than a selective memory recall.

He'd been having a weird dream, where an elderly bloke was asking him, 'What year do you want to live in?', before they landed in Denmark Street and the old man had walked off towards Charing Cross Road, waved and disappeared. As he sat up and felt an Arctic breeze blowing around him, Terry felt very groggy, muddled and unbelievably exhausted.

"Morning Terry old man," Phil said. "Hard night?"

For a few moments, Terry wondered why the lead singer of The Pretty Things should be chatting to him like he knew him. And 'Terry' sounded odd, like Phil was addressing someone else.

"You look like you need a kip and a bath," Phil was saying. "I understand your landlady's thrown you out of your flat. Come back to my place, you can stay in the spare room for now."

"Yeah…" Terry said, still feeling dazed. "That sounds ace."

As he was trying to recall being kicked out of his flat, and wondering where it was, Phil said, "We need you fit and strong for the next set of gigs, man. You're the best roadie we've got, we have to look after you."

Terry had enjoyed the next few weeks, soaking up the atmosphere of the groovy pad in Montagu Square. Pop stars, producers and record company guys were always wandering in and out, smoking a few joints, playing music and putting the world to rights.

One morning, when Phil was sleeping in, Terry picked up a guitar which was leaning against the settee. He began strumming away, singing a song he´d never heard before, but vaguely knowing it was his, when a voice said, "Wow, man, that's a great song. Did you write it?"

Phil was standing in the doorway lighting a cigarette.

"Yeah," Terry replied, a bit embarrassed at being discovered playing one of the band's guitars. "Yeah. It's mine."

"It's fabulous, man," Phil said. "You may be an old bloke and our roadie but you´ve got talent."

A couple of nights later, Phil invited Terry to the 100 Club.

"Georgie Fame's playing," he told him. "There's going to be a lot of influential people at the gig. You never know, they may be looking for songs."

And he was right, fate definitely stepped in that night in the shape of Vicki Palmer.

Chas's voice saying 'we're here Mr. Simon,' roused Terry from his reveries as they arrived at Pye Studios in Great Cumberland Place. Thanking Chas and asking him to pick him up at six o'clock, Terry strode in, ready to start work on what he was sure would be *the* album of the year.

He was making his way to Studio 1 when he saw The Kinks' Pete Quaife walking towards him.

"Terry Simon!" Pete shouted, "I didn't know you were here today."

Shaking Pete's hand, Terry said, "Yeah, we're starting on The Searchers' new album. What are you up to?"

"Just working on Ray's latest song, 'Sunny Afternoon' it´s called. It sounds like a smash to me. Fancy a quick listen?"

Terry checked his watch.

"Sure, I'd love to."

He followed Pete along the corridor into Studio 2, where through the control room window he could see Ray and Dave Davies working on a guitar figure. Ray looked up, waved at Terry and said to the engineer, "Okay, let's try doing an overdub."

The tape op pressed record and, even in its early stages, Terry knew this was going to be massive. It had a great music-hall vibe, and as the follow-up to the recently huge 'Dedicated Follower of Fashion', there seemed no doubt that this new winning streak for The Kinks was going to last for some time.

Terry shook Pete's hand, gave a thumbs-up to Ray and Dave and dashed off to his own session, full of ideas for the first song The Searchers would be recording that day, 'Time Waits For No-One'.

The first person he saw as he entered Studio 1 was Vicki, who got up and kissed him on the cheek. They were fast becoming much more than publisher/

songwriter, and already there were murmurings in the music business about their growing romance.

"The boys are here and all set up," Vicki said.

Terry saw Mike Pender, Chris Curtis, John McNally and Frank Allen obviously running through the song.

"Can you put the studio intercom on?" Terry asked the engineer.

"Sure."

"Hi guys," he said. "Are you ready to try a take?"

"Yep, and good morning, music man," Mike replied.

The four of them looked at each other and nodded, Chris counted them in, and they were off.

With the group's trademark harmonies and jingle jangle guitars – which Terry had no doubt had influenced The Byrds - it sounded fabulous. Vicki leaned into Terry and said that this could be the next single.

"Believe me, Vicki, they will all sound like the next single when the album's finished," Terry replied.

Chapter Seventeen

By 1968, the pop scene had moved away from psychedelia and mind-bending productions. Terry's 'trippy drugged-out' material was considered dated and ending up at most on 'B' sides. Which meant that he had increasingly less involvement in the production, record companies wanting a simpler, pared-back sound to appeal to a new generation of teenagers.

Though he still earned good money from the royalties of one of his songs being on a hit record, albeit not the 'A' side, Terry hated seeing the kudos shifting away from him and began descending into sudden mood shifts and spending late boozy nights in Soho.

To the surprise of many of her friends and colleagues, Vicki and Terry were married in the Autumn of 1970, a photo of them emerging from the registry office appearing on the inside page of Melody Maker. Although the photo showed Vicki beaming at the camera in a trouser suit specially designed for her by gentleman's fashion king Tommy Nutter, Terry's face was blurred as he'd turned to speak to someone behind him just as the photographer had snapped the shot.

During their wedding night in Crete, he began complaining that hardly anyone from the press were at the reception.

"Cilla and Bobby's wedding made the six o'clock news," he moaned, downing his umpteenth glass of champagne.

"Why does publicity suddenly mean so much to you?" Vicki asked him. "It never did before."

"Yes, but I didn't need the publicity when I was making hit records," he replied gloomily. "I do now."

"Oh, so you only asked me to marry you for the publicity?" Vicki said, as the Grecian dawn broke on their doomed relationship.

Terry's refusal to say, instead storming out to the sunrise beach bar, was her answer.

As the months went by, Vicki tried to ignore the situation, unable to admit to herself that she'd made a huge mistake marrying this man. She spent her days at the office and her evenings in meetings with managers, producers and A & R men, while Terry stayed at home, devouring uppers and downers like candy and eating countless packets of jelly babies. His weight began to fall alarmingly and the muscled, fit man she'd met in 1966 was now a shadow of his former self. He was usually fast asleep on the settee when Vicki got home, she'd cover him up and tiptoe up to bed, occasionally hearing him shout in his sleep until the early hours.

Then suddenly, around late '71, Terry seemed to get a new creative lease of life and, over the course of several months, began to make plans for his 'dream album', *A Psychedelic Symphony*. It became an obsession and, when he wasn't knocking back booze and acid, he was banging away on his keyboard in the bedroom, creating something which sounded to Vicki like spoons crashing to the floor.

Vicki tried her best to talk Terry out of the project, but he was adamant. Even when she adopted the slightly harsher tactic of telling Terry that Psychedelia had died with '67, he wouldn't be swayed. He demanded Vicki play his home demos to record companies and, although she did, she would come back every evening with the same response.

"They're simply not convinced, Terry. They won't spend the money on something they don't believe in."

In fact, all the big labels had turned her down.

"Why are you putting yourself in this position, Vicki?" one A & R man asked her, switching off his cassette player before the second song had begun. "I hate saying 'no' to you, you've always had such great taste. But, this really is a load of dated trash. And, you think so too."

It was at that point that Vicki decided enough was enough. She wouldn't allow her reputation to be ruined by a delusional, sick man who needed rehab rather than a hit. She went home and told her husband that the charade, the dream, as Lennon had sung on his debut LP, was over. Of course, Terry threw a strop and slammed out of the house, on his way to get wasted with anyone who would join him at some Soho dive's toilet cistern.

Later that evening, he was seen standing in the pouring rain outside an electrical goods shop in Shepherd's Bush, shouting at the TVs in the window silently broadcasting Top of The Pops for passers-by on their way home. T.Rex were performing their latest chart-topper, 'Telegram Sam', and Terry was shouting that he'd known Marc 'when he was *nothing*! But *I* knew. I *knew* he'd be a star.'

Ironically, it had been The Searchers' Mike Pender who, stuck in a traffic jam on his way home to Acton, recognised his old producer clearly in a bad way. He got out of the car and coaxed Terry into the back seat, settling him in and telling him that Vicki was waiting for him.

"She doesn't fucking care anymore," Terry drunkenly mumbled, as Mike made his way to Kensington, to take the once mighty songwriting legend home to the only person who could help him.

***

Over the next few weeks, Vicki began looking into a selection of top-notch rehab places which had been recommended to her, and eventually chose a clinic out in Surrey. Though it cost the Earth, it seemed to promise the best personal care required for a man who needed the kind of support her world could no longer offer. There was a waiting list, but they agreed to take Terry in the August of '72.

On the eve of Terry entering the exclusive clinic, Vicki took him to the Top Of The Pops studio, as a thank-you for agreeing to give rehab a try. She thought it would be something he could enjoy like the old days, and maybe chat to some of the artists appearing that night, rediscovering a connection to a world he'd looked on as increasingly alien.

It was all going quite well, Terry seeming to enjoy the atmosphere and bopping away to the latest hits by Alice Cooper, Mott The Hoople and Derek & The Dominoes. He even got a real fillip when The Electric Light Orchestra appeared, performing their first hit, the Beatles '67-styled '10538 Overture'.

Terry cheered when they'd finished, shouting, "At last, Psychedelia is back!"

He turned to Vicki, beaming away.

"I told you it was only a matter of time."

He happily followed Vicki backstage after the show, and, much to Terry's delight, Roy Wood was standing by his dressing-room door chatting to Jeff Lynne. The last time he'd seen Roy was when The Move's 'I Can Hear The Grass Grow' was in the charts five years earlier, and he'd met Jeff when he was in The Idle Race, a band Terry had loved.

While Terry excitedly regaled Roy and Jeff about his *Psychedelic Symphony*, 'which I know you'll love', out of the corner of her eye, Vicki saw David Bowie laughing with Ian Hunter, clearly pleased with Mott The Hoople's performance of his song 'All The Young Dudes', which was climbing the charts.

To Vicki's horror, Terry did a loud yelp and, leaving Roy and Jeff looking mystified, he rushed down the corridor, his arms outspread, yelling,

"David! *David*! It's me! Remember me? Terry Simon from the 2i's!"

Vicki ran after him shouting at him to stop while a security guard, who'd heard the commotion, suddenly appeared and threw himself at her husband, wrestling him to the ground.

"He won't hurt anyone," Vicki pleaded, "He'll be fine, honestly. Let him go. Please?"

The security guard reluctantly released Terry as Vicki bent down and rocked him in her arms.

"I knew, Vicki," Terry moaned. "I knew he'd make it."

"You did, mate," a voice said.

It was David. He knelt down beside Vicki and squeezed Terry's arm.

"Terry, me old mate," he said, "of course I remember you. The One-Man Lennon-McCartney. Lovely to see you again. Marc's in New York but I'm sure he'd send you his love. Now, let's get you up on your feet and then your lovely wife can take you home to a nice warm bed."

He helped Terry up and turned to Vicki.

"Have you got a car here?" he asked her.

"Yes, thank you, David, I have. You're very kind."

"No problem, Vicki. Get this great man home. The pop scene has a lot to thank him for."

He grinned again at Terry, those vampire teeth still gleaming as they had back in '66.

"Goodnight, my friend," he said. "Sleep tight."

Watching Vicki escort a sobbing Terry towards the stage door, David went back to join Ian.

"One of the greatest songwriters ever," he said. "There but for the grace of God…"

Chapter Eighteen

Terry was diagnosed as having had a psychotic collapse and stayed in the rehab clinic for three months, Vicki visiting him whenever she could. During one of her visits, Terry told her he was thinking of moving to L.A.

"I know the scene over there is so much more in tune with what I'm into," he told her. "They're such progressive cats in California."

He grabbed her arm and squeezed it.

"Come on, Vicki, let's go find a new life."

She nodded encouragingly, saying that when he was back home they'd talk about it. But by the time Terry had left the clinic just before Christmas he seemed to have forgotten that particular dream.

Sadly, the respite didn't last, and, in the Spring of 1973, Terry announced he was leaving her, saying, "There's clearly nothing between us anymore, except your refusal to help me get my career back."

It had surprised but not shocked Vicki. A music business colleague had recently confided in her that Terry spent most days going from bar to bar, telling whoever would listen that he was relocating to America 'where they'll really get me, unlike my bloody wife'.

On a rainy morning in April, she drove him to the airport, waved him goodbye and watched him wandering through passport control looking like something The Bonzo Dog Band had dragged in. She never saw him again.

Their separation was mentioned in a tiny piece at the back of the NME, but apart from that not a single newspaper or music magazine covered their split.

Terry was killed in a car crash in Laurel Canyon in 1983, driving a friend's beaten up old Cadillac too quickly round a bend. The car plummeted down a ravine close to Cass Elliott's old house, where she'd once entertained the likes of Joni Mitchell, Stephen Stills and David Crosby. So, while Terry may not have reached the heights of such superstars, he ended his days amongst their music still shimmering in the trees, their glorious harmonies humming in the California breeze.

Vicki had Terry's body flown back to the UK and oversaw his sparsely attended funeral in Bouncer's Lane Cemetery in Cheltenham. He was buried, as per his wishes, near the recently-deceased Brian Jones.

"Brian was the psychedelic Stone," he'd once said. "*He* understood me. If he'd have lived we were going to make an album together. It was a promise he made the last time I saw him."

As she'd stood at Terry's graveside, she remembered their last conversation, when he'd called Vicki a few months before his death. Telling her how much he missed her, he said that he was thinking about returning to London. However, it soon became clear why he'd called. She'd recently bought a recording studio in Basing Street which had once been owned by Micki Most, and, having read about the purchase in Billboard, he'd rung her one last time to try his luck.

"Your new studio sounds amazing, Vicki," he'd enthused. "Perfect for me to make my dream album."

As he'd chattered away about what he'd need for the session, the musicians he had in mind and how many months he'd require the studio to be booked for, she sat behind her desk looking at Terry's gold discs on the wall. The last one had been awarded over fifteen years ago, silently marking the end of an era.

When Terry had finally stopped talking, she told him, as gently as she could, that there was nothing for him in London or the British pop scene anymore. It began the usual release of bile and vitriol when Terry couldn't get his own way. As he called her all the names under the sun, it was confirmation that it wasn´t her that he missed, she was simply his only route back to reclaiming those vaulted, long-gone highs.

On the morning of Terry's death, Vicki was parking her Alpha Romeo in her reserved space in Soho Square, outside the building Original had moved to a few years earlier. As always, Radio One was playing and she was about to switch it off when a piece about Terry by Annie Nightingale came on. As she sat listening, she noticed Ginny Taylor running up the steps into Original.

They'd met the day before when Vicki had been walking up the large spiral staircase, which ran down the centre of the building. She'd heard footsteps behind her and turned to see a pretty Audrey Hepburn lookalike dashing up the stairs. She was immediately reminded of Trudi, her old singing partner, and, when Ginny spoke, the likeness was even stronger.

"I'm just on my way to the music copying room," she'd said breathlessly, "to pick up a tape of songs I want to play to Bananarama."

She explained that she'd started at Original a few days earlier as a song plugger and, smiling shyly, added,

"And you, of course, are the legendary Vicki Palmer."

"Guilty," Vicki replied. "And do you know that when I first started out in publishing, I was a song plugger for Chappell's. I absolutely loved it."

"It's such a buzz, isn't it?" Ginny said, introducing herself.

"Very nice to meet you, Ginny," Vicki replied, shaking her hand.

Ginny seemed to hesitate then said, "It's kind of because of my mum that I'm here."

Vicki then knew her hunch had been right.

"You must be Trudi's daughter," she said. "You are *so* like her."

Ginny smiled.

"A lot of people say that."

"How *is* your mum? I haven't seen her for… oh, much too long."

"She's fine. I know she'd send her love. She has fond memories of your times together."

Vicki smiled affectionately.

"The last time I saw Trudi was in 1965. She'd rung to ask me out to lunch at Mirabelle, and told me she was pregnant… with you!"

Ginny did a little curtsy.

"When I told her I wanted to work in music publishing, she suggested I apply for a job here."

"She should have called me to let me know," Vicki said.

"No, Mum was very insistent that I get the job without any special favours. She said you'd respect me much more for that."

"She was right – as always. Your mum is a very wise woman. I always regretted losing touch with her, but our lives became so different, and then she and Andrew moved out of London to…".

"Esher," Ginny said. "They were determined to bring me up surrounded by fields rather than office blocks."

"And yet… here you are."

"I yearned for office blocks."

The two women laughed.

"Dear Trudi," Vicki said. "Helluva voice she had too. Please send her my love?"

"Of course."

As they went their separate ways an idea struck Vicki.

"Er - would you like to come to the A & R meeting on Friday? I think you'd get a lot out of it."

"Oh my, I'd love to, Miss Palmer," Ginny said, eyes widening.

"Vicki, please. All my favourite people call me Vicki. See you at ten on Friday morning. Bring your ears with you!"

Chapter Nineteen

'There was a huge turn-out for Vicki's funeral, many of Original's songwriters and the artists who'd recorded their songs were there, spanning the decades of her amazing career. They packed the chapel at Bouncer's Lane in Cheltenham, to bid her a last farewell.

Vicki and I had only sporadically been in touch in recent years, for the usual reason. She simply didn't want to see Simon. Her meeting him at the I-Candy bash in 2002 had completely freaked her out and, as she couldn't explain it, she instead avoided it. We thereafter only ever met 'a deux' where I would, out of consideration for her, not mention Simon.

However, it became increasingly difficult because, as he and I got closer and eventually engaged, it meant that what would normally be a large part of any conversation between friends, we simply didn't discuss. As had happened with Suze, my relationship with Simon resulted in me losing contact with one of my closest pals.

She'd not attended our wedding in 2007, and our get-togethers over the next few years became even more sporadic. When we did meet up it was usually at Fortnum & Mason's in Piccadilly, the food was good and it was handy for me, about a ten minute walk from the office. But our last lunch there a few months earlier had been an odd mix of enjoyable and confrontational.

We'd just ordered our starters, a melon salad with a ginger and demerara sauce, and were chatting about what she was up to as a retired lady of means, and, of course, my news about the latest happenings at Original were always of interest to her. The atmosphere was actually very congenial, so I decided to broach the subject of

Simon again, though this time to admit that she'd been right about him. But, as usual, before I'd got beyond mentioning his name, she did her dismissive wave of the hand thing.

Feeling rather annoyed, I said, "Please don't do that, Vicki."

She just grumbled and said,

"Let's move on, shall we?"

"To where?" I asked her, rather tetchily. "The past?"

Just then, a fluttery old lady wandered by going towards the door, and stopped to fiddle in her handbag as though she'd lost something.

"Are you alright?" I asked her.

She chuckled, a little embarrassed and said, "Oh yes. I thought I'd forgotten my purse, but it's here. Silly me. Well, good day."

Vicki watched her leave and muttered, "Nosey old dear, I hope I never get like that, a fussy old biddy."

I laughed and told her she looked too fabulous to ever become fussy or an old biddy, and it cleared the air. Now in her mid-seventies, she resembled a very well-kept Dusty Springfield. Her back was still ramrod straight, her blonde hair perfectly coiffured by her favourite stylist in Knightsbridge, her make-up always impeccably applied, and her outfits, from her amazing collection of designer '60s gear, fitting her like a glove.

As the waitress brought our starters, I mentioned that I'd seen Mum a few days earlier and she'd sent her love, and that Dad was writing a book about The Honeybees.

"He wants to interview you for the book," I told Vicki, to which she giggled and said her stories would fill the book alone.

"What's it called?" Vicki asked.

"'Shame On You – They Should've Been Stars'," I replied.

Vicki threw back her head and laughed out loud.

"Fabulous title!" she said. "'Shame On You' was so very nearly a hit. It does sound rather twee now, sadly."

"Do we have the publishing?"

"No, it's with Chappell's. We recorded it in 1960, Johnny Worth wrote it for us. It was a lovely recording session, Hank Marvin played guitar, Jet Harris was on bass, Tony Meehan played drums and Norrie Paramor produced it. We sang it on tour and performed it on *Thank Your Lucky Stars*, and it felt like it was going to be big, but the kids didn't go for it."

Vicki began shimmying in her seat and trilling the hook, 'you're a naughty, naughty boy, shame on you', complete with all the moves. When the waiter arrived to clear our plates, smiling to himself, she pouted at him and said, 'just living some memories, darling. You have all yours ahead of you'.

"I think you're fabulous," he said. "Is your outfit original?"

"Mary Quant, 1965."

"Amazing!"

"She is," I told him.

He beamed at Vicki and, recovering himself with a little cough, asked if we had decided on main courses.

"Yes," Vicki replied, "we'll have the salmon in dill sauce with new potatoes, please."

He looked at me.

"For both you ladies?"

"Yes," I replied chuckling, "I always let Vicki choose what we eat here. She's never wrong."

With another admiring smile at Vicki he went off to

place the order.

We went back to chatting about Dad's book, which he'd shown me a rough draft of, and I told Vicki it really captured the early '60s when everyone felt the future held something exciting.

"We did," she said. "I feel extremely sorry for kids today, the future doesn't look anywhere near as bright for them."

"Dad would love to get some of your memories in there," I said.

"Well, tell him to call me," Vicki replied.

Sadly he left it too late.

The main course tasted delicious and as we munched away, we chatted about some rather extensive new decoration she was planning for her house in Kensington – 'it needs a complete make-over' - and her trip to the South of France later in the year.

After our scrumptious crème caramels with lashings of whipped cream, and two lattes with chocolate chip toppings, I was full to bursting. Vicki asked for the bill but I insisted on paying. Against her nature, Vicki demurred adding, "But I will buy you a little treat… through there…"

She pointed to the Food Hall and got up.

"I have a wander round here every so often," she said, going towards the hall which opened out behind the restaurant. "Usually on my own but as you're here…"

This was the most enjoyable part of our get-together. Chatting about how much she loved the place, she sauntered in and approached an extremely smartly-dressed chap who virtually stood to attention when he saw her.

"Hello, Home Delivery, please?" she said to him.

"Of course, madam," he replied, bowing his head slightly.

"Here's my card," Vicki said.

"Oh, excellent. Yes, Kensington. Marvellous. Thank you, madam."

She then went from counter to counter, pointing out things which she'd bought in the past, and those 'which you should really try, Ginny', while telling me about Fortnum's home delivery service.

"You select and pay, they package everything up and it'll be at my door within two hours of ordering."

"Fantastic," I muttered following her around the hall, feeling like a child out on a magic shopping spree with Mummy.

First she picked a selection of cheeses, then went onto another counter where, licking her lips, she ordered some Scotch Eggs, rolling her eyes at how delicious the caramelised ones were. When the sales assistant offered her a taste of the new Chickpea, Feta and Red Pepper selection, she immediately added it to her order.

"Are you having people to stay?" I asked her, as she moved onto the potted Welsh Rarebit, buying two pots.

"My neighbours are having a big anniversary do this evening," she explained, "and guests are asked to bring something for their buffet. They always spoil me rotten when I go there for lunch so…"

She was suddenly distracted by the fabulous array of hampers by the wall and cooed with delight at the cheese and chutney hamper.

"Oh my," she said. "I must get one of those for Christmas. And they also do a vegan one. Pinky and Beau will love that!"

'Who are all these friends of hers I've never met?' I asked myself.

Then she led me into the chocolate section, a veritable mouth-watering sweet-tooth display, offering nights in alone with a great weepy movie, stuffing oneself in between wiping one's eyes.

"Ginny," Vicki said, pointing at the marzipan and petit fours, "let me buy you some of those. They are to *die* for."

I tried to say no, but she was already picking out several for me, the counter assistant boxing and wrapping them rather beautifully in an embossed gold and green paper and handing the package to me.

She then purchased a box of truffles and a gorgeous-looking selection box of chocolate creams of all flavours.

"Your neighbours are going to love you when you turn up with all this," I said, as she walked us through to the Preserves and Marmalades.

"Oh, this is not all for them, they're my treats too, and one or two old music biz friends regularly pop in for a coffee and a natter and always wolf everything down."

I suddenly felt very saddened by the fact that my relationship with Simon had ended such social possibilities with Vicki. I silently blamed him yet again for spoiling the life I could have had without him.

After a delightful half-an-hour of perusing, tasting and adding to Vicki's 'Delivery Box', we paid a visit to the rather sumptuous Ladies, complete with hot lemon-scented hand refresher towelettes and the air aroma'd by what smelt like Sandalwood and Ginger.

Finally we went outside and manoeuvred across a rather busy Piccadilly. As we stood chatting for a few minutes, I briefly glanced down the road at an elderly couple in the distance walking towards Hyde Park Corner. The gait of the man looked like Jack's, the tilt of his head too was similar, and I was about to mention it to Vicki when she said, "Oh God, it's that nosey old woman from Fortnum's."

I hadn't noticed her, but, sure enough, looking in the window of a Budweiser bar a couple of blocks down the road was the lady who had been fussing in her handbag. She kept looking up at the sign above the door and shaking her head.

"Is she stalking us?" Vicki said. "Come on, walk with me to the tube so we can get away from her."

I glanced down Piccadilly to see if the old couple were still there, but they'd gone, at which point 'fluffy biddy' saw us, waved and began walking towards us.

"Come on, let's go," Vicki said.

"We can't just walk off," I replied, "that would be very rude."

"Well, that's new," the old lady said as she reached us, a little out of breath. "I'm sure it used to be a drapery shop."

She glanced back towards the bar and chuckled.

"Everything in London changes so quickly, doesn't it? I wanted to buy a couple of their rather nice gingham tablecloths, but never mind."

"Time marches on," Vicki said pointedly.

"It certainly does," the old lady said. "But don't let me stop you, you're clearly keen to be on your way."

I smiled to myself as she came a little closer.

"Excuse me being forward, dear" she said to me, "but has anyone ever told you that you favour Audrey Hepburn?"

"Many times," I replied, thinking what a lovely,

rather comforting person she was. "My first husband especially."

She twinkled at me.

"I´m sure," she said and then turned to Vicki. "And you, my dear, are the spitting image of –"

"Ginny!" Vicki almost shouted. "We *really* need to go."

"I´m sorry," I said to the old lady. "We must…"

"Oh yes, time waits for no-one," she replied cheerfully.

She waved a cab down, and, as she got in, smiled at me.

"You didn´t have to be so rude," I told Vicki, waving at the old lady as her cab swept by. "I thought she was a delightful old thing."

"Ginny darling," Vicki said, "you´ve always been excellent with *everyone*, while I long ago accepted that I am not."

When we got to Piccadilly Station, she pecked me on the cheek, said we must meet up again soon and hurried down the steps to the tube.

***

The service wasn't particularly religious. Vicki, a staunch atheist, would have only reluctantly agreed to us gathering in a church to say farewell. She was simply carrying out her ex-husband's wish that she be buried beside him.

As it turned out, the setting and the service were absolutely perfect, full of fun and laughter. There were stories about Vicki's life and career, including some extremely fruity tales which the lady vicar definitely chuckled at.

For me, and I know I'm biased, the best eulogy was from my mum. Trudi looked great that day, wearing an Yves Saint-Laurent two-piece tweed suit that Vicki had given her as a twenty-first birthday gift. The colour, royal blue, perfectly matched Mum's beautiful eyes. Like Vicki, Mum had kept her figure and always looked great in her '60s gear, which of course made her extremely cool to her friends' grand-kids.

She told some wonderful stories about their days as The Honeybees, touring with pop stars of the day, recording at Abbey Road 'when it was still known as EMI Studios and the engineers looked more like research scientists in their white coats', and, a tale I hadn't heard before, having dinner with Eddie Cochran and Gene Vincent during their fateful tour of the UK in 1961.

"I was sorely tempted to become Mrs. Cochran," Mum told a transfixed congregation, "but my dreams were shattered by the fact that Eddie was engaged."

Then she glanced down at Dad and me in the front row and said, "And, of course, I had met the love of my life by then."

A ripple of 'Aahs' rang around the church, Dad giving me one of his proud 'she's mine' smiles.

"Vicki quite liked the idea of tying the knot with Gene," Mum went on, "but decided she couldn't bear the thought of becoming Vicki Vincent. 'Darling!' she'd said at the back of the coach travelling to our next gig, 'I couldn't ever entertain being V.V. for the rest of my life. It sounds like an STD!'"

Everyone burst out laughing and it felt very cathartic. Mum was clearly enjoying the reaction and firmly in her stride.

"Now, 'Vicki Wilde' she wouldn't have minded. But

Marty, gorgeous boy, was already taken –" and here Mum looked over at Joyce and Marty Wilde behind us and winked at them – "and anyway, he wasn't on the tour."

Mum got a round of applause for her fabulous slice of nostalgia, and for reminding us all that Vicki was so many things to so many people.

I had toyed with doing a little speech of my own but decided against it, and anyway I couldn't have topped Mick Fleetwood's outrageous stories of a particular weekend in Glasgow in 1977.

Apparently, Vicki had been there to see one of her singer-songwriters, who was supporting Fleetwood Mac on their 'Rumours' tour. There'd been shenanigans galore at the after-show party, which may make it into Mick's memoirs one day.

"There'd been more bowlfuls of keys than cocaine," Mick had joked, glancing over at the vicar who gave him a 'naughty boy' face, clearly enjoying her church being full of such glamorous and famous people.

As we all gathered outside, Vicki was laid in the ground, dressed, so Mum told me, in an André Courrèges outfit she'd worn for The Beatles´ Royal Variety performance in 1963. It was the night when John had told the rich folk in the audience to rattle their jewellery, winning over a nation watching it on TV.

After everyone had left, Mum and I stood at the grave with its rather grand Gothic headstone bearing Terry's name and the words 'Elusive Butterfly' underneath.

"The engraver's still got to add Vicki's name," Mum said.

"Did you know him," I asked her, "Terry Simon?"

"No, she told me about him on the phone, and to be honest I was surprised to hear her clearly falling in love. It wasn´t something I´d ever expected Vicki to do."

"What? Fall in love?"

"No, not Vicki. That had never seemed part of her plan. She'd had quite a few boyfriends, many of them obviously mad about her, but as soon as things started to get serious she´d end the relationship. Vicki was so ambitious, dead-set on making her own way in life, romance for her just got in the way."

"Was the marriage successful?"

"Not really. I think, from the way she talked about Terry, Vicki was actually in love with his songwriting."

She looked at the headstone.

"Interesting that she brought his body back and had him buried here. It proves that she did care for him, in her own Vicki kind of way."

"I wonder what wording will be added?" I said, as we stared at the mound with bundles of flowers lying across it.

"Probably her favourite motto - 'Stick it to 'em, ladies.'"

As we were both laughing, my vision suddenly blurred. I blinked to clear my eyes and the words, 'Here lie Vicki Palmer 1939-2012 and Terry Simon 1937-1983, together in music at last', appeared on the gravestone as if out of a mist.

When my vision cleared, the headstone was back to normal, just showing the original inscription.

Feeling a bit unsettled, but not wanting to worry Mum, I said,

"Can we sit down for a bit? It was rather hot in the

church."

We wandered along to a bench on the path and settled into a shared silence. Opposite us was the grave of Brian Jones. I'd heard rumours that he and Vicki had once been an item and asked Mum if she knew anything. She chuckled and said, "I once plucked up the courage to ask her about it, around the time The Stones had just released 'Satisfaction'. She just gave me one of her giggles and that wide-eyed look which always meant 'Off limits, darling'."

"I'd loved to have known Vicki then," I said.

"She was a true trailblazer. I was always sorry we lost touch. When I found out I was pregnant with you and we moved out of London, it also meant saying farewell to Vicki."

"It didn't have to be farewell," I said, "you could have seen each other occasionally. London's not that far from Esher."

"I know, but we had different life plans, different lives. We did try to keep in touch, but I think all that domesticity, me nattering away on the phone about building cots and creating a nursery, bored her to tears."

She turned to me.

"I asked her to be your godmother, you know, but she turned it down. 'You need someone who'll be there for your child,' she told me, 'and I simply don't do children, darling.'"

Mum looked into the middle distance and sighed.

"I loved Vicki but… once the crazy days were over, all we had in common were memories."

"She loved you, mum," I said, taking her hand. "She never forgot those good times."

"Good times are not enough though, Ginny, they never are."

She tapped my arm.

"But I knew she'd adore you when she finally met you, how driven you were – just like her. I always thought of her as your 'stardust mother', the one who had planted a kiss of success on you when you were in here."

She tapped her tummy.

"The last time I saw her, she kissed her hand and patted my tummy. 'Be strong and love your life', she'd said to you. I'm sure you must have heard her."

She nudged my shoulder.

"Touched by stardust definitely, my clever girl."

"You know, no-one's told me what Vicki died of," I said. "She looked okay the last time I saw her, a little tetchy perhaps and maybe a bit thinner, but apart from that…"

"A brain tumour, apparently. Very advanced and terminal when it was discovered, quite by chance. Her vision had gone a bit blurred and she went for an eye test. The optician was concerned by what he saw in the scans, sent her to a specialist, who diagnosed the tumour."

"When was this?"

"Just a few weeks ago."

"And you never told me?"

"I didn't know, darling. Not until her sister Alex phoned to tell me she'd died."

"I didn't know Vicki *had* a sister."

"Neither did I. She lives in Boston, has done for decades apparently."

"So how come she knew your number?"

"Clive gave it to her."

"Clive?"

"Vicki's legal adviser, Clive Twomey. I never knew him but Andrew did back in the day. He helped Vicki set up Original when he was working in the legal department at Chappell's. He went freelance when Vicki left the company."

"There's so much I didn't know."

"Join the club. Apparently Clive arranged for Vicki to go into a palliative care and organised her funeral, to her specific instructions. He contacted Alex to let her know Vicki had died, and gave her our number."

"Why didn't Clive let you know?"

"Alex wanted to call me, she knew how close Vicki and I had been."

"So, was she here today?" I said.

"No, she has MS, much too poorly to make the trip, poor thing. But she sounded lovely on the phone. She's quite a bit older than Vicki, in her eighties."

For a moment we both went quiet, then I said, "Vicki never talked about her past or her family."

Mum smiled.

"Once when we were in a bar, shortly after we'd started working together, I asked her if she had any siblings, but she did that dismissive wave thing and just said, 'That's the past, Trudi, let's look to the future.' I never brought it up again."

"I was wondering where you were!" Dad said behind us.

"And I was wondering when you'd appear," Mum replied.

"Catching up with a few old faces," he said, pecking Mum on the cheek. "Getting some more quotes for my book."

Mum and I got up and the three of us linked arms and walked back to their car.

"How's the book coming along?" I asked him.

"Getting there. I wish I'd been able to chat to Vicki before she died, but sadly…"

I nodded and smiled at him.

"Alex told me that their mum was a true blue royalist," Mum said.

"Really?" I asked her. "Vicki's mother? Clearly that didn't run in the genes."

"Think about it - 'Victoria' and 'Alexandra'. They also had a brother called Bertie, but he died when he was a toddler. TB apparently."

"Vicki was a woman of many secrets," I said.

As we reached the car, I told them that Simon and I had split up. Mum's response surprised me.

"He could be a little strange," she said, "but I always found him rather endearing, like a lost child."

"You're the first person who's ever said anything nice about him," I told her.

"Oh, I'm not surprised you've split up. You never wanted children when you were with Jack and I can't imagine you'd want a man-child as your husband. I knew it wouldn't last, but I thought it may do you good, to have someone who needed caring for. Jack was always your equal, that was clear from the start, but sometimes we need the opportunity to nurture the weak and the needy."

"Who was yours, Mum?" I asked her, grinning at Dad. "Your weak and needy person?"

"Certainly not your dad!" she laughed, stroking his arm.

"I guess your mum has her nurturing fix doing

voluntary work at Brinsworth House," Dad said.

"Brinsworth House?" I said. "You never told me that, Mum."

"Mum doesn´t tell you everything, darling," Dad said. "There are some things one just… does."

"It happened by chance really," Mum said. "A couple of friends of mine from the old days were in there, Pearl and Teddy and dear Kathy Kirby, and I used to visit them fairly regularly. We'd chat about the tours and the records and I was always struck by how other people would join in and share their memories with us. One afternoon, I bumped into the lovely Fluff Freeman and he suggested I become a voluntary visitor. I've been doing it for years now."

I stared at Mum, who was still a constant and delightful surprise.

"It's financed by *The Royal Variety Performance*," she said. "And some of the money earned from the phone votes on *Britain's Got Talent* helps pay for its upkeep. I never really liked Simon Cowell until one of the nurses told me that. And the fact that Vicki was a Trustee gave me a nice connection to her, albeit distantly."

"Vicki was? Really?"

"Yes, so Alex told me. She's left the whole of her estate, the house and her entire personal wealth to Brinsworth House."

"That woman is a box of secrets which has only been opened today," I said, shaking my head.

"An enigma in life *and* death," Mum said.

She moved closer to me.

"So… enough about Vicki… you're a single woman again. Any… new plans?"

"Not romantically," I replied, laughing. "But… I'm

putting my house on the market and…"

"Yes, darling?"

"I'm strongly considering accepting the board's offer to run Original's new office in Sydney...Australia."

"Yes, I know where Sydney is, darling," Mum said, smiling, and then added, again surprising me, "Good for you, Ginny. It's about time you tried something new, it's what you need right now."

"How do *you* feel about it, Dad?" I asked him, as he came over to hug me.

"Ginny, you will make a success of whatever you do, wherever you are. *And* it will give your mum and me a chance to finally visit Australia. We've always wanted to."

Mum stroked my face and looking into my eyes, said, "Your dad and I are always here, anytime, as long as you let us know how you are, then we won't worry… at least no more than we've always done."

Dad began crooning the old Perry Como song, 'Father of Girls' - *'When you're the father of boys you worry, when you're the father of girls, you do more than that, you pray'*. It struck me, as it always did when he sang, what a lovely voice he had.

I squeezed Mum's hand.

"Thanks, Mum," I said. "I love you."

"I love you more," Dad said, our usual in-joke whenever we were parting company.

"I know you think of yourself as independent and strong – and you are," Mum said, "but sometimes we just need to talk, let it all hang out, as we used to say when we were groovy."

"You're still groovy, Mum," I said, which prompted another serenade from Dad, this time the Mindbenders' hit, ´Groovy Kind of Love´.

"That was a hit the month you were born," Mum told me, swaying on the spot as Dad reached the chorus. "Your dad put it on the radiogram when we brought you home."

They got in the car and, as he pulled away from the kerb, Dad was still singing it while Mum was doing the backing vocals, waving at me and blowing kisses.´

Chapter Twenty

Jack was coming to very slowly, the sound of the phone ringing in the hall seeping into his consciousness.

"Oh, let the machine take it," he told himself.

As he began drifting off again, he became vaguely aware of Ginny's voice leaving a message. The click as she hung up shook him fully awake, and in a slight panic, wondering why she'd called, he leapt up, rushed into the hall and pressed play.

"Hi darling. I hope you haven't left the house yet. The thing is, Jack, I've just heard on the car radio – Diana's been killed in a car crash in Paris. Please ring me when you get this message. I'm so sorry, darling. Ring me."

He heard someone in the background telling Ginny the screening was about to begin and she said, 'Okay, I'll be right there,' and then with a final 'Call me, Jack,' the line went dead.

He sat down heavily on the chair by the phone table, trying to take in what Ginny had said. After a few minutes, he went into the sitting room and turned on the TV. There it was, the awful, heart-stopping truth. As the presenter told the story, that Diana had been killed in an underpass in Paris, her car crashing into the wall, there was footage of hundreds of people leaving flowers at Kensington Palace.

The phone went in the hall again and he ran to answer it. It was Ginny.

"Jack? Are you okay?"

"I don't know what I am, to be honest. I fell asleep about an hour or so ago and woke up feeling exhausted, very nervous and shaky, and now this awful news."

"I know. We're all in bits here. Such a beautiful

young woman who'd finally seemed to be getting her life together, taken away in an instant. It's – well, it's a fucking fuck-up!"

Ginny always made him laugh when she swore as it never sounded quite natural, more like a child saying a naughty word for the first time. And even at this terrible moment he laughed, then realised that tears were falling down his face.

"Fucking hell, Ginny," he said between sobs.

"Look, Jack, people I've never seen cry, never seen showing a flicker of emotion, are sobbing their hearts out here. So, don't worry, it's not just you. Diana's death seems to have triggered something in everyone. And you're going to feel it even more because, well, you're personally invested. The portrait was such a huge break for you. You're bound to feel like shit."

"I guess so. One thing I do know is I have to ring Isabel, Diana's PA, though I'm likely to start blubbing uncontrollably down the phone."

"Well, look, darling, give me Isabel's number and I'll call her and explain that you're too upset to call. I'm sure she'll understand. It's up to you, darling."

"No, I'm being pathetic, I'll call her. We always got on so well, so I feel I at least owe her that."

"Good. That's good, darling. But first, make yourself a very strong coffee or a sweet cup of tea."

Jack nodded silently, already working out what he was going to say when he rang Kensington Palace.

"And darling," Ginny was saying, "I love you."

"I love you too. Please try and come home early today? I want us to go and lay some flowers with everyone else."

"Of course. I'm not going to the post-screening party.

I've got to make a couple of calls to the office then I'll come home straight away."

Jack put down the phone, made himself a very strong cup of coffee with, unusually, three spoonfuls of sugar and decided seeing crowds of weeping people holding bunches of flowers, toys and hand-written messages were not what he needed right now. The idea of him and Ginny going down there later to join the throng was not such a good one after all.

He steeled himself and rang Diana's office, thankfully keeping it together. As he finished the call, he heard the post dropping through the letterbox and went to pick it up off the mat.

There were a couple of bills, an invitation to a friend's upcoming exhibition in Bond Street, and at the bottom of the pile a very official looking envelope with '*From The White House, Washington DC*' above his name and address. He tore it open, intrigued to find out what the letter said.

Dear Mr. Marlowe,

The President and the First Lady would like to invite you to paint their official portrait at a date convenient to you.

Both the President and his wife have been extremely impressed with your work, which they saw at a Royal Academy exhibition in London recently. They are convinced that it is you they wish to paint them.

The portrait will be hung in their home in Westchester and will be given a 'grand reveal' at a garden party held in the rose garden here at the White House, to which you and your wife are of course invited.

Please let us know how your diary is looking, and when you would be able to fly to Washington to meet the President and the First Lady to discuss the painting.

We will of course offer you first-class flights and the best hotel here in Washington during your stay and any necessary further trips during the progress of the portrait to its conclusion.

All best regards and we look forward to hearing from you,

    Yours,

    Patricia Langham

    The White House Press Office

He'd just finished reading the letter when he heard Ginny arriving home. The thought, 'as one door closes, another one opens' came into his head, as she ran in and threw her arms around him.

Chapter Twenty-One

After waving goodbye to her parents, Ginny drove back home, mulling over the funeral service and saying a private final goodbye to Vicki. Jack's note, which she'd read several times over the last couple of weeks, started floating through her mind. He'd explained that Simon was now 'in a place and time of his choosing, with a new identity and the chance to live out his dreams to the full,' reminding Ginny how Simon had always raved about the '60s.

Did Jack take him there? And which Jack? Presumably it was the older version who'd visited Suze. The note was written by someone who sounded wise, someone who had all the answers.

Was his note leading her to work out who Simon had become? Was it Terry Simon? That would explain Vicki's horrified reaction to meeting Simon for the first time. 'He had Terry's voice', she'd said, but the person Vicki had met that night at The Dorchester looked nothing like the man who Jack had, more than likely, taken back to the '60s. He would still have been the same unstable narcissist, whisked out of Ginny's life and transplanted almost sixty years back into Vicki's, 'a real piece of work,' so her colleague had told her.

One thing that had been troubling her was whether Jack knew 'Terry' would make Vicki's life hell, as Simon had done hers? 'I can't believe he did,' she told herself again. 'Jack would never do that. It was just history repeating itself.'

She'd Googled 'Terry Simon' but came up with very little. His Wikipedia page just listed the biggest hits he'd written and produced in the '60s, with a short paragraph about him being 'married briefly to music publisher Vicki Palmer'. In the ´references´ section, there was something about the wedding, but when she clicked on it there was just a message saying, ´This article has been deleted´.

She'd then clicked on 'Images', but that had brought up nothing except a very pixilated photo of Vicki and Terry coming out of a doorway, with the credit line 'Terry Simon and Vicki Palmer, Marylebone Registry office, 1970'. Terry's face was - conveniently? - blurred as he'd looked behind him just as the photographer had taken the photo. Was his stance similar to Simon's? Could the indistinct profile be his? She couldn't really tell.

Another thought which kept coming into her head, one which first arrived just after reading Jack's note and still nagged at her, was 'what if Jack comes back and I'm no longer there?'. She began once again questioning if she should, after all, sell the house and take the job in Australia. But the answer, which always followed her doubts, was, 'you can't just stay here waiting for Jack, whichever version, to suddenly appear again. It could be years ahead. If he does return at some point, he's resourceful enough to find you. You have to move on, you have to get on with your life. Jack would always endorse that.'

She turned on the radio, a '60s Hits channel, and smiled as a Sandie Shaw track, one which Terry Simon had written, came on. There it was. Jack telling her across the ether that, when you need to, move on to a place that will make you happy.

After a long drive, Ginny arrived home feeling very tired. Parking the car and walking up the path towards the front door, she imagined the house as it used to be, something she'd hadn't done for a long time. As she put her key in the door and walked in, what she found was both a shock and a dream come true.

Chapter Twenty-Two

As Ginny walked into the hall, she had a strange feeling of being out of phase. The sense of a ripple in a pond ran through her like a mild electric shock. Everything looked like a double film exposure, the images before her slowly shifting focus, impossible to define. Then, as the image finally aligned and stabilised, she simply stared in disbelief.

Jack was standing in their old Butterfly Cottage hallway, smiling at her. He looked to be in his fifties, as he would be now, his mop of curly hair shorter and greyer. The thought, 'maybe Suze was exaggerating about his age' passed through her mind.

"Hello darling," he said. "Are you alright?"

"Ye-es, I-I´m just - "

That ripple bubbled through her again and, as though coming round from fainting, her confusion suddenly cleared.

"Yes, I´m fine, darling," she said.

"You look tired," he said. "Difficult day, I guess."

"Yes, quite emotional really."

"I have something to show you but… it can wait till later, I'll pour you a drink."

"No, show me now. I'm sure it'll be something lovely."

She followed him down the hallway, glancing at photos on the wall of their wedding, and one with Vicki, everyone cheering the camera with a poster behind them saying 'Welcome to The New Millennium!'. The one of them laughing behind a giant silver-iced cake in the shape of the number twenty-five momentarily intrigued her. She couldn't recall when it had been taken, though clearly recently.

She was still thinking about it when Jack opened the door of his old studio room and stood aside to reveal, there on the easel, a portrait of her, one she´d never seen before.

"I´ve been working on it at my studio for weeks and finally, I finished it today," he said. "I think it captures you really well."

"I love it, Jack!" she said, her eyes welling up.

Seeing this older version of the girl who smiled from the portrait in the sitting-room made her feel incredibly emotional. She moved in closer to get a better look.

In the background was the summerhouse and in her right hand was a sheet of paper with the word ´Journal´ at the top of the page. There was a slight blurring of her left hand, as though she'd moved it just as a photographer had taken the picture. It was something Jack often did in his portraits, 'catching a moment as it moved by'.

A wave of contented tiredness swept over her and, still looking at the portrait, she sat down on the settee and lay her head on one of the cushions. As she began to fall asleep, Jack lifted her in his arms and carried her into the bedroom, settling her under the covers and stroking her hair.

"Sleep well, my darling," he said. "It's good to have you home again."

Ginny made a kind of happy little girl sound, and in her sleep she murmured,

"Home again."

Chapter Twenty-Three

Sir Jack and Lady Ginny Marlowe stood outside Buckingham Palace holding up their medals for the photographers. Jack had been awarded a knighthood for services to art, and Ginny, while automatically becoming Lady Marlowe, had herself been awarded the O.B.E. for services to the music industry.

Earlier that morning, Jack had woken Ginny with breakfast in bed, and, as she'd munched on her toast and eggs, and sipped her piping hot espresso, she'd looked around the bedroom with a kind of satisfied joy. He'd sat by her and watched her eat.

"Good to be home?" he asked her.

"Always good to be home," she replied.

Jack stroked her hair and looked a little concerned.

"You sure you're okay?"

"Yes, honestly," Ginny said, dunking her toast in the boiled egg. "I must have been exhausted when I got back. I felt very woozy when I walked in but I had a great night's sleep. Things are still a bit hazy though… a little surreal, if I'm honest. Not sure why."

She laughed.

"I feel my age today."

"You've been working very hard lately," Jack said, "back and forth to New York, and sorting out the staffing of the new Sydney office."

"Darren's going to be fantastic at the helm," Ginny said, swallowing her last piece of toast. "He's been wanting to run things for a while – waiting for me to retire basically. But now, he finally gets to do his own thing. He'll love it."

"You also had a long, emotional day yesterday. How

was the funeral?"

"Oh, you know, rather sad and yet strangely joyful. So many people there, it was a real celebration of Vicki's life."

"Quite right too."

"I wish you could have been there."

"I know. But, there was such a lot of Trust stuff to sort out, and the upcoming exhibition in Berlin still needs tweaking."

"I'm looking forward to that. Vicki was too. We were only talking about it a couple of weeks ago."

Jack held Ginny's hand.

"You're going to miss her."

"So much. She's buried in the same plot as her ex-husband, near Brian Jones' grave, his hero apparently."

"I didn´t know she´d been married."

"She never talked about him. It wasn't a great marriage apparently. Mum told me they were divorced in the '70s, he went to live in America and was killed in a car crash in 1983, just before I started working at Original."

She looked into the middle distance and seemed lost in thought.

"Dreaming of meeting the Queen?" Jack said, taking her tray off the bed.

"Absolutely! I'll go have a shower, that'll wake me up."

***

As they left the palace in the MG, Jack told Ginny they were going to lunch at their favourite Greek restaurant in Chiswick.

"Kostas," Ginny said, "we haven't been there for

ages."

"And Suze is joining us. She rang this morning while you were asleep to congratulate us on our awards. She'd seen a piece about it on BBC Breakfast."

"We made the telly?"

"Apparently. Jenny Bond was very excited to see which outfit you'd wear, so Suze said."

"Jenny Bond? I can now die happy."

Jack laughed and glanced across at his wife.

"You look beautiful," he said.

"Not bad for forty-six and no bra."

"Alan Bennett?"

"Victoria Wood."

"Of course."

"Will Suze be on her own, or with the elusive Tee?"

"Apparently Tee's coming."

"At last, we get to meet Suze's mysterious lady."

During what was a delicious lunch, Ginny began to feel a little phased again. As Suze chatted away about how her relationship with Tee was going, she nodded in all the right places, while her mind kept wandering, as though slipping in and out of a dream.

"It's short for Verity," she heard Tee saying to Jack. "Verity Braintree."

"*The* Verity Braintree?" Jack replied. "Good God, you're a genius!"

"Well, thank you, kind sir," Tee replied.

"No, really, I *love* your sculptures. It's great to meet you, I had no idea."

He beamed across at Ginny and mouthed a 'Wow!'.

"Tee shuns publicity," Suze said proudly, "she lets her work speak for her."

Tee nudged Suze.

"It's what you told me," Suze protested.

"I've seen some of your portraits," Tee said to Jack. "Impressionist Realism, yes?"

"That's right," Jack replied.

"Fascinating stuff, beautifully done."

Jack touched his heart and smiled.

"Tee has an exhibition at the Tate Modern next week," Suze said.

"And you must come as my special guests," Tee said, looking from Jack to Ginny.

"We'd love to," Jack said, "wouldn't we, Ginny?"

But Ginny was lost in thought.

"Braintree…" she was saying to herself. "Braintree… Yes! That was the name of the person who we bought the bungalow off."

"So it was," Jack said.

"That would have been my brother," Tee said. "Suze told me you lived at Butterfly Cottage. My parents used to live there."

"I remember now," Ginny said, her face brightening. "You told me about this, Suze."

"Did I? When?"

"Not long ago, when I came to see you… I remember you had a lovely collection of Tee's sculptures."

Suze looked confused.

"I don't think so, Ginny… I don't have any of Tee's sculptures in my flat."

"Yes you do. That was the night you told me that Jack had - "

Ginny stopped mid-sentence. Her eyes dulled over and she put her hand over her mouth.

"I'm sorry! I - I'm not with it today."

She tried a smile as Jack held her hand, which was shaking.

"Are you alright, darling?" he said.

"Y-Yes, I - "

"Ginny's still very tired from yesterday," Jack explained to Suze and Tee. "Vicki's funeral."

"Oh god, I'd forgotten, Ginny!" Suze said, reaching across the table.

"Vicki?" Tee asked.

"Ginny's old boss. Vicki Palmer. She meant a lot to you, didn't she, Ginny?"

"Thanks Suze," Ginny said, and then to Tee, "Vicki started the company I now run, back in the '60s."

Tee lifted her glass.

"Then here's to Vicki!"

"To Vicki!" Ginny said as everyone clinked glasses.

"And to Sir Jack and Lady Marlowe!" Suze added, raising her glass again to the couple.

Tee did a mock tugging of her forelock and smiled at them both.

"So, it was your brother who sold the bungalow to us?" Jack asked Tee.

"Yes. My older brother, Alistair. He's no longer with us, he died last month."

"Oh, I'm so sorry, Tee," Ginny said.

"Don't be," Tee replied. "He was a horrible man."

"He was the last person to see their mother before she disappeared," Suze said, her eyes widening.

"Disappeared?" Jack asked Tee.

"Mum went missing while Alistair was visiting her," Tee explained. "She went into the kitchen - "

"To polish one of Tee's sculptures," Suze cut in.

"That's right," Tee said, "and she was never seen

again."

"Good Lord!" Jack said. "I'm very sorry, Tee."

"You told me about that, Suze," Ginny said.

"Did I?" Suze replied, looking sideways at Jack. "When?"

Ginny stared into the middle distance and flushed up.

"When I - oh dear. Maybe I dreamt that too…"

Shaking her head and trying a big smile at everyone she said, "Please ignore me, I'm all over the place today."

Then, rallying, she asked Tee, "So your mum was never found?"

"Nope. Vanished without a trace," Tee replied. "Eventually declared 'missing presumed dead'. She was a lovely lady. I still miss her."

"How awful," Ginny said then looked thoughtfully at Jack. "Imagine. Someone you love just vanishing. I can't begin to think how I'd cope."

Jack squeezed Ginny's hand.

"I'm not going anywhere, darling," he said. "You're stuck with me, kiddo."

***

On the way out of the restaurant, Suze gently pulled Jack to one side, leaving Tee and Ginny chatting on the pavement.

"Is Ginny okay?" she asked him quietly.

"Yeah, she's just tired after the funeral, and then the ceremony this morning. She's been working all hours, lots of new signings, red-eye flights all over the place, organising a new office in Australia. She never stops."

"Yes, I know she works hard, Jack, she always has done. But this feels like more than that, like she's not quite with us. You would tell me if there's anything wrong?"

"She's fine. Honestly. I'll keep my eye on her, don't worry."

"It's just that Ginny is always spot-on, you know? Never off the boil, always right there, but over lunch she seemed very distracted."

"I'll look after her, Suze, I promise."

He glanced over at Tee.

"Ginny and I approve, by the way."

"She is rather fab, isn't she? I'm completely head-over-heels."

"Couldn't have guessed that for a second."

"We'll get an invite over to you for the exhibition."

"Thank you, look forward to that."

"And Jack, do make sure Ginny slows down a bit."

"Rather you than me telling Lady Marlowe that," Jack replied.

On the way home, Ginny became a little fidgety, taking off her sunglasses, putting them back on, then off again.

"Are you sure you're alright, darling?" Jack asked her.

"No, I'm not," Ginny replied. "I – I've been having some really weird thoughts and feelings all day."

He looked at her and was shaken by how grey she looked.

"Go on," he said, "talk about it."

"Well, it's going to sound ridiculous, like I've flipped my lid or something. But it's these memories which keep coming to me, they're not mine but for a moment they are. You saw me at lunch, I kept remembering things that I was sure had happened, but which clearly hadn't."

"Is that still happening?"

"Yes."

"Such as?"

"Well, I keep recalling how you disappeared fifteen years ago. But you didn't. And that I married Simon Baker... *Simon Baker?*! He wrote one great song and that was it, never heard from him again. It's lunatic! But the memories are *so* real. Like another life I've had."

"Right," Jack said, nodding slowly.

"It all started when I was coming back into the house last night. I felt very odd, as though I were suddenly two people, one walking into a house I knew and the other shocked at what I saw, and since then all these bizarre recollections keep coming into my head."

"Okay."

"But it isn't okay, Jack. I feel like I'm having some sort of mental collapse."

They'd reached the bungalow. Jack turned off the engine and squeezed Ginny's hand.

"Maybe I'm getting early Alzheimer's," Ginny said, looking down at Jack's hand on hers. "Here I am, with you," she smiled at Jack, "but a weird ´other self´, with a different life, one I've lived without you, keeps creeping into my head. It all going on... in here," she tapped her head, "and it's driving me mad."

"Okay, Ginny," Jack said. "I think I know what´s happening. I had a suspicion about it last night when you came through the front door. I felt something, like a ripple effect."

"That's it!" Ginny shouted. "That's exactly what it felt like."

"I believe it´s an overlap."

"An overlap?"

He sighed loudly and stroked Ginny's face.

"This is going to sound completely crazy but... I think two of your time-spaces were somehow synced for a moment when you came into the house."

Ginny looked like a light had switched on in her head.

"Time-spaces, yes! You wrote me a note which explained them."

"Did I?"

"Well, I remember reading it. I´m sure I did, but..."

She stared at him.

"You see? What is happening to me?"

Jack put his hand under her chin, lifted up her head and kissed her.

"Come on," he said. "Let's go inside. I'll pour us a long stiff drink and try and explain it all. I should have told you about all this before, but I didn't know if you'd understand, I thought it might freak you out."

"That you're a time-traveller?" Ginny said casually.

"You know?!"

"No!" Ginny shouted at the windscreen. "But the other me obviously does!"

***

As Ginny knocked back her very strong gin and tonic, Jack sat with her holding her hand, and explained about time-travel.

"Try to imagine that *this* is our time-space," he said, "where we are now, the one we´ve inhabited all our lives. And yet... another Ginny, from a different time-space, a different life, synced with you when you walked into the house last night, leaving you with memories of her existence and experiences, mixed in with your own."

"And will she now be having mine...?"

"Possibly. I think as she walked into the house she was remembering when *her* Jack disappeared. Fifteen years ago, as you said. You must have both coalesced at exactly the same moment coming through the door. It's rare, most time-spaces tend to be a few seconds apart. Hence people's occasional sense of déjà-vu. But for some reason, you appear to be inhabiting two concurrent time-spaces. I'm sure it won't last, I've only come across it once before, and it does go, though I know it must be pretty scary right now."

"It's more a feeling of deep sadness, a real sense of loss - which is so alien to me."

She looked at Jack.

"How do you stay sane, Jack? How do you cope with it all?"

"It's who I am, Ginny. I have to cope. More importantly, does what I've told you help you understand it better?"

"Kind of."

"You know, I feel extremely relieved we've had this conversation. It's like a spy must feel when he finally tells his wife where he's been going off to all these years."

Ginny giggled.

"My husband, the time-travelling spy. How exciting!"

Then a thought struck her.

"Why don't I ever know you've gone... on one of your travels?"

"I usually do it when you're not home."

"Naughty boy," she said, giggling.

He tapped her nose playfully.

"And anyway, I can get back to the exact place and time I left, so it's as though I've never been gone."

"How clever. Where do you go to?"

"Usually to Paris in the 1860s, my favourite period. I meet up with my Impressionist friends and we - "

"You've met the Impressionists?"

"Often. We sometimes paint together and spend hours in various cafés discussing light and colour and how best to attain it on canvas."

"Good God, how wonderful."

"Yes, it is, but it does get a bit lonely… without you there to share it. Claude often asks about you."

"Claude?"

"Monet," Jack said casually. "He thinks you're quite the looker…"

Ginny slapped Jack's arm.

"He *does*. I did a painting of you from memory which he keeps on his sitting-room wall. I'm sure he'd love to meet you."

Ginny stared at Jack in disbelief as he leaned into her.

"We can – if you want to, that is – have some fun travelling together. We'd visit some wonderful places, fascinating times, *different centuries*. Now you know all about it… why not?"

"As long as we're together, Jack, whatever, wherever and whenever, that sounds like fun – if a bit scary."

Jack got up to pour them refills.

"Y'know, all these memories you have of the other Ginny and the time-space overlap, I think you should write them all down, while you still have them. Like a journal, preserve it for posterity."

Ginny smiled at Jack.

"In your new portrait of me, I was holding a journal in my hand. But how could you have known about it? You've only just suggested it."

"Time-travel is a strange mistress," he replied, bringing their drinks over and clinking Ginny's glass. "Ready for a few adventures?"

"Bring it on!" she said.

Chapter Twenty-Four

Jack watched his younger self walk through the bedroom door and back into his proper time, where he could begin his own journey, to this moment, to this day, in his own time-space.

He stood and listened for a few seconds, went to check the bedroom and found it empty.

"Bon chance," he murmured to Young Jack, then wandered into the sitting-room.

Glancing at the mantelpiece, he smiled sadly at the silver urn standing beside the digital clock which read Monday 12th August 2047. His eyes moved to the framed letter from The White House, the one he'd been reading when Ginny arrived home after Diana's death, the letter which had changed his life.

Flying many times over several weeks to New York and then onto Westchester by stretch limo, where he worked on the early stages of the portrait of Bill and Hillary Clinton, was a huge consolation for him at the time. While not replacing the excitement he'd felt when he got the commission to paint Diana, the Clintons' personal invitation to do their official portrait had given him goosebumps, and did even now.

The Clintons were kindness itself and seemed to truly enjoy sitting for the portrait together. Ginny got on with them both, even when she occasionally asked her always direct questions.

"How do you cope with the Republican Party hating your guts?" she had asked Bill once, prompting a gentle glare from Jack.

Bill had waved away Jack's concern.

"Good question, Ginny," he'd said. "Being a

Democrat means you have several hundred powerful enemies who are just waiting for you to fall – how do you Brits say it... ?"

"Arse over tit?" Ginny ventured.

Bill burst out laughing.

"That's it! Arse over tit! Interesting image..."

Hillary giggled.

"Tits and ass," she said, "my favourite number from *A Chorus Line*."

At which they both started singing the song like two Broadway veterans.

On their first night in Washington, where the painting would be completed at the White House, Ginny and Jack had gone out to dinner at Martin's Tavern in Georgetown, which the President's assistant, Iris, had suggested they try.

"The best food with the most connected crowd in this political Tinseltown," she'd said. "I'll book you Booth Three where JFK proposed to Jackie."

Ginny had looked around the restaurant, wide-eyed that she was 'sitting right where Jackie sat'.

As they'd tucked into the delicious food, a conversation from the next booth started to seep through the noise around them.

"So! Bill and Monica, eh?" they heard a woman say. "It's been going on for *two years*!".

"Does Hillary know?" another woman said

"When you're married to a guy like Bill, gorgeous and randy as hell, it kind of goes with the territory."

"I wouldn't say no."

"It's JFK and Jackie all over again."

"I wouldn't have said no to him either!"

At which point both ladies burst into a fit of loud dirty giggles, and Ginny and Jack decided not to stay for coffee or dessert.

***

The painting was completed in mid-October and was officially unveiled in the White House rose garden one chilly but sunny November morning. Jack and Ginny were special guests at the garden party, along with former Presidents Bush and Carter.

"I'm surprised George Bush is here," Ginny said to Jack. "I thought he hated Bill."

"It's usually the backroom guys who do all the hating, all the scheming," Jack said. "Nixon knew nothing about Watergate, it was his election team who dreamt that one up."

"And he paid the price."

"As Bill said, 'it goes with the job.'"

After the unveiling ceremony, champagne was brought round on silver trays, Barbara Bush gently pulling Ginny away to meet some friends of hers. Jack stood alone for a few moments, looking around the chattering crowd and noticed Jimmy Carter talking to a chap who he recognised from several years earlier. Albert Rothwell, who'd been a lunchtime guest at Jim and Esther's when Jack and Ginny had stayed for the weekend, saw him and excused himself from Carter's group.

He came bundling over, big Cuban cigar in hand.

"Jack!" he shouted, clearly delighted to see him again.

As they shook hands, Jack was aware of some kind

of connection between them, an intangible sense of brotherhood flashed through him, as though he'd known Albert for a lifetime.

"I'm loving today, Jack," Albert said, puffing on his cigar. "Really great to see you've made it so big. Jim and Esther knew you would."

"Thanks Albert. And by the way, I never thanked you for putting them onto the Pauser painting."

"Oh yeah, as soon as I saw it in the auction catalogue, I was sure they'd want to buy it for you."

"It still has pride of place in our house."

"You and Ginny, eh? Congratulations. Great to see her here today. She's as beautiful as ever."

Ginny was a few yards away still chatting to Barbara Bush who waved at them both and mouthed 'Hi Albert!'.

Albert waved back while saying to Jack, "I'd like to have a private chat, if that's okay?"

"Sure," Jack said, wondering if Albert was going to ask him to do his portrait.

"Let's go over there," Albert said, putting his hand on Jack's back and gently manoeuvring him towards a quiet spot at the corner of the terrace.

Checking that no-one else was around, Albert said, "I know you felt that… that spark of connection just now when we shook hands?"

Jack laughed uneasily.

"I thought it was just me," he joked. "It reminded me of the old days of nylon shirts."

Albert grinned as though brushing off the joke and said, "Look, son, it's time we talked."

Jack's unease grew as he wondered where this conversation was going.

"I've been keeping an eye on your career," Albert

said, "which I know is only just starting, and it's going to be amazing. But I also know that you are destined for a life you may not have yet imagined."

Jack wondered if this was one of those recruiting moments, like Philby and The Cambridge Five.

"The truth is, Jack, we are gifted folk, you and I."

He tapped Jack on the chest.

"Your gift is particularly special."

Albert moved in closer.

"There are some splendid adventures ahead for you, Jack. You just need to grasp them…"

He grabbed the air like he was catching something.

"Remember when Esther and Jim were prodding me to reveal who my film actress girlfriend is?"

"Yes, Ginny was very impressed you didn't spill the beans. She thought that was extremely gentlemanly of you."

"It had nothing to do with being a gentleman, Jack. The fact is, I couldn't tell them who she is."

"Why not?"

"My girlfriend is Veronica Lake."

"Veronica Lake? But she's…"

"That's right. She died almost twenty-five years ago… and yet, this evening, I will be taking her for dinner to the Cocoanut Grove in Hollywood."

Albert read Jack's mind.

"No, Jack, I haven't lost my marbles. I never will. Just think about what I've said, and I promise you, all will start to become much clearer. Very soon."

He beamed at Jack.

"You should go back and join the party now. Say hello to Ginny for me."

He shook Jack's hand and, once again, that bizarre

sense of connection fizzled through his body.

"Bon voyage, Jack. Make every journey a good one."

Albert saluted and walked away. As he reached the end of the terrace, he sauntered round the corner and disappeared into thin air.

A voice behind Jack said, "Can I help you, sir?"

Jack spun round and a burly security guard, who resembled a character from *Men In Black*, was smiling at him in a benignly threatening way.

"Er – no," Jack said, "thank you, I-I thought I saw someone moving over there, but I was mistaken."

The security guard glanced over Jack's head.

"I'll check the area, sir, just in case," he said, "but perhaps you should go and re-join the party now."

"I will, thanks," Jack replied, feeling a bit like he'd been politely but firmly sent on his way.

As he turned to make his way back towards the crowd, the guard said, "Oh, by the way, sir, I think your portrait of the President and the First Lady is terrific."

"Thanks," Jack said. "Appreciate that."

"Not a problem sir. Enjoy the day."

The guard walked off towards the side terrace and Jack made his way back towards Ginny, who was now chatting to Jimmy Carter. As she turned and smiled at him, he felt like something within him had jolted awake, like a seventh sense, something indescribable, some kind of 'old knowledge' now inhabited him.

For most of his life, he'd known that he was different, special even, but he'd always assumed it was his artistic talent. Now, he realised exactly what it was. And it went way beyond painting portraits.

"Excuse me, sir."

It was the guard again.

"Just thought I'd tell you, you were right, someone *had* been there, at the side terrace. Whoever it was had gone, but I found this in the grass."

He held up a cigar butt and Jack smiled to himself, murmuring 'Albert'.

"I'm sorry, what was that, sir?"

"Oh nothing, a friend of mine smokes those."

"Was he here, sir?"

"Yes, but he's… gone now."

***

Jack smiled at the memories of that day outside The White House, when his life had taken a wholly different turn, then his eyes went back to the urn glinting in the afternoon sun.

He recalled how Ginny had been complaining of severe headaches for about a month. Finally, she made an appointment to see a specialist. The X-rays showed an advanced brain tumour, further tests proving it was inoperable.

"How ironic," Ginny had said in the car on the drive home from the diagnosis. "It's what killed Vicki. All those years ago, and it's still a killer disease."

On their 60th wedding anniversary, she'd asked Jack to carry her through the garden onto the summerhouse veranda. She was as light as a feather, smiling at the garden full of bloom as he'd cradled her in his arms and settled her on her favourite rocking chair.

"Do you want anything, darling?" he'd asked her.

But she'd just shaken her head as she watched the swaying freesias and bluebells, the cornflowers, chicory and the wild cosmos, all which she'd planted so many years ago. It was a blanket of colours, and as usual the butterflies were loving the wealth of nectar on offer.

They'd both remained silent for a long time, Jack occasionally glancing over to see if Ginny looked uncomfortable or needed anything. But he was struck by how happy she'd looked that morning, in her favourite place with her favourite human being beside her.

Out of the silence he heard Ginny's voice, almost a whisper now.

"Jack? I want you to promise me something."

"Yes, my love?" he said, pulling his chair closer and holding both her hands.

"I want you to go to wherever your heart takes you, when I'm gone, with whoever makes you happy."

She'd looked at him and smiled.

"Because I know there is someone… out there…" she waved her hand vaguely in the air, "who will make you happy."

"There's only you, Ginny, you know that," he'd replied, tears pricking his eyes.

"But I'll be gone, darling, very soon, and I don't want you to be alone. You have too much love still left in you to let it go to waste on… on someone who'll no longer be here to return it."

She nodded her head and rested it on the back of the chair, gently rocking herself into a slumber.

"Promise me," she said.

"I promise."

As Ginny's breathing grew quieter and the rocking ceased, Jack knew that his wife was slipping away. He leaned over and kissed her forehead.

"Sail safely, my love," he said.

Chapter Twenty-Five

A young couple, Stephen and Bella Mainstay, were standing at the gate of Butterfly Cottage, smiling at the cute period property they'd received a letter about that morning.

"It's very pretty," Bella said.

"Yeah, it is. Think you'd be happy here?"

"Absolutely. It's saying 'Live here' already."

"I still don't know why we've inherited it," Stephen said.

"It was in the letter," Bella replied. "It said someone would be here to meet us…"

She turned round and an elderly man with a head of short grey curls was standing on the pavement, grinning at them both.

"Hi, my name's Jack," he said, "you must be Stephen and Bella."

He shook their hands.

"Your grandfather and I were great friends," Jack replied.

"Grandpa Harry?"

Jack nodded as Bella's eyes lit up.

"I know who you are! You're the famous painter." she said. "Jack Marlowe."

She looked in her shoulder bag and took out the letter.

"We got this from The Marlowe Trust. That's you, isn't it?"

Jack laughed.

"Guilty."

"And Gramps' portrait," Stephen said, "that was done by you."

"That's right," Jack said. "Harry was about your age

when I painted it."

"Wow," Bella said, "this is amazing!"

"So… this house…?" Stephen said. "Was it yours?"

"Yep, and now it's all yours."

"But why are you giving it to us?"

"After my wife, Ginny, died," Jack replied, "I decided it was time to move on. But I wanted to make sure the house went to someone who would look after it, who would love it as we had. I know how much your grandparents thought of you, Stephen. They were very special people, as were Harry's parents, Jim and Esther, who were extremely kind to me when I was just starting out."

"I didn't know them," Stephen said, "but Gramps spoke about them a lot, especially after Grans passed away."

"The beautiful Hannah," Jack said.

"Yeah, she was a real looker, right into old age."

Jack and Bella both chuckled.

"Well she *was*!" Stephen protested.

"So," Jack said, "here are the keys, the deeds to the house are now in your names. This is my solicitor's card, he's waiting for you to get in touch and collect them. There's one proviso which I've written into it."

"Here's the catch," Stephen said.

"No, no catch, just a promise to me and for Ginny, that you won't make any major structural changes to the house. It must stay as Butterfly Cottage while you live in it, and the back garden, which Ginny created, will remain as it is. Any alterations you need to make will have to be submitted to and approved by the Trust. Of course, decorate it as you please, you'll probably find it a bit old fashioned for your taste! But it is now your home to enjoy."

"Stephen and I love the bungalow just as it is," Bella said.

Satisfied, Jack nodded.

"Okay then, come and have a look round."

"It's adorable," Bella said, wandering in behind Jack, who walked off down the hall, calling over his shoulder, "I'll leave you to it."

"Thanks Jack," Stephen said, as Bella went into the sitting-room.

"Oh, Stephen, come and look at this!"

Two portraits were propped up on the mantelpiece.

"That one's a sketch of Gramps," Stephen said.

"You sit just like that when you're reading," Bella said.

Stephen pulled a face then peered at the other portrait.

"Not sure who this is…"

"Is it your Granny?" Bella asked.

"No," Stephen replied, "it's not her, I don't think so anyway."

He looked at the small plaque on the frame.

"It's called *Portrait Of A Lady* by someone called… Sergius Pauser."

He picked it up and turned it over.

"There's an inscription… it says… 'From Jim and Esther to our dear friend Jack. By your favourite painter, for our favourite painter.'"

"Wow," Bella said, "it's like a slice of your family history bundled together in two portraits. We'll have to hang them side by side in here."

She took Stephen's hand and squeezed it.

"We're home," she said.

Jack stood alone in the kitchen, looking out the window at the garden where Ginny's ashes were spread, amongst the plants which she had cared for so lovingly. He could hear the excited conversation down the hall of the young couple who he had just handed the keys of the bungalow to. It was clear they adored it as much as he and Ginny had when they'd first seen the house so many years ago.

As he was musing over the past, he heard the familiar tinkling sound and there, walking in from the hallway, was an elderly lady he vaguely recognised. She was about his age and holding a small bronze sculpture in her hand.

'The brilliant Tee,' Jack thought, as the old lady smiled at him and said, "Oh, it's you again!"

Stephen and Bella walked across the hall into the first bedroom, where they found two paintings on the wall of a very pretty lady from different periods of her life.

"God, she looks like Audrey Hepburn," Bella said.

Stephen went over and studied them.

"The inscription on this one says, 'Ginny by Jack, 1985' and… on this one… 'Ginny by Jack, 2012'."

"She was so beautiful," Bella said. "Jack clearly loved her very much."

"By the way," Stephen said, "where *is* Jack?"

"He went down the hall," Bella replied.

Stephen went out of the bedroom and looked towards the back of the house.

"Maybe to the kitchen," he said. "Shall we go and see?"

They walked down the hall, looking in the other rooms as they went, but found the kitchen empty.

"Maybe he's in the garden…" Bella said, then yelped with delight. "Oh, Stephen!" she cried, staring through the window. "Look, it's beautiful!"

She opened the door and stepped out into yellows, lilacs, reds and blues in full bloom.

"It's like a nature reserve," Stephen said, "what an amazing place."

"And a summerhouse!" Bella cried. "I've always wanted a summerhouse. This just gets better."

***

They walked round the bungalow again, but it seemed that Jack had gone. Stephen checked outside the front door, glancing down the street, but there was no sign of him. He shrugged and walked back into the house.

"Guess he had somewhere he needed to be," he said.

"He's probably feeling sad about leaving," Bella said, "too many memories. I can understand that."

Then Stephen saw a note on the hall table.

"It's addressed to us," he said, unfolding it. He read it out.

Dear Stephen and Bella,

I hope you're very happy here at Butterfly Cottage. I know the house will love you as much as it did us.

Take care,

Jack

Chapter Twenty-Six

One Sunday morning, three years after moving into Butterfly Cottage, Stephen and Bella were sitting on the summerhouse veranda reading the papers over coffee and croissants.

They'd kept their promise to Jack, making very few changes to the bungalow. Bella had at first suggested they turn the back bedroom into a dining-room, but the arrival of the twins, Matthew and Sarah, eighteen months after they'd moved in, had put paid to that plan. With an eye to the future, and the permission of The Marlowe Trust, the Mainstays had built a ground-floor extension at the back of the house, incorporating a third bedroom, for when the twins grew too big to share one room, and a larger kitchen giving space for a proper dining area.

"Hey Bells," Stephen said, looking up from his Sunday Times magazine. "I'm just reading an article about Sergius Pauser, and it says there's an exhibition of his work at the Tate, opening next Saturday for two months."

"Then we have to go," Bella said. "Can we take the twins?"

"I'm sure kids are allowed in, especially as ours are still pram age."

He read on.

"It also says the exhibition is showing some works by Jack Marlowe '*who publicly stated that Pauser was one of his biggest influences*'."

"So, decision made," Bella said.

***

The exhibition was clearly popular, with a long

queue outside, though, from what Stephen and Bella overheard as they waited with the others, it was Jack's paintings which were the biggest draw. The fact that the world-famous painter, who would now be in his late eighties, had disappeared from view gave his name extra kudos. The many unproven rumours that he'd been seen in Paris, Berlin and Florence, amongst many other sightings, also made the enigma of 'reclusive genius' grow into a cultural fascination.

"And to think this guy gave us his house," Stephen said, finally getting to the head of the queue and pushing the twins' pram through the door.

"Let's visit Jack's exhibition first," Bella suggested, pointing at the room ahead of them.

It was a huge space, given over to several of Jack's portraits of the likes of the Clintons, the Obamas, Bishop Tutu and Bill Gates, along with the first public viewing of a painting of King William and Queen Catherine. Bella particularly felt an instant connection with Michelle Obama, sitting at her desk in The Oval Office, Barack proudly standing beside her.

Hundreds of people filed past, stopped, studied, commented and then moved onto the next painting. It made the back of Stephen's neck tingle.

"I can't believe that *the* Jack Marlowe painted my grandpa," he said.

"And there he is!" Bella shouted.

She pointed over the heads of the crowd at a huge study in oils of Harry Mainstay, looking to be in his forties. They rushed towards the painting.

"Er - excuse *me*," a lady ahead of them said, "wait your turn."

She glared at them and Bella glared back.

"Excuse *me*," she said, in a tone of voice which even impressed Stephen, "that painting is of my husband's grandfather, whose son was Jack Marlowe's godson, so I think he has earned the right to push ahead of *everyone* here."

The woman looked at Stephen, then at the portrait of Harry, and nodded.

"Mm, I can see the likeness, so, yes, I agree with you, go ahead, son."

Stephen bowed his head in thanks and pushed the pram towards the portrait.

"It's like I can actually touch him," Stephen said, welling up. "I've never seen this one before, it's enormous."

"Stephen," Bella whispered.

He followed her gaze to a painting of Ginny and Hannah.

"Grans!" Stephen gasped.

"With Ginny," Bella said.

The two women were arm in arm, clearly great friends, their eyes bright with contentment. Hannah was looking straight at the viewer, while Ginny's eyes were obviously twinkling at Jack as he painted them.

The final painting in the room was a mix of self- and-group portrait, featuring Jack looking out from his easel to the left, paintbrush in hand, and sitting behind him, Ginny with Hannah and Harry. Harry was looking at Jack and Hannah was smiling at Ginny. In her hand, Ginny was holding a sketch of Harry.

"I think that's the sketch Jack did of Gramps," Stephen said. "The one we have on our wall."

"How amazing," Bella said, "and to see them all together, so young, so happy. Thank goodness we can't travel forward and see what age does to us all."

As they made their way out of the Jack Marlowe Room, Stephen said,

"I can't believe we met this guy, who painted my grandparents and now there they are, *in there*, for all the world to see."

"You should be very proud, young man," a voice said behind them.

Stephen turned round and there was an elderly lady, smiling at him.

"It's very nice to meet you at last, Stephen," the lady said.

"And you... but – er – how do you know my name?"

"A very good friend of mine told me you'd be here. He wanted to come as well but... things to do... you know how it is."

She turned her attention to Bella.

"And it's lovely to meet you too, Bella," she said, bending into the pram. "Oh, and your babies, they are adorable. They're so gorgeous at that age, aren't they? Sadly, I didn't get on with my brood very well... except one of them, now *she* was special."

The lady nodded at them both and, bidding them good day, wandered towards the exit.

"You didn't tell us *your* name," Bella said.

"Alice," she replied. "I'm Alice. My friend will be sad to have missed you."

They found the Pauser gallery surprisingly empty, which gave them more time to stand and study the paintings.

Suddenly Stephen stopped in his tracks.

"Oh my god," he said, staring at one of the paintings, "it's a portrait of Jack."

Bella said,

"But it can't be. Pauser died in…" She looked at the exhibition guide in her hand. "… in 1970. When was Jack born?"

"Early '60s I think, he was about four years older than Gramps."

Bella looked at the signature.

"It's got '1955' beside Pauser's name…"

"And it's called 'My friend JM, Vienna'."

She looked at the guide again.

"Hm," she said, looking confused.

"What is it?"

"Well, it's not listed in here. The one after it is, but not this one."

They walked on and, as they reached the end of the final row of paintings, there was another portrait of Jack sitting with...

"Alice!" he cried. "That´s her, the lady we just talked to."

Bella read out the inscription.

"*JM and Alice, by Sergius Pauser, Vienna, 1956.*"

Then she looked in the brochure again.

"And this one´s not listed either," she said.

"Come on," Stephen said. "Let's find somewhere to sit down. We have some checking to do."

They found a bench out in the foyer and, as Stephen played with the twins, Bella looked for the gallery's website on her phone, finding the page for the Pauser exhibition. After studying it for a few minutes she said, "I've looked right through it, and the two paintings we saw aren't mentioned."

"But we saw them, both of us did," he replied.

He got up and walked back into the Pauser room. Moments later he emerged looking ashen.

"They've gone," he said. "Neither of the paintings are there anymore. And there are several people in there. It was empty when we left... and now..."

"Well, we both know what we saw, and we both met Alice... and we are not going crazy..."

"We are not. But what we *are* doing is going home. This is all doing my head in."

The following morning, a courier delivered a package to the bungalow, which Bella signed for. She went through to the kitchen, where Stephen was feeding the twins in their high-chairs.

"This just arrived," she said, handing him the parcel. "There's no sender's name or address on it."

"It feels like a painting," Stephen said, opening it while Bella took over feeding the kids.

It was an oil painting of Jack and Ginny, probably in their fifties, sitting on a park bench. It was dated 1867, Paris, and signed by Paul Cézanne.

Stephen stared at it and showed it to Bella.

"It's beautiful," she said, "But - "

"I know... Cézanne painting Jack and Ginny? It's mad."

A small white envelope dropped from the wrapping onto the floor, which Stephen picked up and opened.

"It's from Jack," he said.

As Bella wiped the twins faces and sat back to listen, Stephen read it out.

Dear Stephen and Bella,
Alice told me you were at the exhibition yesterday

and I'm sure you've got a lot of questions.

The painting you're looking at was done when Ginny and I were hanging out with the incredible bunch of artists we now call The Impressionists. It's yours to keep. It could make you millions but will more likely be called a fake because of the subject matter: Jack Marlowe and his wife sitting in a Parisian park in the late 19th Century, painted by Cézanne? 'Must be a forgery!'. But it's not. Paul was a great friend of ours.

Stephen glanced up at Bella.

"Bloody Nora," he said.

"I *know*," Bella replied.

Stephen went back to the letter.

Keep your eyes peeled on the internet over the next day or so for a painting by Van Gogh, which Christie's has declared a forgery. It's a portrait of me and Ginny. A reclusive American collector has purchased it for ten million dollars. Vincent adored Ginny and she was especially kind to him when he became very poorly. She helped nurse him before he passed away.

Now, check the summerhouse. There is one more gift for you there which I know you'll enjoy.

Take care, I hope Butterfly Cottage is treating you well. There's no other house like it. If it offers adventures, embrace them.

All my best to you both,

J.M.

P.S. Alice sends hugs and said I should promise that we won't keep popping in like this! And, by the way, those paintings by Sergius of me and Alice are genuine, done during one of our trips to Vienna in the 1950s.

As yet, no-one except you two has seen them, but Alice wanted to make sure you did. Apologies for the intrigue. Adios mis amigos! x

They picked up a twin each and walked outside, through the garden and into the summerhouse. There leaning against the wicker sofa was a large oil painting. It was a scene set in a café where a group of people were chatting and laughing together. Painted in the Impressionist style.

"Oh Stephen," Bella said, "it´s your grandparents… chatting to… Claude Monet… and next to him is Edouard Manet. And there's Berthe Morisot, and Renoir, and Pissarro!"

Stephen gave his wife an impressed 'get you!' look.

"I got an 'A' in Art History, thank you very much," she said, nudging him and leaning into the painting.

"It's called 'Impressionist Friends' and it's signed *Jack Marlowe, Café Guerbois, Paris, 1863*. That's the café where the Impressionists used to meet up and discuss plans for exhibiting their work, and that was the year that Manet's 'Le dejeuner sur l'herbe' was rejected by the Salon de Paris."

She looked at Stephen and shook her head.

"Stephen - this painting was done at a really crucial time for Impressionism. Manet's rejection by the Salon was basically what led to The Impressionist Movement being formed."

She laughed.

"Your grandparents had coffee with the Impressionists!"

"I *know*! How crazy, how fucking wonderful is that?"

Chapter Twenty-Seven

On a bright Spring day in 2012, on what would have been her husband's eightieth birthday, Sally Braintree sat in Fortnum & Mason. The waitress was serving her lunch of Dover sole, new potatoes in garlic butter and chives, with a delicious green leaf side salad in a balsamic dressing, topped off with a large glass of chilled chianti.

She cheered the air with her glass, saying, "To you, Alistair dear."

She chuckled at the waitress who smiled back at her, thinking what a delightful old lady she was.

Sally shivered with pleasure, thanked the waitress and tucked into her meal. As she looked around her favourite eaterie, her mind wandered back to when she'd first met Alistair while working as a secretary at Braintree & York in Dean Street. Within a few days of her starting work he'd asked her out, and had proposed to her within just a couple of weeks of their first date.

However, in spite of his promised ardour, Alistair turned out to be rather a cold fish. He was very practical, which was useful as she couldn't even change a plug, and he was clearly under the impression that he loved her. However, showing his affection with a quick peck on the cheek as he left for the office, and a brief smile when he returned home every evening to a warm meal and a clean house, were clearly sufficient for him.

The two occasions when she had fallen pregnant were the results of tipsy nights whilst on holiday in Torquay. Otherwise, sex was rare and always felt like a duty, never with the unbridled passion she'd dreamt of when reading romantic novels at typing college.

But, Sally mulled, she'd been quite contented. She

was comfortable, untroubled most of the time, and entirely without ambition, the perfect wife for a man like Alistair. And being needed suited Sally. It was the first time in her life she'd felt necessary to someone. Her parents had been distant and cold to their only child, not abusive or cruel, just rather dismissive of her feelings and only abstractly aware of her existence most of the time.

The shared relief at home when Sally announced she was getting married was tangible – hers at the chance to get away at last, and her parents' at the realisation they no longer had to think about their daughter's welfare.

When she'd finished her meal, a young, smiling waiter, who was, Sally thought, ′a little too thin′, arrived at her table, cleared the plates and asked if she wanted dessert.

"Do you know, I think I will," she told him. "Could I see your cake trolley please?", almost suggesting he should get a few cream buns down him.

Ten minutes later, she was enjoying an utterly wonderful lemon drizzle cake, licking the cream off her tiny shiny spoon and chuckling at how her mother used to scold her for doing it at the dinner table. Finishing it off with gusto, she glanced over at two ladies sitting near the window by the door.

The younger one looked rather like Audrey Hepburn, very pretty, petite and dressed exquisitely simply. The older lady was stick-thin, wearing what was clearly a vintage 1960s dress. With her heavy dark mascara and obviously bleached hair she looked like a cross between an aging Dusty Springfield and a starving panda.

They were deep in conversation and, as she waved at the dessert waiter for the bill, she wished her sister-in-law

Verity had been with her so they could have had a good old giggle about it. Dear Verity, it had been ages since she'd seen her, and she decided to give her a call when she got home. Mobiles had never been her scene. Sally hated their intrusiveness, and how everyone on trains and buses were glued to them now. She'd always loved conversation with strangers, having a knack for getting people talking, but that had become quite impossible lately. No-one even looked at you anymore.

The skinny boy brought her bill on a silver salver, and, as she got a fifty-pound note out of her purse she asked him how long he'd worked at Fortnum's.

"Just a few weeks," he told her. "I'm actually an actor."

"I bet you can dance," she said to him.

"Yes, I *love* dancing," he said. "I'm auditioning for a musical next week, a revival of *Singin' In The Rain*. My agent says I stand a good chance of getting a part in the chorus."

Sally beamed at him.

"Oh, *Singin' In The Rain*, I saw the Tommy Steele production in… it must have been 1983. I absolutely *loved* Roy Castle. What a talent. Sadly missed."

She could see that the boy, who couldn't have been more than twenty, hadn't a clue who Roy Castle was.

"What's your name?" she asked him.

"Marlon," he replied. "Marlon Carter."

"Well, Marlon, if you have a spoonful of the talent that Roy Castle had, then you will go far."

She left a satisfyingly large tip, wished Marlon good luck, and, joking that he'd 'better not break a leg!', got herself together to go.

As she checked she had everything, she glanced over

at the two ladies again and noticed that 'Audrey' seemed a bit annoyed with 'Dusty' who was shaking her head, apparently trying to explain something. Wandering past their table as slowly as she could, Sally overheard 'Dusty' saying, "Let's move on, shall we?"

To which 'Audrey' replied,

"To what? The past?"

Dying to hear a little more, Sally opened her handbag and pretended to look for something. 'Audrey' noticed her and said,

"Are you alright?"

"Oh, yes," she replied breathlessly, "So sorry, I thought I'd forgotten my purse, but it's here."

She held it up and beamed at them both, noticing 'Dusty' giving her a real glare. Sally said a jaunty 'Good day' and left, hailing a black cab which did a nifty U-turn and swept her up Piccadilly towards Shaftesbury Avenue.

As she watched all the bright and busy stores speeding past her, Sally recalled how Alistair had never joined her for her Saturday trips to London.

"London," he used to say, "is where I travel to every morning for work, so I see no reason to go back there for pleasure."

She used to feel a bit guilty going off on her own for an afternoon, imagining him getting increasingly more disgruntled at being left to make his own pot of tea, or search high and low in the kitchen for biscuits or cake. Even leaving him a casserole simmering on the hob annoyed Alistair, but then, as his mother had once told her, he actually enjoyed feeling hard done by.

At least, she thought, as the taxi went past the Shaftesbury Theatre, which was showing *Hairspray* starring that rather lovely Michael Ball, Alistair hadn't become violent or angry when Alzheimer's had struck. He'd turned into rather a sweet man, in fact, always grateful for any little thing she did for him. He particularly loved her combing his hair, when he no longer knew what a comb was for, and when she handed him the Daily Mail and his reading glasses, he'd look at them like a little boy delighted to be given something he'd never seen before, but which looked like jolly good fun.

Their children, James and Christina, had tutted around him whenever they'd paid occasional visits, blaming her for the fact that 'Daddy' couldn't remember what day it was. Now a widow, they visited much less frequently, probably assuming she'd miss them and ring to ask when they were coming over. The fact was, while they expected her to need them, she had no need of them whatsoever.

Sally's reveries were interrupted when the taxi turned left and parked outside Braintree & York's office. She gave the driver a tip and wandered in, climbing the short flight of stairs into the reception area. She greeted Dina, the office manager, who offered her a cup of tea and asked her to take a seat.

Lawrence York had called that morning and invited her to come in and go through all the legal matters concerning Alistair's passing, and to 'sign a few pieces of paper'. She was now, he'd told her on the phone, a wealthy single woman with a substantial house - which she had every intention of selling as soon as possible – and that just a couple of signatures would 'dot all the i's and cross all the t's'. As she picked up one of the Homes & Gardens magazines off the coffee table, she thought that she rather fancied buying a one-bedroomed apartment by the sea.

Chapter Twenty-Eight

"Mother!" Sally's son James said, as he walked out of his office and came towards her, beaming in that artificial way she'd always disliked.

"Darling, lovely to see you," she replied, standing up to kiss him on each cheek and gaze into his always watery eyes. She also noticed his cheeks were getting increasingly more flushed. 'Drink or blood pressure?' she wondered.

"I haven't heard from you since Daddy's funeral," James said, instantly throwing the blame onto her.

"Yes, dear, it's been a couple of weeks," she said, "but you know where I live."

James did one of his annoyed little coughs, and said as pleasantly as he could, "Lawrence said you were coming in. You know I'd have been more than happy to save you the journey and deal with all this myself on your behalf."

"I'm not an invalid or gaga, dear," she replied, "and anyway it gave me an excuse to have a wander round London again, which I always enjoy."

She glanced over at Dina, remembering that she'd only recently returned to work.

"Dina," she said, beaming at her, "I should have asked you, how's the baby?"

"Oh, he's doing great, thanks Mrs. Braintree. He said his first word last night – 'sit', though it sounded like something rather more rude!"

The two women chuckled while James looked either puzzled or disgusted, it was never clear which. Dina's phone rang, she tapped her earpiece, murmured, 'Yes, Mr. York,' and smiled at Sally.

"Mr. York is ready now, Mrs. Braintree," she told her. "Go right through."

James watched his mother cross the landing, walk into Lawrence's office and close the door.

"I don't see why I can't deal with this," he said like a stroppy little boy. "After all I *am* her son."

"That's probably why, Mr. Braintree," Dina said, immediately picking up the phone to 'call a client'.

"If that's Mr. Pettifer you're calling," James said, "put him through to me."

"It is, Mr. Braintree, and your phone should now be ringing."

James looked momentarily confused, then dashed into his office and shut the door.

***

Lawrence York stood by his desk and shook Sally's hand warmly. She'd always liked him, and watched him grow into an excellent solicitor with a constantly expanding client list, outdoing her son in every area, especially in customer relations. Now in his late fifties, he was as handsome as his father, Derek, had been, with the same intelligent sea-blue eyes and, also like his dad, the ability to make everyone feel welcome.

Derek York had been the one she'd noticed on her first day at the company. Thrilled that he was the partner she'd be mainly working for, Sally had secretly hoped that he'd ask her out. He was single and seemed to like her, without being in any way touchy feely. But though he'd smiled rather gorgeously when she'd brought him his chamomile tea on the dot at eleven every morning, and bid her a friendly good evening at the end of each day, it was Alistair who'd been bold enough to suggest he take her to see *An Affair To Remember* in Leicester Square.

Derek had eventually married a solicitor at another company, and their professional competitiveness was clearly the glue which held them together. Sylvia was dynamic, ambitious, charismatic and exceedingly bright. But, Sally had thought at the time, not a little jealously, she was not in the least bit good-looking, although Alistair had once referred to her as 'handsome'.

Derek and Lawrence seemed to be the perfect father and son and clearly enjoyed working together. James, on the other hand, was always combative with his father. At home, Alistair was the boss, but at work there was a rivalry, a need to prove who brought in the wealthiest clients. It was never an attractive look, and was no doubt why Derek and Lawrence had the biggest client base. They were simply much more fun to deal with. Of course, there was a huge turn-out for Derek's funeral the previous year, compared to just family and a few neighbours at Alistair's.

She'd sometimes scolded herself for imagining being at home waiting for Derek to arrive back from the office, rather than Alistair, who never suspected her longings and imaginings. The fact that she could never be in love with her husband, while not disliking him enough to leave him, left Sally in a kind of emotional limbo.

She felt that she didn't deserve the comfortable life he provided for her, but, as she watched Alistair wolf down everything she served up, it meant, at least, that she could go off to bed knowing that he was contented with her as his wife.

Now here she was, sitting opposite the man she wished was her son, with the inherited smile of the man she wished she'd married, to discuss the situation created by the loss of the man she wished she'd never said yes to.

"Now, Sally," Lawrence said, his voice always so warm and kind, "I have a couple of things for you to sign, to make sure everything, your bank account, household services, your tax status, your assets, everything, will henceforth be in your name only."

He slid the pieces of paper across to her and she duly added her signature at the bottom of each one. Lawrence signed and witnessed them, then, grinning at her, handed her an envelope.

"And there's this," he said, "hand-delivered this morning."

She read her name on the front and, intrigued, tore the envelope open. It was an invite, a personal invite, with her name handwritten on the embossed dotted line, to attend an exhibition that afternoon at The Royal Academy.

She looked up at Lawrence and shook her head.

"Why would the Royal Academy invite me? I've occasionally wandered in and had a look at a few things and even lunched in their Courtyard Café, but…"

Lawrence beamed at her.

"Dina said the chap who delivered it was probably in his eighties but very well-kept, and rather handsome as she told it."

He laughed and added,

"Sounds like my kinda guy."

Sally had guessed that Lawrence was gay from quite early on, and loved the fact that both Derek and Sylvia had embraced his coming out when he was fifteen. Alistair had done his usual tutting about it and she'd hated James' unfunny jokes like 'watch your back!' whenever his name was mentioned over dinner which she'd once challenged her son about.

"I'm not homophobic, mother," he'd protested, "as long as he doesn't creep up behind me at the office or join me in the showers after a game of squash, I'm fine about it."

He'd giggled unattractively and she'd felt like saying, 'Lawrence wouldn't give you the time of day, dear,' but she'd bitten her lip and cleared the table for dessert.

As she stared at the invitation, wondering who could've known she'd be at the office today, Lawrence said, "You should go. It could be fun."

Chapter Twenty-Nine

Sally walked into the Royal Academy and produced her invitation for the lady sitting behind a desk marked, 'Private Showing'. Florence, as her name-tag revealed, checked her list and, writing a big tick next to 'Sally Braintree', handed the invitation back with a beaming smile.

"This will also give you a ten percent discount at The Courtyard Café today, madam," she said brightly. "And, er, I was told to give you... this."

She held up an envelope addressed to 'Sally' and handed it over.

"Oh," Sally said. "*Another* envelope. First the unexpected invitation and now this."

"Is it your birthday, madam?" Florence asked her. "All these lovely surprises."

"Well, no, but it feels like it," Sally replied, looking at the envelope. "Who left it for me? An elderly man, perhaps?"

"It was actually an elderly lady. She didn't give her name, but asked me expressly to give it to you before you went inside."

"Hm," Sally said, wondering who that could have been.

"If you go into the main exhibition hall behind me, madam, there are several comfy seats dotted around where you can relax and view the paintings at your leisure... and read your..."

She waved her fingers at the envelope.

"Yes, that sounds like a good idea," Sally said. "Thank you."

Florence wished her a nice time and gestured towards

the exhibition hall door.

"Please stay as long as you like. There is a lot to enjoy!"

Following the sign for 'Invitation Only', Sally wandered in and sat down, opening the envelope and taking out a handwritten note. The spidery script, clearly indicating it was written by an older person, meant she'd need her reading glasses. She got them out of her handbag, intrigued by how her day was unfolding.

Dear Sally,

I'm so glad you made it to the exhibition. Jack and I wanted you to see the lovely painting which is at the far end of the room on the right. We not only wanted you to see it, but to also have it. There's a little stick-on tag beside the painting, peel it off and take it to the lady you spoke to at the door. She will arrange for you to either take the painting today or have it delivered to you at home.

Squinting at the far wall, Sally got up and continued to read as she walked towards it.

I was always fond of you, Sally, and wished you'd been my daughter rather than simply my son's wife. At least he brought you to into my life, so I have something to thank him for.

"Alice!" Sally said to the room. "But that's impossible. She'd be… no, it's impossible."

She sat down again on another settee and continued to read the letter.

I am now sharing my life with my 'ghost', Sally. The man I told you I used to see in Butterfly Cottage from time to time. He's a time-traveller. I know that must sound utterly bizarre, but it's true. And, as it turns out, so am I, sort of anyway. I am what Jack calls 'a latent traveller', someone with the gift but it's dormant 'until necessary', as Jack described it. One minute I was taking Verity's sculpture to the kitchen for a quick scrub, the next I'm in the kitchen decades into the future looking at Jack. And it felt so natural, Sally. Meant to be.

As you know, it happened on the day that Alistair was visiting, trying to persuade me to move into Carstairs Lodge. I simply couldn't face the possibility of living with him (though I never would have hated living with you, darling). Like my knight in shining armour, Jack held my hand and whisked me away. It's all been rather divine.

We have been very happy, time-slipping hither and thither like ancient star-crossed lovers. He's such great company, and my, the places we've been.

The most bizarre thing, which I have to try and forget about, is that, while Jack was born fifty-eight years after me, we are now around the same age. Jack calls me 'a cradle snatcher' when he's getting frisky, and even at my age I certainly don't mind that.

Anyway, to get back to the reason you are here. Go and look at the painting with the red and gold tag beside it and all will be clear, or at least clearer. I do hope you will enjoy it and hang it on the wall of your new home. I have missed you and Verity, but no-one else, except of course my dear Arthur who made me very happy during our long marriage.

Yours in another time and space,

Lots of love,
Alice xx

Sally sat for a while, and then, smiling to herself, she put the note in her handbag and walked towards the painting with the red and gold tag beside it. She actually chuckled when she reached it. There was Alice next to a rather good-looking elderly man with curls and a dashing smile. She looked at the small plaque on the frame: *'Friends Through Time' by Harry Mainstay.*

"Good for you, Alice," Sally said to the painting.

She removed the red and gold tag from beside the portrait and walked back through the room, her heart fluttering like a butterfly.

She handed in the tag to Florence who said, "It is *definitely* a special day for you, Mrs. Braintree!"

She checked down her list, holding the tag as she went down the page.

"Here it is. 'Friends Through Time'. I *love* that painting. Such a happy-looking couple, aren't they? I don't know the artist, but he has really got a Fauvist flair about him, wouldn't you agree?"

Sally nodded, not sure what 'Fauvist' meant but feeling sure it was a good thing.

"Now, Mrs. Braintree. Would you like to take the painting today or shall we send it to your home?"

"Well, I will be moving soon, so is it possible to leave you my phone number, just in case you need to contact me, and I will let you have my new address as soon as I have it. If you could send the painting to me there, that would be most kind."

Sally wandered out into the sunshine chuckling to herself.

"My oh my," she said. "What an amazing day."

She was thinking she'd walk up Piccadilly as she wanted to pop into one of her favourite draper's to buy a couple of their gingham tablecloths, when something struck her. In Alice's note, she'd referred to 'your new home'.

"How the heck did she know…?" Sally murmured, shook her head at the whole surreality of it and wandered off into a sunny London afternoon.

Sitting towards the back of the Courtyard Café were two elderly figures, sipping their coffees and watching Sally walking away. Alice turned to Jack and said, "She looks very happy."

"She does."

"Happier than I've ever seen her."

"I wish I'd have known her," Jack said.

"You'd have liked her."

Jack stood, left some money on the table and said, "Home?"

Alice stood up and grinned at Jack.

"Home," she said.

They held hands, walked towards Hyde Park and disappeared.

***

Sally stood outside what had been her favourite London draper's, disappointed that it had been turned into a particularly gaudy bar. She looked up Piccadilly and saw the two ladies from Fortnum's. She put on some pace and, as she reached them, started nattering some fussy nonsense she knew would annoy 'Dusty'.

As she'd thought, 'Audrey' was rather lovely, happy

to chat for a few minutes but 'Dusty' was clearly keen to get away. As 'Audrey' bid farewell and they made their way towards the tube, Sally waved down a cab.

"Waterloo Station, please," she said to the driver, loving the sense of independence it always gave her.

'Audrey' smiled and waved as the cab drove by, Sally wishing she'd had more time to get to know her.

At the station, she checked to see if her train was on time and realised she had half-an-hour to kill. So she took herself off to Costa Coffee, bought one of their tasty lattes and a delicious-looking cream doughnut, and found a small table by the door.

'My,' she thought, as she licked the cream off her fingers. 'Sally Braintree. Who'd have thought life would end up being *such* an adventure?'

Chapter Thirty

One evening in 1924, Jack and Alice walked towards the imposing front door of Lockton Manor. They had just got back from seeing Noel Coward's smash hit play *The Vortex* at The Royalty Theatre in Soho. Its storyline, featuring drug addiction and younger-man-older-woman romance caused critical outrage and public delight, making headlines in many of the newspapers and becoming the cause célèbre of the day.

The theatre that night had been packed to the rafters with fans of the great playwright who all stood and cheered when the play ended. Many people had been looking forward to Noel Coward doing his famous final bow speech, but sadly he had been unable to play the part of Nicky that evening. His place was taken by 'a fascinating young actor', as the slipped-in note in their programme read, one John Gielgud. It had amused Jack and Alice that they had also enjoyed the older Gielgud's performance in the 1970 production of *Home* at the Royal Court during one of their recent travels.

Lockton Manor was an early Victorian Gothic pile, with various substantial wings that no-one had visited for years. The central part of the house was still inhabitable, though with more basic amenities than certainly Alice had been used to. Even as a small child, her parents' house in Surrey had hot and cold running water. Jack, of course, took it in his stride, having inhabited many primitively-plumbed dwellings during his trips back to the 19th century with Ginny.

Jack had always been fascinated about what the Manor had looked like, wondering just how 'Gothic' it had been in its day. For him, buying the deserted mansion answered so many questions and he could at last know first-hand what had stood here before it had been demolished and replaced by the bungalows.

With its long pointed arches, flying exterior buttresses, stained-glass windows, ribbed vaults and tall spires, it was impressive. Jack had particularly liked the fan-vaulted ceiling in the great hall, the beautiful lacework carving like layered butterfly wings.

One evening, he and Alice were sitting by the fire in the Great Hall, chatting about their recent trip to 1950s Monaco. Alice had loved the dinner party they'd attended with several Hollywood stars, including Gary Cooper, Ava Gardner, Cary Grant and Gloria Swanson, and had been particularly taken aback at how beautiful Grace Kelly was 'with skin like porcelain'.

A slight breeze suddenly ran through the room and the flames in the grate shifted as the movement of air got stronger. Jack sat up and murmured,

"Oh Lord, it's happening."

The image of a girl appeared in the doorway, sitting in a rocking chair and glancing out ahead of her.

"Good God," Jack whispered, "it's Bella."

"Bella?" Alice asked, staring at the slowly wafting image before her.

"Young Bella Mainstay, I'd given Butterfly Cottage to her and Harry's grandson, Stephen, minutes before you appeared in the kitchen."

"Can she see us?" Alice asked.

As the image faded, Jack said, "No. It's a reflected time prism."

"A what?"

"It's when an image from the future or the past, in an area which has a time portal, connects with another nearby portal. This one's connecting from where the bungalow would be, across the grounds outside."

"I wonder," Alice said to herself.

"What?"

"I remember something happening at the bungalow, shortly after Arthur and I had moved in. It makes sense now."

"What was it?"

"I saw a young kid in what looked like Edwardian clothes trying to climb the wall at the back of the house, then when he saw me he ran off through the hedge and disappeared. Arthur thought I'd imagined it, of course."

"It happened a lot?"

"Quite a lot, and, of course, I also saw you from time to time. My handsome ghost."

***

Watching the image of young Bella appearing in the doorway became a regular nightly pastime for Jack and Alice. Sometimes she was alone, sometimes with Stephen.

"I do feel rather like a voyeur," Alice said once, as Bella and Stephen were chatting quietly to each other.

"It's harmless." Jack said. "I hoped they'd love it there and that seems to have come to pass."

One evening, however, the image changed. This time it showed an old lady, rocking gently on the veranda and smiling down at a scarf she was knitting.

"Matthew!" she called. "Why not come and join me? I've made some lemon and elderberry juice."

"Matthew," Jack said. "That's the name of one of

Bella's and Stephen's twins."

He leaned forward.

"Then that old lady must be Bella, from many years later."

They watched as Bella suddenly stared ahead of her, looking horror-struck.

"It can't be!" she cried. "Stephen? Oh my god, it's Stephen!"

She tried to stand up but fell backwards onto her chair and fainted. A man in his fifties rushed onto the veranda.

"Mother?" he said. "What's wrong?"

The image seemed to go out of focus, ripple and scan across to the kitchen window.

"It's as though someone's moving a camera," Alice said, fascinated.

"Time prisms are rather like the old camera obscura," Jack said, "you get a kind of panoramic view of a scene. Quite fascinating."

There inside the kitchen stood the young Stephen, looking shocked as he stared out at the garden.

Jack turned to Alice.

"Well, you know what *this* means?" he said.

"Yes, I know. Jack to the rescue."

***

Jack closed the door of Lockton Manor, patting it fondly and murmuring 'So long, old friend'. He linked Alice's arm and together they walked down the front steps, sauntering along the wide, sweeping drive and past the now dry marble fountain featuring nymphs and angels riding a dolphin.

They turned right towards a large group of sycamores which opened out into a narrow clearing. Just as the clouds made way for a beam of sunlight which drenched the field in a golden glow, the two of them disappeared.

Chapter Thirty-One

Sally accepted an excellent offer on Carstairs Lodge, and, during a long weekend in Little Haven looking at properties in the area, she found a lovely one-bedroomed apartment in a small stone-built block of flats on the sea front of Broad Haven. Number Six, Golygfa O'r Môr, or Sea View in English as the estate agent had explained, was just what she was looking for.

She'd first come to this lovely seaside town as a child with a weekend school outing, and then again shortly before she married Alistair. It was a girls' trip with the friends who would be her bridesmaids, celebrating her last fling as a single girl.

They'd had a terrific time, staying in an ancient old holiday cottage from where they took trips out every morning to various bays and places of interest, the highlight being when they'd visited Marloes, pronounced Mar-las by the locals, where they sat on the clifftops and watched the baby seals frolicking on the rocks below.

By a strange coincidence, her apartment building was situated where the old holiday cottage used to stand and, as she'd entered the flat on her first viewing, she got a strong feeling of déjà-vu. It felt like she was coming home.

She hadn't got to know her neighbours yet, although she'd had a pleasant chat with an elderly chap called Peter at Number Four. He seemed rather a complicated fellow, but he'd been very kind to offer to take her for lunch to the nearby Galleon Inn, which she was looking forward to.

As they were nattering, a middle-aged couple from Number Three went out to their car in the reserved parking bay. Peter had told her it was Pamela and Mark who ran a bistro in Little Haven, which became another eaterie he said they should visit.

And there was the extremely handsome, beautifully-dressed man from Number One. She'd been standing by the window enjoying her early morning Earl Grey and seen him sauntering towards the open-topped Ford Consul she'd spotted a few times.

'I must get chatting to him,' she'd thought, as he coasted by. 'I'd love a spin in that!'.

One afternoon, as she was admiring the painting of Alice and Jack, which the Royal Academy had delivered just a few days after she'd moved in, a large parcel arrived by courier, containing a substantial gold-embossed book called *Crossing Time Spaces - A Journal of Recollections and Adventure*. Inside the first page of the book was a short note which Sally had read over her cup of Darjeeling:

Dear Sally,

I think you will enjoy reading this. It's a journal which my late wife, Ginny, wrote. Our story will I hope help to make recent occurrences clearer. There are also my occasional additions to the narrative and a short addendum at the end by Alice. I know she is especially pleased that you and she were friends and often speaks about you very fondly.

Be happy in your new home. Who knows, we may pop in sometime - only joking!

All best,

Jack Marlowe.

'More intrigue,' Sally thought, and, taking the journal

out onto the patio, settled herself in a sunny spot and opened it at the first page.

***

As Jack had predicted in his note, the journal answered so many of the questions she'd been asking herself ever since her visit to the Royal Academy. What had seemed like a surreal involvement in others´ unexplained adventures at last made sense. Even if it made her head spin a little, just understanding things a little better made the unbelievable seem entirely credulous.

But there was one extra thing about the journal which utterly delighted her. On the last page, Jack had included a reproduction of a painting he had done of Ginny. At last, she could put a proper name to the pretty girl she'd seen at Fortnum's.

"I knew you were special," Sally said to the girl who smiled out of the painting, as she had done that day at the restaurant.

She wasn't sure why, but there were occasional sections of the journal, such as the flowery scent Ginny smelt whenever she'd travelled with Jack, and the sound of wind-chimes which filled the room when they were thrust forward or back in time, which resonated with her.

Maybe it was just a memory of Verity's pretty garden in Holland Park, with its array of beautiful aromas and the comforting sounds of bells and chimes which hung from various walls and branches.

Smiling at the thought of Verity, she walked into the kitchen and put the kettle on. As she dropped her lemon and ginger teabag into the mug, she decided there was something she needed to do. She got her address book from out of the drawer and found who she wanted to call.

***

Lawrence York put the phone down and looked at Dina, who was making notes about the business of the day ahead.

"Is everything alright, Mr. York?" Dina enquired, as he stood behind his desk mulling something over.

"What? Oh yes, sorry, Dina. It looks like I'm driving to Broad Haven this morning. Can you cancel all my appointments for the day?"

"Can I tell people why?"

"Just say I've been called away on urgent business. The fact of the matter is, Mrs. Braintree wants to change her will and said she needed it doing today. So, that's where I'm going."

He grinned at Dina and winked.

"And… better not tell James where I'm off to, and definitely not why!"

Chapter Thirty-Two

Two years later, Tee Braintree was leaning on her walking stick outside the apartment which Sally had left to her in her will. She didn't know Broad Haven, had been never been, but it certainly appealed. She breathed in the smell of the sea and smiled.

When Lawrence York had phoned to tell her of the inheritance, Tee had asked him, "But why me?"

"Sally said you'd say that," he replied, "and she told me to say on her behalf... because she knew you'd ask that question."

Tee had laughed at that, knowing Sally's ambivalence towards her children, aware of their presumptions. She turned to Suze.

"Do you like it?"

"I think it's lovely," Suze replied.

"So do I. I think it's rather darling. Would you like to live here?"

"The two of us? Together?"

Suze and Tee had maintained their own properties throughout their relationship. Neither of them had ever raised the possibility of living together, both enjoying their independence while ensuring they saw each other several times a week.

"I think it´s time we considered it," Tee said, squeezing her hand. "This could be our new life together."

"But what about your studio in London?"

Tee smiled at Suze.

"I haven't been there for ages."

She waved her stick and laughed.

"I'm a little too old for climbing over scaffolding and frames now, and I'm sure I'd find a small studio space to rent nearby for when I get creative. This area seems very artisan, there were lots of little galleries and workshops as we drove here. We can check it out together."

"And your lovely flat in Holland Park?"

"It's time for a change, don't you think?"

"Well, if you're sure."

"Never been more sure. Come on, let's go and look at our new home."

As they wandered in, Tee stopped dead, staring at Sally's painting on the wall.

"Good God," she said. "It's mummy."

Suze walked with her to get a closer look.

"Who's she sitting with? It looks a bit like Jack, but it can't be, he's too old."

"And that's my sculpture, the one I did of Mum, on the table behind them."

"Who gave the painting to Sally?" Suze asked.

"I have no idea."

"She never mentioned it?"

"No."

Suze squinted at the small plaque on the frame.

"'Friends Through Time' by Harry Mainstay. Do you know him?"

"Never heard of him."

"That does look like Jack. Maybe it's his father?"

"With my mum?"

The two ladies shook their heads at each other.

"It's rather wonderful," Suze said, "but..."

"Unsettling?"

Suze nodded.

Tee felt the need to sit down and, as she approached the settee, she saw a large book on the coffee table, with two envelopes lying on top it. She fell heavily onto the settee and pulled them towards her.

"Lawrence mentioned there was a book here with a couple of notes which Sally wanted us to read. She said they would explain everything."

"Explain what?"

Tee read out the title of the book.

"*Crossing Time Spaces - A Journal of Recollections and Adventure.*"

"I'm feeling just a little spooked out," Suze said. "First the painting and now this."

"Lawrence said there's a bottle of gin and some tonics in the fridge, why don't you make a couple of large ones and we'll settle down to have a ganders."

Suze glanced again at the painting and shivered slightly.

Chapter Thirty-Three

"My God," Tee said, taking off her reading glasses.

While the notes had been intriguing, the one from Alice especially emotional for Tee, the journal had been absolutely mind-blowing.

The two ladies sat in silence for a few minutes, looking at the painting and drinking their G & Ts.

"What an incredible story," Suze said eventually. "I do wish Ginny had told me."

"Would you have believed her if she had?"

"Well, the whole thing *is* bonkers, but yes, I'd have tried to understand," Suze said.

"'Understand' and 'believe' are two entirely different things."

"The weirdest thing – amongst so many – is how a much older Jack came to see me, well, not me, another me."

"I think as Jack says in the journal, you just have to accept it as fact and not keep trying to make sense of it."

"Voices from the past speaking from the future..." Suze said. "What am I going to say to Ginny next time I see her? 'Oh hi, darling, I know all about the other you and I even know when you're going to die!'"

Tee chuckled and put her arm round Suze.

"You'll be fine. If you love Ginny, just keep schtum."

Suze looked rather unconvinced.

"I don't know if I'm strong enough to do that."

"Of course you are. Now, let's put on our warm cardies, have another G & T and watch that storm coming in over the sea. I love a good storm."

As Suze took their glasses into the kitchen, she felt her day had been turbulent enough already.

***

A couple of weeks later, Suze was reading the Guardian while Tee was opening the mail.

"Ah, this one's from Lawrence," Tee said. "He said the estate agent has had a couple of offers on our properties, and is asking if the higher offers are acceptable to us."

"I don't mind what King's Court goes for, as long as it sells," Suze said.

"My feelings entirely. I'll ring him to tell him to accept the higher offers. Good. That's that sorted."

"He's very efficient isn't he?"

"Yes. Sally had a lot of time for him."

Tee looked off through the window.

"I do wish I'd have come over to see Sally, rather than just phoning her occasionally. I feel very guilty about that."

Suze squeezed Tee's arm.

"You always said the two of you laughed a lot when you spoke."

"We did. She was like a sister to me. I did love her."

"And she loved you." Suze waved her hand around the room. "Clearly rather a lot."

Tee picked up her mobile to call Lawrence about the offers, when she heard a loud tinkling sound which rang around the room.

"What was that?" she asked Suze.

"It's what happened in the journal!" Suze cried, as the door to the bedroom suddenly opened and a young woman came rushing in.

"So, girls," she said, "where are we going to today?"

"Sally!" Tee gasped.

The young woman stared at the two old biddies.

"Who the hell are you two?"
She looked around the room.
"And *where* is this?"
"Oh God," Suze said, "now what do we do?"

Chapter Thirty-Four

Charles Lockton closed the front door of his Broad Haven apartment and wandered down the main path which led onto the seafront promenade. He was planning a pre-lunch power-walk before popping into the Galleon Inn for a plateful of their delicious prawns in garlic, his mouth watering just thinking of it.

As he passed Number Six, he felt the air move rather oddly, a shimmer he recognised immediately. He stopped, wondered if he should intervene, then, putting the prawns in garlic out of his mind, walked up the path to the front door.

He hadn't properly met the couple who'd moved in after Sally had passed away. She'd told him that she had left the flat to her sister-in-law and her partner and, as he rang the bell, he reminded himself of their names.

"Tee and Suze, that's it," he said to himself. "I'm sure that's what Sally said."

The door opened and a rather handsome, if slightly dishevelled, woman in her seventies stood there looking completely flustered. She ran her hand through a mane of grey hair, which was trying not to tumble down from a loosely-pinned bun.

"Er- this isn't a good time, actually," she said, about to close the door.

"Really?" said Charles, peering in. "I am inclined to disagree."

He slipped past Suze and wandered through the hallway.

"My name's Charles," he said, as Suze ran after him.

"But who *are* you?" she said, fluttering her arms like an escaped bird.

"I've already told you that," he replied a little tetchily.

As Charles entered the sitting-room, he found another elderly lady sitting with a visibly upset young girl staring around the room like a lost child.

"I live at Number One," he said to the old lady, "and I'm guessing you are…"

"Charles," she said.

"No, that's my name, dear. You must be Tee?"

Tee smiled.

"Yes, I am. Sally told me all about you."

She looked at the young girl sitting next to her, eyes as wide as saucers.

"Not you, dear, the other Sally, that is the one who -"

Charles stepped forward and spoke to the girl.

"You're due to be married soon," he said. "Correct?"

"Well, yes, as a matter of fact I am. To Alistair, Alistair Braintree, next week…"

"Oh Tee!" Suze cried. "That's your brother. So, this *is* Sally."

"Well of course I'm Sally," the young girl said. "Will someone tell me what is going on?"

Charles sat on the arm of the settee.

"Tell me what happened, Sally," he said, his voice amazingly calming.

The girl heaved a large sigh.

"Well, I'd just been to the rather primitive loo outside, and was coming through to ask the girls what they fancied doing today when… when I was suddenly *here*. Wherever this is. With you two. Whoever you are."

Charles patted her on the shoulder and smiled reassuringly.

"Now, Sally, listen to me. I'm going to put this right. Okay?"

The girl wiped her nose on a hanky and nodded.

"I'd like you to come with me," he said, holding out his hand. "Everything is going to be tickety-boo."

Turning to Tee and Suze, who looked in shock, he said, "You two, stay here. I won't be long."

Then to Sally, "Now, let's get you home, darling. You have a wedding to prepare for."

Tee and Suze watched them walk through the bedroom doorway and disappear.

Chapter Thirty-Five

One Summer's morning in 1968, Charles stretched out in the sizeable bed he'd come to love on these occasional visits to Swinging London, and looked around at Cass Elliott's hippy-esque Chelsea apartment. With its Che Guevara posters and oriental wall coverings, it reflected King's Road in its grooviest period.

As he got up and padded into the bathroom, he remembered his last visit, when Paul McCartney had come over to play them the acetate of *Sergeant Pepper*. Cass had turned the volume up full, so it blasted out of the open window at passers-by below. No-one who looked up and heard the music floating down recognised the glorious strains of 'Lucy In The Sky With Diamonds' or 'Fixing A Hole'. Very soon, of course, they, and the rest of the world, would.

"This is the best thing I have ever heard," Cass had said, taking a drag from the joint she'd been rolling.

"And you are two of the first people to hear it," Paul replied.

"What do you say, Charles?" Cass said, handing him the joint.

"I say, 'It's getting better all the time,'" he'd sung along with the track.

"Better, better, better," Cass harmonised with the chorus.

Cass was now touring the States so Charles had the place to himself, and, after a long soak in the delightfully deep bath, he decided he'd take a wander to the recently-opened Chelsea Drugstore for a late breakfast. He recalled when it was the White Hart pub and he'd popped in for a drink en route to the home of Sir Carol Reed. It was in 1948 and, having just received his second Bafta Award for *The Fallen Idol*, Reed was starting work on his future classic, *The Third Man*.

Grahame Greene, who'd written them both, was there with his friend Alexander Korda and Charles had watched them all heatedly discussing how to put the novel on the screen. Most excitingly, Orson Welles was also there.

"This guy got me the role," Welles told Charles. "Selznick wanted Noel Coward, but Carol here insisted I get the part."

The evening had ended with Reed putting on a disc of the music of Anton Karas.

"I discovered this zither player outside a courtyard restaurant in Vienna," he told everyone. "His music will be the sound of *The Third Man*."

"I *love* that sound!" shouted Carol's ten-year-old nephew, Oliver, who had arrived with his mother Marcia and was running round the dinner table miming the zither.

"He's a little devil," Carol laughed, "but already, what star charisma."

Carol could not have foreseen that twenty-three years later his nephew would make one of the most controversial movies of all time. Charles had been a guest at the premiere of *The Devils* and, at the after-screening party, Oliver had told him,

"We never set out to make a pretty Christian film. Charlton Heston´s made enough of those... this film is about twisted people."

He'd smiled wickedly.

"Two of my favourite scenes were edited out. One was a two-and-a-half-minute sequence featuring naked nuns sexually defiling a statue of Christ, while Father Mignon looked down on the scene masturbating."

Charles had involuntarily widened his eyes at that, which made Oliver burst out laughing.

"I know, dear," he'd said, "imagine what the Vatican would have made of *that*! The other cut scene showed Sister Jeanne – darling Vanessa - masturbating with the charred femur of my character, after he'd been burned at the stake."

Oliver had raised one of his eyebrows naughtily while nibbling on a canapé.

"Tasty," he quipped.

"You're a very bad boy," Charles said.

"And that's why you adore me, Charles," Oliver replied, giving him a peck on the cheek.

Chapter Thirty-Six

Lawrence York was sitting in the garden of Bridesview, looking out on its acre of fruit trees and various varieties of roses, wondering why he hadn´t done this years ago. While he would always regret not seeing Sally again before she died, he was thankful that she had, indirectly, led him to this great house and to the rather wonderful Tee and Suze, who'd become good friends since he'd moved here. For the first time in a long time, Lawrence felt a sense of peace, along with an innate sense that the future promised something wonderful.

Always a city boy, he'd found himself becoming increasingly – and surprisingly - bored of London. He'd loved the scene when he was younger but he'd now reached an age where he'd grown out of – and felt increasingly too old for - visiting bars and clubs, and his circle of friends, who had once fascinated and amused him, were beginning to bore him, something he'd never expected to happen.

Even his second-floor flat in Bayswater, which he'd bought twenty years earlier, no longer appealed. He'd begun to feel hemmed in when he got back from work, with just a tiny balcony overlooking a busy road, and the anonymity he'd once craved, not knowing any of his neighbours beyond a quick nod in the lift, now felt like loneliness.

It had taken over a year to organise, but he'd finally sold his share of Braintree & York to a typically pedantic and difficult James, and ensconced himself at a pretty B´n´B in St. David´s, from where he could drive out to view various properties and get to know Pembrokeshire better.

Lawrence had fallen in love with the large, honey-coloured detached house just outside St. Bride's, made an offer which was instantly accepted and within a couple of months had moved in.

One morning, he was chatting to Tee outside her apartment after a delightful brunch of cheese and warm crusty bread baked by Suze, when a great-looking guy drove past in a fabulous classic car and waved at them both.

"*Who* is that?" Lawrence said.

"Charles, Charles Lockton, he's a neighbour of ours, immensely helpful as it turned out."

"Does he help out when we're busy?" Lawrence said.

Tee laughed.

"Oh, more than helps out, fully employed, darling. *And* he's single. Why don't Suze and I arrange a dinner for four here? Soon."

Lawrence arrived first for Tee and Suze's matchmaking dinner party, feeling a little apprehensive. Suze had not helped by nattering on about how special Charles was, how socially at ease he was, how surprised she was that no-one 'had snapped him up earlier'.

He kept his nerves in check by telling himself that, at most, Charles would be another enjoyable fling, and, sniffing the rather delicious aroma of the vegetarian 'crispy crust casserole' Suze had prepared, he was pleased to see another distraction, several framed photos of different varieties of butterflies which had been hung since his last visit.

"Those are lovely," he said, impressed by the various iridescent hues captured brilliantly by the photographer.

"We finally got round to hanging them," Tee told him, handing him his gin and tonic which as always was heavy on the gin with just a splash of tonic. "They were taken by my mother in the '60s."

"She was very talented," Lawrence said, taking them in.

"It must be where Tee gets her artistic talent," Suze said, bustling out of the kitchen and pinning up her loosening bun.

"Alistair was ready to throw them in the skip until I nabbed them," Tee said.

"Yes, I can´t imagine them being to Alistair's taste," Lawrence said wryly.

"I keep forgetting you knew Tee's brother," Suze said, her bun resisting any attempt at being tidied into place.

"He was a complete Philistine," Tee said.

"Alistair was a perfectly good solicitor," Lawrence said diplomatically, "but not so good at discussing anything to do with the arts with clients who were on the boards of museums and galleries. Dad always directed them to me."

The doorbell rang and Suze went to answer it, all aflutter about 'the divine Charles'. His nerves returning like the butterflies on the wall, Lawrence went to look at a grouping of small sculptures, figures in different stages of movement, on a shelf unit by the door which he also hadn't seen before.

"I love these," Lawrence said.

"Yes, something else we finally unpacked," Tee said.

She was explaining that they were the first stages of much larger sculptures, which were now in various public spaces around the world, when Suze came back into the room shouting 'Here he is!', followed by one of the most charismatic men Lawrence had ever seen. He'd fancied Charles when he'd seen him drive past, but now, close up, he looked like an aristocratic Terence Stamp.

His beautifully fitted grey mohair suit over a black silk polar neck top added to the 1960s stylish allure which was completed by the highly-polished Beatle boots. The laughter lines around his sea-green eyes crinkled gorgeously as he smiled and stepped forward to introduce himself. For the first time in his life, Lawrence felt his heart being stolen away.

Within days of the extremely successful 'Cupid's Bow Dinner', as Tee called it, Charles became a regular visitor to Bridesview, where he and Lawrence would lie in till eleven and have a late breakfast in the garden. Most afternoons they took trips around Pembrokeshire in Charles' car, parking in a quiet spot off the road or on the edge of a deserted bay, sharing picnics, stories and a growing romance.

"I love this car," Lawrence said one blazing hot afternoon, as they tucked into pitta bread, houmous and tzatziki. "A real classic. And it's like new."

He stroked the mauve leather seating and the inlaid satinwood dashboard.

"I bought it from Cliff Richard," Charles said casually.

"He kept it all those years?" Lawrence asked.

"No. He sold it to me in 1963."

Lawrence glanced over at Charles and pulled a face.

"I know you're well-kept for your age, darling, but -"

Charles just chuckled, cheered Lawrence with his glass of Perrier and said, "I'm going back to the apartment this evening, so I'll drop you off en route. I need to prepare for our outing tomorrow."

"What outing?"

"I'll pick you up at ten o'clock and take you on a little trip," Charles replied. "and don't bother getting dressed, I'll bring an outfit for you. Something fitting."

"Fitting? What's wrong with the clothes I've got? I have some perfectly lovely suits if we're going somewhere 'posh'."

"Hm, 'posh' is not the word I would choose for our destination," Charles said, packing the leftovers in his cool case.

"Is it a fancy dress party?"

"That's for me to know and you to find out," Charles replied tapping Lawrence on the nose.

He turned on the ignition and, smiling across at his bemused boyfriend, sped off.

Chapter Thirty-Seven

Charles arrived at Bridesview at five minutes to ten the next morning, with a cream and red leather suitcase which reminded Lawrence of the luggage he and his parents had taken to Torquay each year when he was growing up. Charles opened it grandly and lifted out an outfit on a hanger like an assistant in a high-class couturier's.

"I can't wear those!" Lawrence protested, staring at the red and white zip-fasten cashmere cardigan, sky blue and cream Rayon T-shirt and lilac check slacks. "I'll look like some aging hipster sixty years too late."

He quickly added, "*You* always look great in vintage clothes, but me?"

"You will look fabulous," Charles said, handing him the clothes. "Now get changed and let's have a look."

Ten minutes later Lawrence was looking at himself in the mirror pulling a face.

"Talk about mutton dressed as lamb. This is ridiculous!"

"Dear boy," Charles said, "you look gorgeous. You still have a great figure, so why not flaunt it? Age is merely a number, it's how you carry it that matters."

He handed Lawrence a pair of slip-on cream leather loafers, which were probably the most comfortable shoes he'd ever worn.

"What a dashing pair we are," Charles said, doing a little twirl in his red, white and blue striped shirt with a zip-up collar, mohair grey trousers and red leather winkle-pickers. "Prepare yourself for a fabulous time."

"But where are we going?"

"London, of course!"

Chapter Thirty-Eight

As Charles drove along Marylebone Road, Lawrence tapping his hand to Pharell Williams' 'Happy' on the car radio, The Landmark Hotel came into view.

"Is that where we're going?" Lawrence said. "I bet it is. I knew it was going to be some kind of theme party."

Charles murmured 'not quite The Landmark' and turned left into Harewood Avenue, parking the car outside what looked like an old café now closed down and boarded up.

"Follow me," he said, getting out of the car and walking towards the derelict old shell.

"In there?" Lawrence asked, staring up at the peeling sign above the door.

"Doreen used to do the best eggs and bacon I've ever tasted here," Charles said. "I can taste them now."

Smiling at Lawrence, he grabbed his hand and, with a breezy 'Come on', opened the door and walked in. Loud wind chimes rang around them as they stepped into a busy café, dimly lit by three unshaded lightbulbs hanging from the yellowing ceiling. The air was full of cigarette smoke and, around small wooden tables, groups of people looking like extras from *Billy Liar*.

A lady who reminded Lawrence of Hattie Jacques was standing behind a Formica-covered counter, wiping it down with a dishcloth. When she saw Charles her face lit up.

"Charlie boy!" she shouted. "Nice to see you again."

"Doreen," Charles replied, going up to the counter and giving her a peck on the cheek. "Two plates of your fabulous eggs and bacon and a pot of your excellent tea, please."

"Alright, lovie. We're a bit busy, but there's a nice table by the window over there. I've just given it a wipe."

Lawrence followed Charles to the table and stared around him.

"So, what do you think?" Charles asked as they sat down.

"Where the fuck are we?" Lawrence replied. "Is this some kind of period party?"

Charles wiped the steamed-up window with his sleeve and said, "Look out there."

What Lawrence saw resembled one of the *Look At Life* films he used to watch as a child at the Roxy. Men wandered by in bowler hats atop suits and ties while younger men strode past in collarless jackets, Terylene crotch-hugging slacks and all sporting Beatles haircuts. On their arms were girls with Mary Quant bobs, baby-doll dresses and mini-skirts. It was like a scene from *Take Three Girls*.

"We are in the year when Britain found its own look, its own music and its own culture," Charles said. "The beginning of the new age."

Lawrence's eyes were on stalks.

"Did you drop some acid in my tea this morning?"

Charles smiled at Lawrence.

"This has nothing to do with drugs," he said. "It's as real as you and I. Welcome to 1963!"

Doreen arrived with a tray and began laying out a surprisingly lovely tea set, blue china teapot with matching milk jug, sugar bowl and two cups and saucers.

"Only my best china for Charlie," Doreen said.

"It's lovely," Lawrence said.

Doreen winked at Lawrence.

"I bet you were expecting two chipped old mugs,

weren't you dear?"

"Of course not, I - "

"Thank you, Doreen," Charles said, "you're a gem."

Doreen blushed up slightly then gathered herself together.

"Now, gents!" she said. "Eggs and bacon will be ready in a jiffy."

She beamed at Charles.

"So lovely to see you again, Charlie."

"You too," Charles replied, as she busied off singing along with 'From Me To You' which was playing on a small transistor radio on the counter.

Charles saw his boyfriend's gobsmacked expression and leaned forward.

"All I ask, my lovely confused man, is that you simply listen to what I have to tell you. Will you do that?"

"If it explains this…" Lawrence waved his hand around the room.

"It will," Charles replied. "Will you be mother?"

As Lawrence poured the tea, his boyfriend began telling his barely believable life story.

Born in 1897 into the wealthy Lockton family, Charles had always felt there was more beyond the confines of his privileged life.

His first time-slip had happened when he was nine, while wandering around the family mansion in Turnham Green. As the young lad had aimlessly gone from corridor to room, from room to corridor, he saw a door he hadn't noticed before.

"It seemed to wave and billow like a dream-image," Charles said to Lawrence, looking above him as though seeing the doorway again.

Being an inquisitive kid, he opened the door and, accompanied by the sound of wind chimes and a sweet scent, found himself outside. To his amazement the manor had disappeared, along with the grand sweeping drive and the endless grounds in which he often played. Only the fountain, with its nymphs and angels playing with the laughing dolphin spouting water into the air from its mouth, remained, surrounded by an area of parkland hedged in the distance by a line of laurel trees.

"Didn't it freak you out?" Lawrence asked Charles. "Everything changing like that in a second?"

"Oddly no. I was more fascinated, thrilled even. I felt like a character in a novel, an adventurer. I guess my natural instincts kicked in."

Doreen arrived with their meals, plonking a bottle of HP sauce on the table.

"Enjoy, my lovelies," she said, winking at Lawrence and pulling a 'he's nice' face at Charles.

Thanking Doreen, Charles put a slice of the thick crispy bacon in his mouth, savoured it for a moment then continued his tale.

He walked across the parkland towards the hedge and pushed through a gap in the foliage. A low stone and flint wall ran along what looked like a row of one-storey brick dwellings. Wondering if they were workers' cottages his father had built for his staff, Charles decided to climb the wall and see for himself.

With a lot of huffing and puffing, he scrambled to the top and peered around him. There stood a lady, who looked to be about the same age as his grandmama, smiling at him from the veranda of a small timber-clad summerhouse. She looked kind, he thought, but was dressed most oddly, her skimpy one-piece dress looking more like a pinafore. It shocked him that a lady would wander around in public in her undergarments.

It was only when she spoke to him that he panicked. He jumped down and ran through the hole in the hedge, galloping as fast as his legs could carry him. He shot across the parkland and spotted the wafting doorway in the distance. The sound of wind chimes rang around him again as he ran through it and found himself back in the corridor of the mansion.

Curious to see what was outside, he climbed onto one of the stone window-ledges and looked through the large mullioned window. The mansion's grounds, the marble fountain in the middle and the sweeping gravel road were back.

"I'd have been terrified," Lawrence said.

"Oh no. I was intrigued and I wanted to do it again. I went searching for the wafting door every day, and whenever I found it, always in a different part of the house, I went through it, and my, what I found was always wonderful!"

By his early teens Charles had become an expert time-traveller, arriving anywhere he chose and always getting back to exactly the moment he'd left. What fascinated him the most was how he could mix easily with people in any period, able to discuss anything and everything, as though he'd always lived there. He had money and was dressed in the fashions of the year in which he'd arrived.

"Hold on," Lawrence said. "Why then did you bring us these '60s clothes to wear?"

Charles laughed.

"I'm afraid the time portals' taste in high fashion leaves much to be desired. So, as I wanted to be dressed to impress, as I did on this trip with you, I brought our wardrobe with us. Don't you approve?"

"Yes, I feel completely 'in period'," Lawrence said, smiling. "Pretty cool, in fact."

"Good."

Lawrence poured out more tea for them both.

"What did your parents think," he said, adding a dash of milk, "you disappearing off all the time?"

"Well, Daddy left us when I was ten and never came back, and Mummy was only ever vaguely aware of anyone outside of her own thoughts, which was probably why my father decided to fly the coop and have a few adventures of his own."

"So… your father was… ?"

"Also a time-traveller? I have no doubt about it."

"And… silly question I know, but… is he still alive? Somewhere?"

"I'm sure of it. I sometimes have a feeling that he's quite nearby. I can feel his presence, if you know what I mean."

"Like he's watching you."

"Yes. I did once shout out, 'I know you're there, Daddy!', and got the oddest glances from a couple of old biddies walking by."

"I find it really hard to grasp, I'm afraid," Lawrence said. "It would blow my mind. Just accepting this -" – he looked around the room, "is hard enough."

"It's amazing how the brain soon learns to deal with the initial shock, and to see it as a gift, not something to be afraid of."

He carried on scoffing his meal and, taking a large sup of tea, said, "I mean, look at us now, inhabiting what became the most momentous month in British pop culture. September 1963, when The Beatles released 'She Loves You' and soaked into the mass British consciousness, about to become the biggest pop group in the world. Tomorrow, we could be meeting Noel Coward in his dressing room in Las Vegas. There are no limits. Just endless adventures!"

"Don't you ever miss your old life at Lockton Manor?" Lawrence asked him, surprised that he was enjoying this wholly unhealthy meal so much.

"No. Draughty old place. Though it was tastefully decorated. My grandfather, Reginald, was a great friend of William Burges, knew him from architectural college. He commissioned him to design the stained-glass windows at the front of the house, and he came up with some truly gorgeous wallpaper. Before I left for good, I cut out my favourite designs, rolled them up and took them with me. I eventually gave them to Michael… Michael Fish."

"The weatherman?"

"No, you ding-dong, the fashion designer."

Lawrence looked non-plussed.

"Mr. Fish?" Charles prompted him, which still garnered the same puzzled expression.

With a sigh, and a look of 'My dear, where *have* you been?', Charles explained.

"Michael was one of the premier fashion designers of the '60s and '70s. Jagger, Hendrix, Keith Richard, John Lennon, all wore his clothes. Lord Snowdon was a regular customer as was Peter Sellers, even Jon Pertwee when he was Dr. Who… those ruffled shirts he wore were designed by Michael. He created the kipper tie, and even designed dresses for men. He used one of the Burges wallpapers I gave him as inspiration for the dress Bowie wore on the *Man Who Sold The World* album cover."

"That's one of my favourite Bowie albums," Lawrence said, wishing he'd known all this when he'd bought the LP.

***

"Did my little talk help?" Charles asked Lawrence as they left the café.

"It was fascinating," Lawrence replied, "and what a great pla -"

He sniffed the air, then his sleeve and pulled a face.

"Oh, I *stink* of cigarettes!" he said.

Charles laughed.

"In 1963, everyone stank of cigarettes."

They got into the car.

"I've got a bottle of Brut in the glove compartment. Splash some on."

"Haven't you got anything better?" Lawrence asked him. "Tommy's Summer Cologne, perhaps?"

"Tommy Hilfiger is twelve in 1963, dear," Charles said. "Stay in period, the key to successful time-travel."

Lawrence opened the glove compartment and splashed the Brut onto his face.

"Oh my god," he said, "now I really smell like my dad!"

Charles hooted with laughter, turned the ignition and set off, the car radio blasting out 'She Loves You'.

"Even the car's in 1963," Lawrence said.

"Of course, darling. Where I go, she goes."

They passed a news kiosk where the headline 'Christine Keeler Arrested' was drawing lots of buyers for the Daily Mail.

"I remember watching that on the news," Lawrence

said.

"The old post-war establishment was finally breaking down," Charles said. "No more National Service, no more rules, there was a new game being played by an entirely different breed of people. So exciting!"

As they headed north, Charles glanced over at Lawrence, who was happily singing along to Billy Fury's 'In Summer'.

"So…" he said, "I'm guessing Tee and Suze haven't told you about their… experience?"

"What experience?"

"How I saved the day for them?"

"Well, that doesn't surprise me, but I have no idea what you're talking about."

"Interesting. They clearly didn't think you were ready."

"Ready for what?"

"For the fact that a young Sally time-travelled into their apartment."

"Sally? A time-traveller?"

"When she was much younger she had the gift – a reluctant traveller, as I call them. Poor lamb had been propelled forward sixty years. Luckily I was on hand to take her back to her proper time, just in time for her wedding."

"So… if you hadn't been 'on hand', she'd have never married Alistair. That could've been her lucky break."

Charles chuckled.

"Yes, Tee said he was rather a dull boy."

"How did Sally deal with it?" Lawrence said. "She seemed such a calm, untroubled person."

"She didn't remember it. Involuntary travellers

always forget the first time. Her subconscious clearly couldn't handle it and she never travelled again. For her, it was as though it never happened."

Charles pointed ahead of them where a group of excited girls were making their way across the Abbey Road zebra crossing, autograph books clutched in their hands.

"Ah, the early Apple Scruffs," Charles said, pulling into the studio car park.

"We're going in? To Abbey Road?"

"Of course," Charles replied. "We're expected. And, period check, in 1963 it was known as EMI Studios."

He got out and walked towards the famous steps up to the main door.

"Now, let me do the talking," he said, as Lawrence followed him in like an excited teenager. "And remember what year we're in. That's very important."

"Mr. Lockton," the receptionist said. "Nice to see you, sir. Go straight through to Studio 2."

Lawrence felt his heart beating double-time as they went down the corridor and through a thick, heavy door.

"Hi George!" Charles shouted, as he strode in and shook the hand of The Beatles' producer standing by the mixing desk.

"Charles!" George Martin said, bidding a pleasant 'Hi' to Lawrence, who stepped forward to be introduced to the great man.

"Let me introduce you to our engineer, Norman Smith," George said.

"Oh my God," Lawrence blurted out, "you produced Pink Floyd's -" then froze on the spot.

Charles was glaring at him as Norman looked

puzzled.

"Pink who?" he said.

"Oh, s-sorry," Lawrence stammered. "I-I-I was mixing you up with…"

"Another Norman Smith?" George said wryly, raising an eyebrow at his engineer. "Hope you've not been moonlighting, Norman."

Norman laughed,

"Not me, boss," he said, then smiled at a reddening Lawrence. "Pink Floyd, you say? What kind of a name's that? It'll never catch on."

On the large speakers, they heard The Beatles breaking into 'I Wanna Be Your Man'.

"Sounds great," Charles said.

"Yeah," George shouted back, "it's the first of the new songs the boys have written for the next LP. It's Ringo's number."

The Beatles stopped playing and Paul's instantly recognisable voice said, "How's the mikes, Norman?"

"Great," their engineer said, "do you want to go for a take?"

"Yeah, let's do one. Ready Ringo?"

"As I'll ever be!" Ringo's droll voice replied.

George smiled at Charles and said, "John and Paul actually wrote the song for a new group Andrew Oldham's managing. It'll be their next single."

"The Rolling Stones!" Lawrence said excitedly.

"Yes, do you know them?" George asked him, rather incredulous. "John told me they had a minor hit with a Chuck Berry song a couple of months ago. Are they any good?"

Charles quickly jumped in, "We've seen them a couple of times at The Orange Tree in Richmond, *haven't we, Lawrence?*"

Lawrence nodded gratefully.

"Yeah, they're very good," he said, wishing the floor would swallow him up.

"Okay boys," Norman was saying. "Let's go for one. The Beatles, 'I Wanna Be Your Man', Take One."

And off they went, playing like their lives depended on it, Ringo's voice full of the joy his legions of fans loved as he sang, *'I wanna be your lover baby, I wanna be your man'* while John and Paul sang along in unison.

Lawrence looked through the control room window at the vast Studio 2 below, clearly entranced.

"He's really taken with them, isn't he?" George said to Charles.

"Oh yeah, a Beatles fan through and through."

"Tell you what, which hotel are you staying in?"

"The Savoy," Charles replied.

"Good choice. Okay, I'll get a copy of the boys' *Please Please Me* LP sent over there, signed by all four of them, as a gift to Lawrence. How'd you think he'd like that?"

"He will be *beside* himself," Charles said.

As the song ended, they heard John say, "How was that?"

George went to the desk mike.

"Sounded okay, boys," he told them, "but I think we could do another take?"

"Nah, let's move onto 'Little Child'," John replied. "We'll come back to Ringo's number, it still needs some work."

Charles went over to Lawrence and quietly said, "Time to go, my dear."

Bidding farewells to George and Norman, he

opened the door and strode out, followed by a reluctant Lawrence.

"Aren't we going to stay and *meet* The Beatles?" he moaned.

"*I* have already met them," Charles replied. "I think we should wait until you've learnt the art of keeping in period."

He winked at Lawrence.

"I had to get you out of there, just in case you started nattering to John about 'Strawberry Fields Forever'."

He pushed the swing doors open and shouted, "Norrie!"

A man with thinning hair and horn-rimmed glasses walked over and shook his hand warmly.

"Lawrence," Charles said, "let me introduce you to the great Norrie Paramor."

As Lawrence shook Norrie's hand, a young, tanned chap with a brylcreemed quiff, who'd been sitting behind Norrie, stood up.

"Cliff!" Lawrence shouted.

"Charles," Cliff said, grinning, "do introduce me to your excited friend."

Lawrence watched the three of them chatting easily about the song Cliff and Norrie had just completed recording in Studio 1, the title track of *Wonderful Life*.

"The *Summer Holiday* album sold a million," Norrie said, "even more than *The Young Ones,* so this one is likely to be enormous."

"Except," Cliff interrupted him, holding up his finger and then pointing towards Studio 2, "the rumours are, those four lads down the corridor are also due to make a movie. It's bound to have a soundtrack album, so I'm just hoping they don't bring it out at the same time as mine."

Cliff laughed ruefully.

"They're wiping out all my rock 'n' roll mates."

"But you're still here, Cliff," Norrie said. "Their bubble will burst. They're just a fad. You're an established star and, mark my words, 'On The Beach' is a sure-fire chart-topper."

A uniformed chauffeur arrived in the doorway.

"Your car's ready, Mr. Paramor," he said.

"Thank you, Ed. Er - Cliff? Need a lift?"

"Great, Norrie. If you could drop me off at Peter Gormley's?"

Norrie turned to Charles.

"I trust you're coming to the party at The Marquee tonight? It's the big send-off for Vicki and Trudi. They're officially retiring The Honeybees, and I'm throwing them a big farewell do."

"Love to," Charles said. "The end of an era."

"Indeed it is," Norrie replied, as the four of them went outside and down the steps together. "Okay, see you gents at nine. Just give your names at the door, you'll be on the guest list."

"How's the car behaving, Charles?" Cliff said.

"Runs like a dream, doesn't it, Lawrence?"

"Beautiful car," Lawrence said. "Charles told me it was yours before he bought it off you."

"Yeah, I'm looking for something a bit zippier. The Consul's for the older gentleman these days."

He winked at Charles, grinned that famous crooked smile, saluted them both and jumped into Norrie's Rolls-Royce, which moved off stately as a galleon out of the gates. The group of girls who'd been clutching autograph books on the zebra crossing were now waiting by the gate and peered through the car window. Looking disappointed they started singing 'She Loves You' at the tops of their voices.

"So, when did *Wonderful Life* come out?" Lawrence asked Charles, who was staring beyond the studio gates, craning his neck as though he'd seen something. "Charles?"

"What?"

"I was asking you when *Wonderful Life* came out?"

"Oh… sorry. I thought I saw… hm… never mind."

He shook his head as if to say 'Silly me' and walked towards the car.

"Cliff's movie," he said, "came out the same week as *A Hard Day's Night*."

He opened the door and jumped in.

"Fate, thou canst be a cruel mistress."

"And 'On The Beach'?"

"It peaked at No.7, as 'A Hard Day's Night' was enjoying its third week at the top of the singles charts."

"Ouch!" Lawrence said.

"Ouch indeed."

Lawrence got in and Charles turned the ignition.

"Now, a hearty meal at the Savoy Grill is in order, followed by a divinely hot bubble bath!"

They swept out of the car park, Charles singing *'Can't buy me love, everybody tells me so, can't buy me love,'* to the Beatles fans who stared at him as though he were crazy.

"Naughty," Lawrence said.

"I know, aren't I?"

He burst into *'Money can't buy me love, can't buy me love,'* and turning to Lawrence they both yelled *'No, no, no, no!'* at the tops of their voices.

***

Charles was enjoying his promised soak while Lawrence was lying on the Kingsize double bed in their suite, mulling over the day's events.

"Isn't everyone very gracious and gentlemanly?" he called through to the bathroom.

"How do you mean?" Charles called back, sipping his champagne and luxuriating in the steam.

"Well, Cliff and Norrie, George Martin and Norman, they're all such charming people, real gents in a very old-fashioned way. I always thought the '60s was the revolutionary decade when common courtesy died out."

"Ah! You're talking about the *late* '60s. If you met Mick Jagger or Keith Richard on the street today they'd be quite shy, friendly young chaps, nothing like the drug-taking uncouths most people remember."

Lathering the soap and rubbing his arms with the generous suds, he said, "The happy-go-lucky '60s became much more militant later on. I was in Paris during the '68 riots, though luckily I had the Hotel George V to escape to when things got a little unnerving. My friend Francois Dupré had bought it and very generously gave me a permanent residency, which I use from time to time."

Lawrence got up and went and perched himself on the edge of the bath, massaging Charles' back with a loofah.

"Can I ask you something?" he said.

"You can ask. You may not get a reply... though if you keep that up, I'll tell you anything you want to know."

"Well, I know you're a Lord and all that, but how

come you seem to always have an endless pit of money. I mean, you said there's always ready cash wherever you travel to, but, to stay in a place like this, it cost a fortune even back in '63."

"It's called 'who you are' not 'what you have'," Charles replied. "I have made a point of always mixing in the best social circles, wherever and whenever I am. Everyone loves a Lord in their midst, even if they haven't a clue which Lord he is." He stood up. "Pass me my towel, darling."

Lawrence handed Charles a large white towel off the door, watching him dry off what was still a very good body.

"I stay here completely free of charge," he continued. "Richard D'Oyly Carte, who built The Savoy, gave me a lifetime free membership to his 'Club of Good Friends', as he called it. I've managed to stay afloat all these years through the generosity of rich, powerful people."

He put on the ankle-length white dressing gown and wandered through to the bedroom.

"I have breeding and understand etiquette perfectly. Even the rich, royal and famous need like-minded friends they can rely on. *And* who they enjoy being with. Voila! I fit the bill."

He lay back on the bed and smiled at Lawrence.

"Now, my darling, come and give a happy old man a gorgeous massage with those *fabulous* fingers."

He stripped off his dressing-gown and rolled over on his tummy.

"And while you manipulate my aching muscles, I'll tell you about the time Noel Coward and Judy Garland once drank me under the table in The Grill."

He chuckled to himself.

"And there was that time I beat Oscar Wilde at chess in the foyer, with a rather delicious prize for the winner. You've heard of Bosie, I assume?"

"Lord Alfred Douglas? Wilde's lover?"

"One and the same."

"You *didn't*!"

"Didn't what?" Charles said, laughing his head off.

Lawrence slapped his bum, which elicited a delighted yelp.

"*'The love that dare not speak its name!'*" Charles shouted.

"Wilde wrote that," Lawrence said.

"No, it's always wrongly attributed to Oscar. It's from Bosie's rather juicy poem *Two Loves*."

He turned over and cried,

"*'And he came near me with his lips uncurled, and caught my hand and kissed my mouth, and gave me grapes to eat and said, 'Sweet friend, come, I will show thee shadows of the world, and images of life.'*"

He stroked Lawrence's face.

"*'Have thy will, I am the Love that dare not speak its name.'*"

"Please don't tell me that was written to you?" Lawrence said.

"My uncurled lips are sealed," Charles replied.

Lawrence leant down and kissed him.

"You are simply amazing."

"How true!" Charles murmured into his ear.

Chapter Thirty-Nine

The Marquee was packed. Lawrence stood in a corner with his gin and tonic watching one pop icon after another arriving. They'd mingle and chat and always find their way to Charles, who would natter away so easily to these huge stars of their time. Lawrence recalled how as a young kid he had watched many of them performing their latest hits on *Thank Your Lucky Stars*. And now here he was, a man in his sixties, sharing the very air with them in the year when he had been that awestruck child.

As he'd grown up, he'd become someone who rarely got wide-eyed about anything. He came from a successful, upper middle-class family which had given its name to one of the best and longest-lasting companies of London solicitors. Many of Braintree & York's clients had been well-heeled, well-bred types who would spend most of their weekends at their country retreats, wining and dining their similarly rich friends. But pop stars? No, that was never the company's client base, somehow its reputation never spread to the famous, only the rich.

Now he watched the likes of Brian Epstein, Larry Parnes, Dusty Springfield, Gerry Marsden, Billy Fury, Tony Meehan and Helen Shapiro chatting away together just feet away, with the slightly unsettling feeling that not one person there, apart from Charles, had a clue who he was.

As he was deep in thought about it all, Charles appeared out of the melée, accompanied by a small chubby guy and a handsome blonde hunk he vaguely recognised.

"Lawrence," Charles said, glass of champagne in hand. "Meet Joe Meek and his new prodigy."

Meek proffered a rather limp, clammy hand, while his friend thrust forward a satisfyingly dry, meaty handshake, introducing himself as Heinz.

"Heinz is gonna be *massive*!" Joe said excitedly, eyes popping out of his head. "He's already in the Top Ten with 'Just Like Eddie' and the kids *love* him."

He beamed at Heinz, clearly besotted.

"I mean," he gushed, "who wouldn't?"

"Heinz was in The Tornados," Charles told Lawrence.

"Oh, I loved 'Telstar'," Lawrence said.

"My first smash," Joe said, still staring at Heinz. "I persuaded this luverly boy here to leave the group and go solo and we're set to do great things. He's in my new film, *Live It Up!* - which stars David Hemmings - and we're gonna be working on the next single in my home studio tomorrow. It's called 'Country Boy' and it's going to be *huge*. Just like Heinz."

Joe screeched a girly laugh and looked from Charles to Lawrence.

"You should come along to the session. See my boy in action. He's quite a performer."

Charles thanked Joe and explained that, unfortunately, they were leaving that night.

"Okay, maybe another time," Heinz said, with just the hint of a German accent. "It was nice to meet you guys."

"You too," Lawrence said, "best of luck with the new record."

With his arm firmly around Heinz's waist, Joe went back into the crowd, looking for someone else to impress.

"Was 'Country Boy' huge?" Lawrence asked

Charles, watching Joe introduce his prodigy to a clearly enthralled Larry Parnes.

"Didn't even reach the Top 20," Charles replied.

"Didn't Joe commit suicide?"

"Yes, he shot his landlady in 1967 then killed himself. Poor guy, he was a genius, but by then the hits had dried up."

Lawrence thought how odd it was, knowing the future of people whose present he currently shared. He realised that that was why he felt so disconnected from everyone there. He could never be 'one of them' or even a friend to anybody in the room, knowing their fates, even the dates some of them died. He was on the point of asking Charles if that ever bothered him, when a small, skinny lady spotted Charles, waved and walked towards them.

"Vicki, darling," Charles said, hugging her. "You look *fabulous*!"

Lawrence thought she favoured Twinkle, with her dark mascara, pink and white PVC outfit and knee-length red boots, but reminded himself, with a private pat on the back, that Twinkle didn't have her first hit until 1964.

"Very nice to meet you," Vicki said, as Charles introduced Lawrence.

She reached up to give him a peck on the cheek, the scent of Chanel pervading the air.

"I am so pleased Charles has *finally* found someone who's not only gorgeous, but also *his own age*."

She burst into a flurry of giggles and covered her mouth in an exaggerated 'little girl' way.

"Was that too rude, darling?" she said to Charles.

"Not at all, Vicki," Charles replied. "I consider it a compliment to my favourite man."

"Adorable," Vicki said, beaming at Lawrence.

"Vicki and her partner Trudi have sung on more hits than Cliff Richard has had gold discs," Charles told Lawrence, as the noise of chatter began building.

"But no more," Vicki shouted above the din. "Those days are – as of tonight - officially over."

"You're retiring, Norrie told us," Lawrence said.

"Yes, Trudi's going to become a doting housewife and I – well, I have plans, shall we say?"

Vicki blew them a kiss.

"Well, boys, gotta go. My final encore awaits."

As Vicki disappeared into the throng, Marty Wilde bounded on stage.

"Don't worry folks," he said. "I'm not going to sing!"

It was met with several 'Hoorays'.

"Gee thanks," Marty laughed, then turned towards the wings.

"Ladies and Gentlemen, these ladies need no introduction, two of the greatest female singers British pop has ever enjoyed…"

Already people were applauding.

"Here for the very last time, I give you… Vicki Palmer and Trudi Beauchamp, The Honeybees!"

As the girls ran on to a chorus of cheers and whistles, Lawrence was immediately struck by Trudi's resemblance to Audrey Hepburn. She was dressed in a very simple white cotton dress with a wide cream belt which emphasised her tiny waist and matching high-heels. As what was clearly a record suddenly blasted out, Vicki and Trudi shimmied in rhythm with the track, walked to their mikes and began miming to a song he didn't know. As the girls camply pointed at various men in the audience singing, '*Shame On You, you great big little boy*', Lawrence asked Charles, "Was this a hit?"

"No, but I never understood why not," Charles replied. "It's so *camp*!"

He vamped at Lawrence and started singing along with everyone else, batting his eyelids on the line, '*You never do what I tell you, you're a naughty, naughty boy*'. Lawrence laughed and joined in, thinking this would have made a great drag number.

The song faded to massive applause and Marty rushed back on, grabbing the girls' hands.

"Now, literally for one last time," he shouted, "these wonderful ladies are going to accompany Adam Faith on his latest smash hit, 'The First Time'. Come on folks, a big hand for Adam Faith and The Roulettes – with the *fabulous* Honeybees!"

The four-piece band rushed on, guitars and drums burst in and Adam, dressed in white T-shirt, black leather jacket and tight-fitting jeans, followed the girls on stage. He took the mike and began miming energetically to the song which Lawrence immediately recognised.

What amused Lawrence was, though there were no female backing vocals – it was The Roulettes who were chanting, 'Is it love?' as Adam replied, 'I don't know' – The Honeybees happily mouthed the words along with Adam's backing group. 'Live On Stage' clearly meant something different in the year when everyone mimed on shows like *Ready, Steady Go!*.

At the end of the number, one of The Roulettes stepped forward and gave a large bunch of flowers to Trudi, while another member of the band did the same for Vicki. To cheers from the crowd, they all bowed and ran off stage.

"That was Russ Ballard and Bob Henrit!" Lawrence

shouted over the cries for 'More'.

"Well spotted," Charles said.

"I loved Argent!"

Charles smiled indulgently at him.

"Come and meet Trudi" he said and led Lawrence through the crowd.

Trudi was carefully stepping down from the stage, glancing around her like a lost baby deer, saw Charles and ran towards them.

She seemed very demure and more reticent than Vicki, someone you could at first miss in a crowd, but the more you looked at her, the more a gentle charisma shone through.

"Darling, you were fabulous," Charles said. "We're actually on our way out, but I had to come and say what a great show."

"Yes, not a bad ending to a career, was it?" Trudi replied.

"Vicki told us you're getting married," Lawrence said.

"Yes, Andrew has promised to make an honest woman of me."

She looked around the room.

"He's here somewhere, no doubt gabbing to some poor pop star about their investments."

At that moment, Adam arrived with a chap Lawrence couldn't place.

"Trudi!" Adam shouted. "Why, oh *why* are you deserting me?"

Clearly the worse for wear, he threw his arms round her waist and kissed her.

"Because, my dear sweet silly boy, I'm ..."

She began singing 'Someone Else's Baby', one of Adam's early hits while Adam held onto her and joined in, his face almost touching Trudi's.

"Don't worry everyone," he shouted when they'd finished, "I'm not going to start singing 'Poor Me'."

Trudi leant forward and got hold of his companion's hand, gently pulling him forward.

"Everyone," she announced, "meet Chris Andrews, the composer of Adam's latest single."

Chris looked suitably shy as everyone applauded, while Lawrence looked star-struck.

"Chris Andrews?" he said. "You wrote 'Girl Don't Come' for Sandie Sh -"

"We *really* have to go, darlings!" Charles shouted, yanking Lawrence's hand and pulling him towards the exit. "See you everyone, 'bye Trudi, give my love to Vicki."

Back in the cool night air of Oxford Street, Lawrence said, "What was *that* all about?"

"My darling, what the fuck year is it?"

"Nineteen sixty-three."

"That´s right. And *you*, dear boy, were about to have another Norman Smith moment."

"Oh *shit*!" Lawrence said, banging his forehead. "Chris Andrews hasn't written 'Girl Don't Come' yet."

He pushed his hands through his hair like an embarrassed teenager.

"I'm not very good at this, I'm afraid. Maybe you should leave me behind next time."

"That would feel very lonely," Charles said, leaning in to kiss Lawrence.

"What the fuck year is it?" Lawrence said, holding

up his hand.

Charles did an exaggerated bow.

"Touché, mon ami, and thank you, mein liebe. The Savoy, I think."

***

Walking into the hotel's reception, Charles asked for their key and, handing it over, the receptionist also gave him a parcel.

"This was delivered this evening, sir," he said. "From EMI Studios."

"For you," Charles said, handing the parcel to Lawrence, who looked delightfully puzzled.

"For me?"

"Yes, for you."

Lawrence stared at him.

"Well, open it," Charles said.

As Lawrence tore the brown paper off and the LP emerged from the parcel, Lawrence stared in wonder.

"Wow! It's a signed copy of *Please Please Me*!"

He read the inscription.

"'*To Lawrence, all the best from John Lennon, Paul McCartney, George Harrison and Ringo Starr*'."

"George Martin's idea," Charles said. "I knew you'd love it."

"Love it?" Lawrence cried. "I love *you*!"

He was about to launch into a passionate hug when Charles held up his hand.

"What the fuck year is it?"

The two of them burst out laughing.

Chapter Forty

As Charles was pottering around, getting ready for bed, Lawrence was on the chaise longue staring happily at his Beatles LP.

"Don't you ever feel tempted to change things?" he asked.

"How do you mean?" Charles replied, going into the bathroom and studying his face in the mirror.

"Well, you can travel into all these time-spaces, into so many lives. Don't you ever want to, well, make more of a difference?"

"One learns not to very quickly," Charles said, opening his tube of moisturiser and rubbing it into his cheeks and forehead. "It isn't advisable, indeed it's wholly inadvisable. We are merely occasional voyeurs having fun, and then we quickly move on."

"But if you tweaked things now and then to, say, prevent something awful happening…"

Charles came out of the bathroom.

"I once tried to talk John Lennon out of going to America," he said casually.

"Really?"

"During one of my shopping trips in 1971, I was sauntering down Kensington High Street, thinking I might pop into Biba and shoot the breeze with Barbara Hulanicki over a coffee and a joint, when a white Rolls-Royce stopped, the window rolled down and there was John, shouting 'Charlie Lockton! Need a lift?'. Of course, never one to refuse an ex-Beatle, I got in."

Lawrence jumped up and went to the drinks trolley.

"I *have* to hear this," he said. "Fancy a nightcap?"

"Love one," Charles replied. "Cognac, I think."

As Lawrence poured their drinks, Charles sat down, assumed a Cowardesque pose and continued with his story.

"Well, it turned out John and Yoko were en route to do an interview on the *Parkinson* show, and I naturally decided to blag a front row seat. When we arrived at BBC Studios, Yoko said she needed the loo."

Lawrence handed him his cognac and sat down.

"So there we were, me and the great man, alone together in the Green Room, and, against my better judgement, I suggested that, instead of moving to America, he should stay in the UK. I told him it was his home and where everyone loved him."

"What did he say?"

"It didn't go well. First of all he said that his British fans hated Yoko – which was kind of true at the time - and then he told me to mind my own business. He began pointing his finger at me, saying that if this was another British Establishment attempt to split him and Yoko up, I could go fuck myself. Peace and love disappeared rather sharpish."

Charles downed his cognac in one.

"Anyway, when Yoko came back in, John declared I was not a friend after all and accused me of being sent to spy on them. I tried to argue that was nonsense, reminding him that it had been *he* who had stopped the car and offered me a lift. But he just clammed up. Refused to say another word. In fact, neither of them spoke to me again, ever."

"Oh, baby," Lawrence said, stroking Charles' arm. "You were only trying to save his life."

"Well, although that does sound rather melodramatic, it's true. But it ruined our friendship."

"That's very sad."

"I did try to see him when I was in New York in the Spring of 1980 for Blondie's show at Hurrah's. I went to the Dakota with this rather silly idea that I might turn John onto time-travel, and so avoid him being anywhere near New York on the 8th December."

"What a brilliant idea!"

"I know. He loved anything off the wall, and the chance to go for a spin around a few time-spaces would have blown his mind. But when I rang the bell and gave my name, I was told by a rather stern-voiced chap that 'Mr. and Mrs. Lennon are not available for visitors.' I never tried again."

He wandered off to the drinks trolley and poured another cognac.

"Life has a strange way of moving us towards our fate, no matter who tries to intervene," he said wistfully.

"But you tried," Lawrence said. "Just think, if John had listened to you…"

"He might have made an album which was a damned sight better than *Sometime In New York City*."

Lawrence pulled a ´Really?!´ face as Charles held up his glass and said, "Another?"

Chapter Forty-One

On 19th April 1977, Lawrence and Charles were sitting on the patio of the Haven Fort Hotel in Little Haven, enjoying the sound of the sea below.

"Great hotel," Lawrence said. "And the suite's lovely."

"Neo-Gothic," Charles said. "My favourite style. And it has a ghost story…"

Lawrence sipped his glass of Dom Perignon.

"Do tell."

"The legend is that a young lady in a long white dress haunts the corridors, smiling at passers-by. Of course, it's nonsense. She's just one of those careless souls who keeps slipping through time-spaces. Dorothy Charming, she's called, a precocious and extremely unpleasant little creature. I first met her when I was about eight during one of the family excursions here. She was with her mama and governess, and looked as if she was about to burst into laughter at something only she knew. Infuriating! When I came here again several decades later, there she was, little Dorothy floating on the stairs like some abandoned fairy. I gave her a piece of my mind and told her to get a grip. But she just giggled, tapped her nose and faded off through the wall. Silly girl."

He sighed loudly and then suddenly cried out.

"There it is! I *knew* it! Look, over there!"

Lawrence squinted at the sky and saw an oval-shaped light hovering above the sea. It slowly moved towards fields on the right, finally disappearing behind a large mound on the horizon.

"Now, let's just wait shall we?"

"For what?" Lawrence said, thrilled that he'd seen

his first UFO.

"The story goes – and this is one which Sally told me, after she'd been out for lunch with old Peter the ex-priest…"

"Old Peter the who?"

"One of our former neighbours in the block of flats. Nice old chap. He was an army chaplain in the early '50s. He told Sally he lost his faith when he was in Korea and never relocated it. It sounded to me rather like losing a handbag in Dorothy Perkins, but there you go, flippant old moi. Anyway, when Sally died, the game old bird went on a trek through India, looking for Vishnu."

"Did he find him?"

"No idea, never saw him again. His sister put the flat on the market and Lucy the librarian bought it. Quiet little mouse, hardly ever see her. Too busy reading books, I suppose."

He filled Lawrence's glass.

"But *much* more importantly, Peter told Sally that on this particular night in 1977, a UFO had been seen by the owner of the hotel, or rather his wife, landing in a nearby field. She'd said that two 'humanoid creatures' had stepped out of the craft, walked away into the distance and disappeared."

"Then what?"

"That's it, but I always wanted to see it for myself – and here we are."

"Well, we saw the UFO."

"Yes we did."

"What happened to the spaceship?"

"Dunno. Locals say there was a kind of shallow crater where the woman saw it land. It's too dark to look now but we'll have a gander tomorrow morning before we leave."

Just then a voice from the terrace below them shouted, "Did you see it?"

Charles got up and peered over the patio.

"Hello?" he shouted, cupping his hand. "Who's that? Oh!"

He turned to Lawrence and said rather more quietly, "It's what's-'is-name… Granville, the owner of the hotel."

"Good evening!" Granville shouted back. "My wife woke me up saying she'd seen a spaceship of all things. She's in quite a state. It must have been a dream. Sorry to bother you. Good night."

"We did see something!" Lawrence shouted, coming to join Charles at the edge of the patio. "A craft of some sort."

At that moment a lady in a candlewick dressing-gown and nightcap ran out onto the path.

"Did you see it, Henry?" she shouted.

"No, dear, but these two gentleman say they did."

She looked up at them, Mr. Granville shining his torch in their direction. Then Charles suddenly gasped.

"Good *Lord*!" he said, staring at where the torch had lit up the field.

Lawrence could just make out two figures, walking away from them along a path.

"It's impossible!" Charles said.

"What is?" Lawrence asked.

"The walking stick… and the hat… it can't be…"

As the figures disappeared into the darkness, Charles went and sat down, shaking his head.

"Are you alright?" Lawrence asked him.

"Will you gentlemen be around tomorrow morning to

confirm the sighting?" Granville shouted.

"I'm afraid we have to leave first thing," Charles called back, getting up and walking into the hotel.

Lawrence followed him in.

"What did you see?", he asked Charles as they climbed the stairs to their room.

"Nothing. I'm clearly more tired than I realised. Let's get some shut-eye."

"What about what Mr. Granville asked us, to confirm the sighting tomorrow?"

As they reached their room, Charles put the key in the door and turned to Lawrence.

"As I've said before, we are merely voyeurs. We don't intrude, we don't get involved, we simply have fun and move on."

Chapter Forty-Two

Lawrence was in the rear sitting-room at Bridesview, enjoying the sound and the always evocative smell of the rain through the open French windows. He watched Charles pouring them a drink, walk over and hand him the Scotch and water before sitting down next to him on the settee.

"Can I ask you something?" Lawrence said.

"Always," Charles replied.

"Well, why does such an urban creature as yourself want to live in such a quiet out-of-the-way place as here?"

"Kettle, pot, black, dear, I'd say."

"True, but go on, tell me, why here for you?"

Charles drank his Scotch and smiled.

"I've always loved Pembrokeshire. As you know, I used to come here as a child with my family on regular breaks and I've visited it many times since then. There's something about this area, it sort of speaks to me, I feel a strong connection, like an old-time empathy, if you know what I mean?"

Lawrence nodded.

"I felt that too the first time I came."

"It's as though the landscape is in my bones. About five years ago I decided I needed a proper base of my own, instead of staying at friends' places and hotel rooms all over the time-continuum, fun though that is. My age perhaps? I came to look at the apartment in Broad Haven and felt immediately at home."

He glanced out at Lawrence's lovely garden and then smiled quite beautifully at his partner.

"Even more now," he said, and clinked Lawrence's

glass. "Maybe for our next trip, I could take you to Lockton Manor."

"Your old home?"

"Yes, why not? Show you where it all began, and you could see my butterflies."

"I'd love that," Lawrence said, and squeezing Charles' hand added, "are you going to tell me what you saw at the hotel?"

Charles stretched and stood up.

"For another day, my sweet," he said, knocking back the dregs of his drink.

He leaned over and kissed Lawrence on the forehead.

"I'm feeling rather sleepy, my dear. I think I need to go to bed."

"I'll be up soon, I'll just finish my drink and wash up the glasses."

"Till later, my darling," Charles said, and wandered upstairs.

***

Charles woke with a start, the room in partial darkness. He was aware of Lawrence busying in the kitchen downstairs and smiled to himself at how lucky he had been to meet such a kind and gentle man at this point in his life. With Lawrence by his side, he no longer needed to continually be travelling in search of new thrills.

As he lay there looking at the gently swaying shadows of the magnolias making animal shapes on the wall, he tried to lift his head from the pillow and realised he couldn't. It felt as heavy as lead.

Then he saw the bedroom door open and, thinking it was Lawrence, said, "Darling boy, I'm afraid I don't think I am very well."

The voice which replied was one he hadn't heard since he was ten years old.

"Hello, Charlie boy," his father said.

"Papa! I'm afraid I can't get up to greet you, the old body won't allow it."

Edward Lockton, in his long caped coat, large fedora hat and holding a silver cane, smiled through the half-light at his son.

"I know," he said. "This blasted gift destroys us all in the end. It certainly destroyed any possibility of my being a good husband and father, I hope you understand that now."

"I do. And I feel both blessed and saddened, Papa, that I have found the love you couldn't."

"Well, my boy, I consider you fortunate indeed for that."

Edward stroked his son's now greying hair, leant forward and kissed his cheek.

"Sail safely, Charlie," he said, walking back through the shadows. "I am so pleased we spoke again. Goodbye, son."

As he had done many years before, Charles watched his father walk out the door and, without looking back, disappear. Smiling into the space where his father had been, he gave in to the inevitable and passed away.

Chapter Forty-Three

The impeccably-attired commissionaire, George Sawyer, looked at his pocket watch. It was nine-twenty-five, just a few minutes before Mr. Cairnforth would emerge as usual from the lift in the lobby of King's Court. The dapper old gentleman would tip his hat at George then take his daily walk round the block, before picking up his scarlet MG roadster and roaring off into town.

He'd arrive back home at around one-thirty, spend the rest of the day in his ninth floor apartment sketching, before a final evening perambulation across the road to his favourite Greek restaurant, Kostas, which had opened just a few months earlier.

Finally, at around ten p.m., he would wander back in through the windowed double doors, sit down in one of the red leather lobby armchairs, and join George for their always interesting chat about his day and the portrait he was working on at the moment. At around eleven, he'd get up, bid George 'good evening' and board the lift, 'ready for my trip to Dreamland'.

He'd drawn George a couple of times while they were chatting, gifting him a particular favourite sketch. It showed off Sawyer's wonderfully waxed moustache to its full splendour, his spotless grey uniform with red piping on the seams and collar, along with his shining war medals proudly displayed on that impressive chest. As Mr. Cairnforth sketched, George would tell stories of his wartime escapades in Egypt, which the old gent was always interested to hear.

George had been commissionaire of the prestigious block of flats since it was built twenty years earlier in 1935. He'd started there at the age of twenty-one, and loved his job. King's Court was such an elegant building, with a variety of tenants who would pass through the lobby several times a day, all beautifully dressed and, George imagined, always en route to somewhere entirely exotic. He had seen many people over those twenty years, some who had moved in when the block was first opened and stayed, others who only remained for a couple of years before moving onto a new life, a new job, or to a large house in the country with their newly-betrothed.

The lobby area boasted a long, sweeping reception desk, all chrome and polished satinwood, with several vases of white and pink lilies dotted around on shining mahogany stands, which scented the area wonderfully. The beautiful Parquet flooring, over which ladies' stilettos would click and their tiny dogs would trot, had been reclaimed from the ballroom of Lockton Manor.

Every morning at seven on the dot, George would arrive at King's Court, looking spotless and smart. He'd greet Doris, the receptionist, who had also been there since the block opened. She was a single lady, quite stern in appearance, which belied an occasional wry sense of humour, usually at the expense of a particularly unkempt resident, the kind who rarely stayed very long at King's Court. Times may have been changing, standards clearly dropping everywhere, but Doris and George could be relied on to maintain the polish and refinement their employers, and most of the residents, expected and appreciated.

On cue, the lift arrived, and George stepped forward to open the gates for the impeccably-suited Mr. Cairnforth. They compared the time on their watches with a knowing smile at each other, before the old gentleman wandered towards the exit, ready for his morning.

This time, however, instead of marching out into King Street and striding off to his car, he checked a parcel in his hand and glanced at George.

"Is everything alright, sir?" George enquired.

"It is, thank you, George, but I wonder… would you call me a cab? I have a delivery to make in Gower Street and I've decided I would prefer not to drive today. I've been sketching rather a lot during the night and my eyes are a little cloudy this morning. Would you mind?"

"Of course not, sir."

George turned to Doris, who was already lifting the receiver off her phone. She spoke quietly into it and then, smiling over at Mr. Cairnforth, said, "Your taxi will be here in five minutes, sir."

"Splendid," the old gent said, "thank you, Doris."

He went across the lobby and sat in his favourite armchair, checked his parcel again and began tapping his foot in time to a melody in his head. As he swayed in his seat, he began to sing quietly to himself, "'You can't start a fire, sitting 'round crying over a broken heart… '"

"I don't know that song, sir," George said.

"'Dancing In The Dark'," Mr. Cairnforth replied, "great song."

"Ah yes, my wife and I loved that film, *The Bandwagon*. We went to see it at the Empire in 1953. Fred Astaire and Cyd Charisse. Wonderful!"

Mr. Cairnforth smiled at George and chuckled to himself.

"But I didn't recognise those words you were singing to yourself, sir," George said, "the words I remember are…"

He stood stock still, as though at a microphone, and

began to croon in a not disagreeable way, "'Looking for the light of a new love, to brighten up the night, I have you love, and we can face the music together, dancing in the dark.'"

He beamed across the lobby at Mr. Cairnforth's gentle applause, just as Doris said, "Your taxi's arrived, sir."

Mr. Cairnforth thanked them both, gave his usual sprightly salute and went on his way. Checking he'd got into the cab safely, George turned to Doris and said, "I don't what song the old gent was singing there, but it certainly wasn't 'Dancing In The Dark.'"

***

Jack Marlowe, aka Jackson Cairnforth, arrived at the Slade at ten o'clock and looked around the pristinely-kept lawns surrounding the entrance to the North wing of the building where he had studied and taught. Students and tutors wandered by, unaware who the octogenarian in their midst was. It wasn't surprising, Jack thought, he wasn't born for another seven years.

As he entered the building, he smiled at the Lucian Freud portrait of his wife Kitty Garman, *Girl With A White Dog*, which was hanging in the reception area, part of an exhibition of previous tutors at the school. He wondered how he would have got on with the legendary and often controversial portraitist, who had taught there until 1954.

As he was mulling over such a possibility, he heard the lady behind the reception desk saying, "Excuse me, sir, can I help you?"

"Why yes, if you could," Jack replied, and walked towards the efficient young lady who he recognised as Tessa Goulden. She would bid good morning to many art world legends during her time behind that desk, until her retirement in 1980, the year he had begun studying at the Slade. He remembered her retirement party, and had seen how fond many of the tutors and some of the older students clearly were of the woman who had become, in the words of dear old Craigie Aitchison, 'the always welcoming face of our workplace.'

Smiling now at the young Tessa, he noticed that her auburn hair cascaded attractively around her shoulders, rather than being held in a tightly netted bun of silver grey which had become her daily look when he'd studied there.

Jack handed his parcel over to her.

"I wonder if you could make sure this is delivered to a student here, Yolanda Sonnabend?" he asked her.

"Of course, sir. Miss Sonnabend isn't in today, but will be back tomorrow, I believe, and on her return I will give this to her personally. Could I ask – who is this from?"

"It's a gift from me, my name isn't important, but please just tell her the parcel contains a selection of drawings which I think she will appreciate."

Tessa looked at the parcel, then at Jack, nodded slowly and said, "I do usually like to get the name of anyone who leaves a parcel for one of our students or tutors, sir."

"Yes, I can appreciate that, but I am leaving the UK very shortly, so would not be contactable, I'm afraid. Just tell Miss Sonnabend it's from a friend, if you could?"

Tessa looked at Jack and seemed to make a decision.

"Thank you, sir," she said, making a note on her pad. "I can do that. Is there anything else I can do for you?"

"Er – just one more thing… would you mind if I did

a quick sketch of you?"

Tessa looked a little puzzled, reflexively pressing her impeccably coiffured hair into place with her hand.

"Well, I don't know if I –" she said, flustered at suddenly being the centre of attention.

"It won't take more than five minutes," Jack assured her. "I will sit…" he saw a settee by the window… "over there… and you can just get on with your morning. You won't know I'm here. Is that alright?"

"I suppose it is, but if anyone complains or objects then you will have to stop."

"Of course."

So, as Tessa pretended to be busy, checking her appointments diary and occasionally writing something in there, Jack sketched away. After a few minutes, he walked towards the desk and handed it to her.

"There, that is for you, Miss – er… ?"

"Goulden…" Tessa said, staring in awe at the drawing. "Oh my! It's… well, it's wonderful, sir!"

She felt her face blushing up and the back of her neck tingling.

"I can't believe you did this so quickly. So much detail, and the colours. Mother will really love this, thank you!"

"My pleasure," Jack said, doffed his hat and walked towards the door.

Tessa looked down at the drawing again.

"But, sir!" she shouted. "You haven't signed it."

The old gent just waved, saluted and left.

Jack had had to make a quick exit, having just seen his mother, Nancy, approaching reception. Chuckling to himself at his narrow escape, he walked towards the taxi rank at Russell Square station.

As his cab whisked off, he imagined Tessa showing the sketch to Nancy and wished he could have seen his mum's expression. But, of course, he knew she'd absolutely loved it.

***

A few days later, as the King's Court lobby was bathed in sunlight streaming through the glass doors, Doris looked over at George who was becoming increasingly agitated. He'd checked his watch several times in the last half-hour, pacing up and down and glancing over at the lift every time someone arrived.

His eyes lit up a little when he saw old Mrs. Higson, who lived on the ninth floor, appearing out of the elevator with two other elderly residents, the sisters Jemima and Charlotte Cleverly. The three ladies were in a busy conflab as they wandered towards the exit, the scent of lavender and mothballs wafting around the lobby in their wake. George stepped forward and, tipping his hat, asked as casually as he could, "Excuse me, Mrs. Higson, but, I know your apartment is next door to Mr. Cairnforth's, and I was just wondering if you'd seen him this morning?"

Mrs. Higson glanced up over her fox fur wrap at the broad-shouldered man she'd always had something of a fancy for, tittered at her two friends and put on her most coquettish smile.

"Oh, George," she said delightedly. "I didn't see you there, what with chatting to my friends here about a WI function we've been invited to. What to wear. That is the issue."

She fluttered her eyes at George and giggled.

"I'm going for a pink tweed suit and a grey silk shawl,

what do you think?"

"I'm sure you'll look extremely smart, madam, as always, but… Mr. Cairnforth? Have you seen him at all this morning?"

Clearly disappointed by the lukewarm response to her planned attire, she said, "No, I'm afraid I haven't. Were you expecting to see him this morning?"

"Well, the thing is," George began, trying to ignore the heavily mascara'd eyes batting away at him, "Mr. Cairnforth is always, on the dot, out of that lift at nine-thirty every morning. But, it's ten fifteen now and there's been no sign of him."

Mrs. Higson winked at George and said, "Perhaps… he has company?"

George coughed into his gloved hand and looked quite taken aback.

"Mr. Cairnforth? I'd consider that extremely unlikely… if you don't mind my saying, madame."

"Oh, do call me Melissa, George. We've been seeing each other every day for ten years now, and I'm getting a little too old to worry about fuddy-duddy politeness."

As the three biddies edged closer to George, purring and tittering at each other, Doris decided he needed rescuing.

"Excuse me, ladies," she called over. "I'm very sorry to interrupt but… George… why not go and check on Mr. Cairnforth yourself?"

"Do you think I should?" George asked Doris.

"If you're concerned, then yes, I do. Try knocking a couple of times first, and if there's no answer, then you're within company rules to use your spare key and respectfully open the door to make sure everything is OK. Mr. Cairnforth may be poorly and needs help."

Mrs. Higson beamed over at George.

"You have a spare key to *every* apartment?"

"I have access to every spare key, yes, madam, which I have to sign out to use if I think the necessity has arisen."

"And I have to counter-sign it," Doris assured the old dame.

"Well," Mrs Higson said, whinnying at her friends and pouting at George. "I must have a dizzy spell soon, so you can use your key to open *my* door and come and check on me."

His face reddening and with just the hint of a few specks of sweat on his moustache, George politely excused himself and went towards reception. Mrs Higson sniffed rather loudly, nodded meaningfully at her friends and led them outside, en route to catch a bus to the Lyons Corner House in Coventry Street.

Standing in the heavily-scented lift, his heart beating a little faster as it rose upwards, George arrived at the ninth floor, got out and walked briskly to Number 184, knocking gently on the door. After getting no response, he said, as calmly as he could, "Mr. Cairnforth? Mr. Cairnforth, are you in, sir?"

Again, there was no reply, and, after his second, rather louder knock, followed by a more urgent enquiry, got no answer, George put the key in the door. Trying not to panic about one of his favourite gentlemen in the world, he slowly walked inside.

Chapter Forty-Four

The RMS Queen Elizabeth arrived at Southampton docks on November 15th 1965. George Sawyer and his wife Phyllis stood together on the deck with hundreds of other passengers, feeling the warmth of the winter sun on their faces, still excited about their trip of a lifetime to New York.

While there, they'd enjoyed several shows on Broadway, Phyllis particularly enjoying *Half A Sixpence* as she was a big fan of Tommy Steele, while George had been impressed by Anthony Newley's emotional rendition of 'Who Can I Turn To?' in *The Roar of The Greasepaint, The Smell of The Crowd*.

The couple had stayed in a suite at the Hotel Edison, George being fascinated that Thomas Edison himself had turned on the marquee lights of the hotel when it opened in 1931.

From their fifth-floor window, they could see Radio City Music Hall and, as they sat each evening on the roof deck sipping cocktails, the whole of Manhattan filled their eyes and lit the sky.

Now back in Blighty, as their ocean liner docked and they waited for the announcement to disembark, George reflected on how he and his wife were able to live this entirely new life.

Ten years earlier, when he'd opened the door to Mr. Cairnforth's apartment, he'd found it empty. At first alarmed, his fears were allayed when he noticed two envelopes on the mantelpiece addressed to 'George, from your friend Mr. C.', beside which was a medium-sized brown paper parcel. George took the envelopes and the parcel and, sitting on the rather attractive pink sofa by the window, which Doris had told him was delivered personally to Mr. Cairnforth by its designer Carl Malmsten, he opened the first envelope. Inside was a folded note on Basildon Bond paper. It read...

Dear George

You will have been no doubt concerned about my sudden disappearance this morning, but worry not, I am absolutely well and simply needed to move on. I have thoroughly enjoyed living here in King's Court these last eighteen months, much of that pleasure having been derived from meeting and getting to know you. I feel we became friends, and always looked forward to our nightly chats in the lobby.

You give a remarkable service to all the residents, always polite, impeccably turned out, and there to give a helping hand when needed. However, between you and I, there is a great probability that at some point in the future King's Court will be sold to a company who no longer have need of the services you provide. It is with great sadness that I tell you this and you will simply have to trust my word on it.

So, with that eventuality in mind, please accept the gift you will find in the parcel. It is a beautiful painting done by a good friend of mine who died only last year. He left it to me in his will, but I have several more works by Henri, so I would like you to have this one. Perhaps you will hang it on the wall of your home - until such time as its sale will fully alleviate any difficulties the inevitable ending of your job will create for you and your good wife.

When that time comes, if you would like to, please

contact a good friend of mine, Joseph Sparrow at Christie's auction house. You may not need to contact Joseph for some time, but when you do, please mention that you were recommended to him by me.

I am certain that the money you receive from the auction of the painting will more than look after you and Phyllis for the rest of your lives. It is up to you, of course, whether and whenever you decide to benefit from the sale of the painting.

With all my very best wishes, I thank you for your friendship and care, I will never forget it.

Yours very sincerely,

Jackson Cairnforth

P.S. I have also left you a much shorter note which you can show to the police, should you need to.

George pondered the note for a minute or so then opened the second envelope, which indeed contained a very simple signed explanation of why Mr. Cairnforth had left his apartment so suddenly – 'an unexpected bereavement' – along with one month's rent which would serve as notice to the building's current owners, and an assurance that the painting was a gift from Mr. C. to George 'in appreciation of his superb work here.'

He sat for some minutes, re-reading the first note and then staring out of the window at the view beyond of the Hammersmith tow path and the Thames. He felt both sadness that his friend had gone, and relief that dear old Mr. C. was alive and well… somewhere.

George then opened the parcel. Inside was a beautiful painting of a room, where, against royal blue walls, stood two wooden chairs next to a small round table on which sat a goldfish bowl, which glimmered in the sunlight seeping through the window. In the distance was a market square where several people were milling about.

What struck George immediately were the colours, the vibrant blues of the walls, the turquoise and yellow of the cushions on the chairs, the orange of the goldfish in the light emerald green water. Even the shadows had colour, dark lilacs and mauves. He had never seen such a radiant picture, as though the whole world were shimmering on a late afternoon.

There was an inscription in the bottom right-hand corner, *Intérieur, bocal de poissons rouges, numéro 2,* which he'd ask Phyllis to translate. She'd spent a Summer in Paris when she was on a student swap in the early '30s, where she'd learnt 'enough French to get by.' Below the title was a signature and a date which looked to George like *Henri Matisse, 1914.* He'd not heard of the artist but clearly Mr. Cairnforth rated him very highly, and, again, Phyllis might know of him.

After locking the apartment's front door, he got the lift down to reception, giving the second shorter note to Doris. Although intrigued by his vague and decidedly odd story, and privately unimpressed by the painting in the parcel, she assured George that she would show the note to the policeman who was about to arrive.

"As you were a little while up there, I decided to call the station, but worry not, I'll give the constable a brief résumé and assure him that no foul play is suspected."

Doris suggested to a clearly emotional George that he go home early.

"I can hold the fort on my own perfectly well for one day," she said and, ignoring his mild protests, added, "go home to your wife, George, and enjoy looking at your kind and thoughtful present from dear Mr. C."

Phyllis told George that the title meant 'Interior, The Goldfish Bowl, Number 2' but she was unsure about the artist.

"I didn't bother with art galleries and stuff like that when I went to Paris," she told him. "I was more taken with the cafés, sightseeing and wandering by the Seine with my pals. This chap was probably a friend of Mr. C. when they were art students together and they kept in touch."

"Happen you're right," George replied, knocking a nail in their sitting-room wall and hanging the painting.

Both of them stood back and agreed it was a fine piece of work, one which they'd be happy to glance at each evening as they drank their cocoas before bedtime.

Nine years later, it turned out the old gent had been right. At the age of fifty, George received a letter from Ravenscourt Properties, the new owners of King's Court. It said they were cutting back on costs to adapt to the simpler way of life, and that the block no longer needed a commissionaire nor, as George found out when he arrived at King's Court that morning, a receptionist.

"It isn't the fact I'll be out of work," Doris said, retrieving a lace-bordered hanky from the pocket of the cardigan around her shoulders. "I have a few savings put by and I would have been retiring in four or five years anyway. It's how I'm going to tell mother. She's always boasting to neighbours about my 'prestigious job'. You'd think I worked for the Government the way she goes on."

"My advice, Doris," George said, sitting tentatively

beside her, "is to take your mother on a little break, maybe go to Brighton or Bournemouth for a few days and, while you're there, tell her a little white lie, that you've decided to retire early. That you want to spend more time with her and take some occasional holidays together."

Doris sighed and put the hanky back in her pocket. Nodding briskly, she stood up and brushed herself down.

"Thank you, George," she said. "The redundancy payment *will* come in very handy. I'll pop into the travel agents in Hammersmith during my lunch hour."

Smiling at George, she got to work checking her appointments and visitors book, quietly humming 'Summer Holiday' to herself.

***

George watched Joseph Sparrow looking at the painting he'd brought in to show him. The ironically bird-like little man kept glancing at George and then back at the painting.

"And you say Mr. Cairnforth *gave* you this?" Sparrow said, his eyes widening behind large round spectacles.

"Indeed he did," George said proudly. "He told me if I ever needed some extra income – as I do now – then I should bring it to you, and you would put it into auction for me. Shame really, as the wife and I have grown rather fond of it, but... needs must as they say. Whatever it makes will come in very handy right now."

Sparrow was absolutely incredulous. This was definitely a work by Matisse, though one he had never seen before. It appeared to be a companion piece to the world-famous 'Interior with goldfish', which Matisse had also painted in 1914 and which was housed at the

Museum of Modern Art in New York. Its most recent valuation stood at ten million pounds.

Sparrow put the painting down and said, "Well, Mr. Sawyer, thank you for bringing it in. I will, of course, need to get the painting fully accredited as a work by Matisse."

"Of course," George said loftily, not sure why that was necessary, but accepting Sparrow must know what he's talking about.

"I will also require some documentation which proves that you own this work."

With a flourish, George produced Cairnforth's letter, dated July 23rd 1955. Sparrow studied it for quite some time, and then, nodding decisively, wrote out a receipt and handed it to George.

"Very well, Mr. Sawyer. I will, if that's okay with you, hold onto the painting while I do the necessary due diligence. I will contact you forthwith about the date of the auction, that is, should I receive the full and necessary accreditation. In the meantime, this receipt should suffice as confirmation that we have it safely cared for until then."

George put the receipt in his wallet and, raising his bowler hat to Sparrow, left and went home to tell Phyllis all about it.

The painting received its full accreditation two months later, having been checked by three different Matisse experts. When it was auctioned at Christie's, an event at which the Sawyers were special guests and which made the news around the world, the previously unseen Matisse masterpiece was bought by an anonymous collector for eight million pounds.

Six months later, George and Phyllis moved into their spacious and rather beautiful new home, Cholmondeley Villas on Richmond Green. They took with them Phyllis's eighty-year-old mother and George's seventy-nine-year-old father, for whom George hired two carers. He also took in a housekeeper and a cook, and a gardener to keep the lawns in trim and the shrubs and trees around the walled grounds neat and tidy.

Phyllis always felt a little overwhelmed by it, telling her husband she felt 'a bit like an impostor', but George, who always knew Mr. C. had been a classy gent, enjoyed knowing that his old friend had made sure he would never again have to worry about paying bills or finding another job. Although he'd never expected that friendliness and respectfulness should be rewarded, it was good to know that such an admirable chap had appreciated everything he'd done.

In 1975, the Sawyers' parents having passed, George and Phyllis sold the house in Richmond and downsized to a nice little bungalow in Turnham Green. Being just a few streets away from where they'd grown up, the place felt right.

They enjoyed living at Number One, The Green, but were always saddened as, over time, most of the other bungalows were extended, widened and elevated by sometimes two storeys, to accommodate bedrooms and en-suites, huge conservatories on the back and extra wings on both sides. For the Sawyers, the changes ruined the rather comfy look of the street, which had attracted them to the bungalow in the first place.

In 1991, Phyllis developed a heart condition, which

finally did for her while she was putting out dinner on the small kitchen table at the back of the house. George wasn't sure whether he wanted to remain in the bungalow on his own, but he had no idea where else he wanted to be. Losing his teenage sweetheart knocked the stuffing and any new sense of direction out of him.

His four children had offered to move him into various annexes of their large houses in the suburbs - paid for by Trusts he and Phyllis had set up for them - but he'd always resisted, feeling that he owed it to Phyllis to protect their home from 'the plunderers', as they'd called most of the neighbours, as long as he could. It was his final battle, as he saw it.

Every morning, George would stride out on his perambulation, crossing The Green en route to the newsagent, from where he'd make for the café in Chiswick High Road which did a delicious fry-up breakfast. Once a week, he'd wander into the florist's across the road from dear old King's Court and buy a bunch of dahlias, Phyllis's favourite flower.

"It keeps the memory of my good lady around the house," he'd tell the nicely dishevelled lady who ran the place. "It's such a tidy, compact little thing, the dahlia, isn't it? Just like my Phyllis."

One particular morning, however, he'd decided to change his route and took a walk to the bottom of The Green. It was something he rarely did, but he was in the mood for an enjoyable session of tutting at what his neighbours were doing to ruin the look of the place.

He shook his head at what the solicitor at Number Three had done, all floor-length windows and ridiculous balconies; and Number Four had scaffolding everywhere *again*! Builders were climbing up and down the property, no doubt beginning yet another round of unnecessary excavations and extensions. And Number Five's garden looked like a mud bath. He'd heard from the local butcher that they'd had a swimming pool installed in the basement. Whatever next? He shook his head, hoping one of them might come out of the front door just so he could scowl at them. No-one did, so he scowled anyway.

Finally, there was Number Six, the only house in the street, apart from his, which hadn't been touched. Nodding benignly at it, he was about to cross over when he noticed a very impressive vintage MG being driven towards it. What struck him was how very much it resembled the car old Mr. Cairnforth used to drive. It was even the same scarlet red colour. George slowed his pace as the car was parked rather neatly by the pavement.

A handsome young chap stepped briskly out and walked towards him, causing George to stop in his tracks.

"Hello," the young man said brightly, his long curly hair and paint-stained overalls suggesting he was an artist. "We've not actually met have we? I'm Jack, and you live at Number One, don't you?"

George realised that he was staring rather rudely and, pulling himself up, stepped forward to shake Jack's hand.

"That's right," he said. "George Sawyer. I've seen you and your wife in the distance when I'm pruning the roses, but I don't often pass this far down the street to be honest."

Jack laughed, and it was a sound which caused George's spine to tingle.

"My wife, Ginny, has always felt a kind of distant

kinship with you," Jack said, beaming with a smile which, for George, was quite uncanny. "Like us, you're managing to contain the onslaught of nonsense along here."

Jack waved dismissively at the other houses in the street.

"We are the bookends of these utter monstrosities, aren't we?"

"Indeed we are," George replied, looking at Jack's car and nodding approvingly.

"Unlike this beautiful thing. It's an MG-TF isn't it?"

"That's right, my pride and joy. She was built in 1954. I bought her last week from a dealer in Hammersmith who specialises in vintage cars. A little treat for myself to celebrate... a rather special occasion."

"A *special* occasion?"

"I've been commissioned to paint The Princess of Wales' portrait."

"So you *are* an artist," George said.

"I am. And, with a bit of luck, this commission should make me a little more well-known."

"Well, congratulations, young man," George said. "And I approve of your indulgence. I had a friend many years ago who owned a very similar model to this – the same colour too."

"A man with taste, clearly," Jack said, bid George good morning and, with an eerily familiar salute, went into the house.

'Yes', George thought, 'even his gait is the same.'

Deep in thought, he walked across The Green and made his way to the High Street. Imagining the delicious eggs, bacon and sausages Irene always cooked to perfection for him, something else occurred to him.

When he'd shaken the young chap's hand, just before letting go he'd done a kind of 'double-squeeze'. He hadn't thought about it at the time, but it was exactly what the old gent used to do.

And then it struck him.

Mr. C. had once spoken of 'my late wife *Ginny…*' when they were discussing family one evening in the lobby of King's Court. And the young man's voice… Mr. C's was older, of course, but so similar. His thoughts doing somersaults in his head, George stepped off the pavement.

Carly Newman was fiddling with the hi-fi system in the silver Porsche which had come with her new job in the City. As she selected one of her favourite albums, Nirvana's *In Utero,* she looked up and saw an old bloke walk right in front of her. She jammed her foot on the brake but it was too late. The car hit him full on, throwing him up in the air like a sack of potatoes. Carly watched in horror as, in a kind of slow motion, the broken body fell back down and landed with a sickening thud in the road.

Feeling like she might throw up, Carly rushed out of the car and ran to where George was lying, blood pouring from his mouth. As more people hurried to help, she tried to gather the poor old man in her arms, saying over and over again, 'I'm so sorry, I didn't see you. I'm *so* sorry!'.

George opened his mouth to speak and uttered something. Carly leaned in and asked him to repeat it, but she felt his body go limp and knew instinctively that he'd gone.

"What did he say, dear?" a lady behind her asked, bending down and squeezing her arm.

"I'm not sure... I think he... I think he said..." the girl sobbed through the shock and horror. "He just said... 'It can't be', and then he..."

She threw her head back and wailed to the sky, "Oh God, what have I done?"

"I saw what happened, darlin'," the lady said. "It weren't your fault. He stepped right out in front of you. Poor old bean, didn't even look as he crossed the road."

Whatever memories, questions and unbelievable possibilities had been racing through George's mind as he'd stepped off the pavement, they had now gone forever. No-one else would even consider the similarities between old Mr. Cairnforth and the young man at No.6, The Green. In fact, no-one else would remember Mr. C. at all.

Chapter Forty-Five

Louise Campbell-Sawyer, the youngest daughter of George and Phyllis, was just finishing clearing the bungalow. Two weeks after it had gone on the market, the estate agent had already had an offer on the house, which Louise and her brothers had happily accepted. She didn't like the idea of the new owners carrying out their declared plan to demolish the place and build a five storey family home on the plot - her dad would have been mortified – but what could she do? That's what happened these days, especially with all the property programmes on TV, which celebrated the destruction of the old for the new gleaming mansions people wanted to erect in their place.

The last room she'd done was her father's, and most of the stuff in there would sadly end up on the tip. Her parents' enormous windfall over thirty years earlier had dwindled somewhat, with the luxury cruises, staying in five-star hotels, several trips to the Caribbean and the Greek Islands and the trusts they'd set up for their children.

"Your mum and I have had a ball," Dad had told her once, "but it's your and the boys' turn now to enjoy what's left."

In a trunk at the bottom of the bed, underneath towels and sheets, Louise had found a pastel drawing of her dad, done when he was much younger. It wasn't really to her taste, a bit too colourful and sketchy for her, but she thought it might bring a few quid at Help The Homeless, the charity shop down the road.

Louise put a large plastic bag by the dustbin and

another one full of clothes and odds and ends in the boot and closed the front door of her parents' much-loved home. She carefully placed the sketch of her dad on the front passenger seat and drove off.

Glancing down at the drawing, Louise wondered if her father had known he had terminal cancer. The coroner had told them that the cancer was in his lungs and had started to spread to the brain. Dad had given none of them any inkling he was sick, and she hoped he hadn't known. The awful alternative was that he had stepped out in front of that car on purpose. She saw the sign for the charity shop ahead, pushed her worrying thoughts aside and parked in a thirty-minute bay.

Mrs Laidlaw, who worked at the shop on Mondays and Thursdays, had been thrilled with what Louise had brought her. She particularly admired some of George's military gear from the war, and cooed delightedly over various knick-knacks he and Phyllis had bought on their trips around the world. To Louise's surprise, she was also quite taken with the sketch.

"I'll put that in the window," she said, holding the drawing up to the light. "It's a bit modern art-ish, but some people like that kind of thing. I must say, they are lovely colours."

Louise couldn't tell her who it was by as there was no signature, but that didn't appear to put Mrs. Laidlaw off.

"I think we'd get a tenner for it anyway," she said. "I've got an old frame in the back which I think would be about the right size. Thank you, dear. The folk at the shelter will be very grateful, I'm sure."

A week later, a rather odd-looking gentleman in a

long cape, black fedora hat and carrying a silver cane, walked into the shop. Mrs. Laidlaw thought he looked like some character from a Charles Dickens novel, and was especially amused when he tipped his hat at her and bid her a charmingly old-fashioned, 'Good morning, dear lady!'.

She was listening to the radio at the time, the news full of details about The Princess of Wales' car crash in Paris the previous day.

"Such a tragedy!" Mrs. Laidlaw said to the chap. "And those poor boys."

He nodded and agreed it was very sad, then asked her about the sketch in the window. She told him she had no idea who it was by, but, going to get it, told him that a lady whose late father had lived in The Green had 'very kindly' given it to the shop.

To her astonishment, he offered her one-hundred pounds for it. She considered advising him that the price ticket said '£10', but then decided that, as the homeless shelter needed some extra funds for renovations and the strange bloke looked quite well-heeled, she'd keep schtumm and happily dropped the two fifty pound notes in the till.

"Would you like a bag, sir?" Mrs. Laidlaw asked him, deciding not to charge him the usual 2p.

"No, that won't be necessary," he replied, smiling appreciatively at the sketch. "Arriving at my destination will take but a few minutes."

"So, you're local, are you, sir?"

"A long time ago," he replied vaguely, and, with a rather theatrical bow, he smiled and bid her good day.

She was about to go and make herself a celebratory cup of tea, when she looked out the window and saw the gentleman hover on the pavement, step off into the road and disappear. She blinked, looked again, and sure enough, he'd gone.

"Well, I never!" she said, clasping her pearl necklace. "I think I need something a bit stronger than tea."

Chapter Forty-Six

Imagine Heights, Manhattan, New York, 2062. At 3,500 feet with 250 floors, the apartment block, built in 2040 to mark what would have been John Lennon's one-hundredth birthday, was the tallest building in the world.

The billionaire Edward Lockton, whose personal art collection was rumoured to be amongst the largest in the world, stepped out of the lift into his top floor penthouse and, with a 'Good morning, Marilyn, nice to be home' handed his cane, fedora hat and cape to his android assistant asking her to switch on the revolving floor.

Over the course of the day, it gave him a three-hundred-and-sixty-degree panoramic view, with a vista spread to a one-hundred-mile radius, the sales blurb having boasted, 'On a clear day you can see Philadelphia'. And indeed, as he settled into his two hundred year-old leather Chesterfield, he could see it gleaming in the distance.

Marilyn had been with Edward for ten years, programmed to look and sound like the legendary Monroe, and created by Lake Rothwell, CEO of *Celebrity AI*, who was, like her father Albert, a great friend of Edward's. She had gifted him the android after he had revealed to her one evening, as they watched *The Seven Year Itch* in his cinema at the heart of the apartment, that the Hollywood legend was his favourite film star.

Edward had at first felt uncomfortable having an AI clone of the iconic actress cooking, cleaning and keeping house for him. But when Marilyn had explained very sweetly that she viewed it as an honour to look after 'an actual English Lord' he had relaxed, and over time they had become great pals, Marilyn often acting as his closest and most discreet confidant.

Edward and Lake had met during the Rolling Stones' Hyde Park gig in 1969, sharing a bottle of champagne and dancing with the crowd during King Crimson's set. Their friendship had blossomed through their mutual disgust at the poor treatment of the hundreds of butterflies released before The Stones' first number, many of which were either dead or dying after being cooped up in cardboard boxes for hours.

"My son would have been mortified," Edward said, as they watched the poor creatures trodden underfoot by the audience, and even by Jagger himself as he stomped around the stage.

They crossed Park Lane and went into Les Ambassadeurs for several cocktails and a slap-up lunch, cheering themselves up by discussing what was their favourite live album, Lake's being The Who's *Live at Leeds* while Edward's choice was Judy Garland's 1961 Carnegie Hall show.

"I was there," he told Lake, "sitting just a few seats away from Dirk Bogarde. It's been called the greatest night in show business history. Everyone talks about Beatlemania, well that night I witnessed Judymania."

As Marilyn prepared lunch, the strains of her rendition of 'Heatwave' floating from the kitchen, Edward took out the sketch he'd brought back from the charity shop in Chiswick and studied it with satisfaction. As always, he admired Jack Marlowe's incredible use of colour and light, and though he had no idea who the smart gentleman was in Marlowe's drawing, it was a wonderful addition to his growing collection of the great man's work, much of which the world had never seen.

He put the drawing aside and reflected on his latest trip to his old stamping ground. As when he'd visited Butterfly Cottage in 1961, meeting the Braintrees and sensing the presence of Jack Marlowe, he'd once again used the guise of his old friend D.I. Rush to keep tabs on Ginny's 'missing' husband. An added bonus had been seeing Marlowe's rather wonderful portrait of his wife which Edward would have so loved to add to his collection.

Before visiting Mrs. Marlowe, he'd taken the opportunity to wander into the park behind the bungalow and imagine where his old home, Lockton Manor, had once stood. As ever, he was pleased to see that at least the fabulous fountain, which his father, Reginald, had commissioned the architect Charles Barry to create, still remained as a legacy to the house he'd abandoned ninety years earlier.

Smiling at memories of his time at the manor, he picked up his copy of the latest Paris Match, which lay neatly arranged on the coffee table along with Der Tagesspeigel, El Pais, The Guardian and the New York Times. His eyes were immediately drawn to an article on Page Two of the French newspaper, and, breathing in the delicious aromas of Marilyn's latest culinary creation, he read on, a plan for new adventure beginning to hatch in his mind.

Edward walked through to the kitchen where Marilyn had her back to him checking the oven, looking particularly delightful in the polka-dot headscarf tying up her hair a la Betty Grable. Singing 'She certainly can can-can' to herself she suddenly spun round arms akimbo and gasped, her eyes popping out at the smiling Lord Lockton.

"Oh, my Lord!" she cried, her perfectly manicured hand rushing to her mouth in pure Monroe fashion. "I didn't see you there."

"Clearly not, Marilyn," Edward replied, grinning at her fondly, "but the sight of you today cheers me considerably, and what you're creating in the oven smells delicious."

"Oh, just something I saw on an old Delia Smith programme last night. It looked delicious, so I thought we'd try it."

"Good old Delia," Edward said, laughing. "When you're ready, no rush, could you put a call into Bella Mainstay at The Marlowe Trust, please?"

"Of course, my lord," Marilyn said, glancing into the oven once more before taking off her apron.

She folded it over a chair and, making for the hallway, paused and looked in deep thought.

"My Lord, can I ask you something?"

"Of course, Marilyn, anything, anytime."

"Well, this may sound a little presumptuous but... I have the impression, the sense, that you may be leaving soon. Am I correct in surmising that?"

Edward smiled at Marilyn.

"It's very likely you are correct, my dear, but worry not. I'll ensure you are placed with a good, kind gentleman who I am hoping will move into the apartment when I'm gone. He will take care of you and you will look after him as you have always looked after me. Is that acceptable to you, Marilyn?"

"Of course, my Lord. And, thank you."

"Not at all, Marilyn. Thank *you*."

"For what, my lord?"

"For being my friend."

"Oh, it has been my pleasure, my Lord."

Marilyn pouted a kiss and blew it across the room. Edward caught it, making Marilyn giggle as she went to place the call.

Chapter Forty-Seven

Bella Mainstay ended her call from New York and, as her conversation with Edward Lockton floated through her mind, she sat back and looked around the large Covent Garden office she had inherited when she took over the running of The Marlowe Trust three years earlier. On the walls were various prints of Jack Marlowe's most popular paintings and behind her was the viewing gallery of original works which had been created from Jack's old studio.

The job had been offered to her by Karl Taylor, the current manager of the Trust who was soon to retire. At first she had been unsure about it. Bella had been a widow for two years, after her husband Stephen had suffered a shockingly massive heart attack one morning coming out of the bedroom. He had been so young, only thirty-two, and she had been left with the young twins to care for alone.

"Well, I'm very flattered, of course, Mr. Taylor," Bella had said, "but I couldn't possibly give my time over to what I imagine is a very pressurised and extremely time-consuming job. Who would look after Matthew and Sarah? I am always here at home when they return from school, and I would never allow for them to become latch-key kids."

Taylor coughed lightly and said, "That has been taken into consideration, Mrs. Mainstay. As you know, Sir Jack left a large sum of money to provide for you and the children, and an extension of that is the necessary childcare which would be paid for, should you take the job. The twins can either have a live-in governess at your home or we can offer an excellent private school which is partly funded by the Trust. Both options would ensure that your children receive top-notch education, in not only the sciences and business, but also in the arts, and that their every need is seen to while you are at the office."

He paused, letting Bella have a moment to think things through. Her 'We-ell… ' response encouraged him to add, "Take a few days to think it over, Mrs. Mainstay. But I do urge you to consider our offer seriously. It really is – and I speak from personal experience – a most satisfying and enjoyable job. Most rewarding."

Bella had sat and mulled the whole thing over, the idea definitely intriguing her. It had been extremely kind of the Trust to take such an interest in the twins' welfare after Stephen's death. Although Jack had disappeared from view after he had given the bungalow to her and Stephen, she knew that his wishes were constantly in operation. He had always felt like a distant beneficent uncle, making sure she was looked after, as Stephen's grandparents would have hoped for.

Finally, she discussed it with Matthew and Sarah, who were ten going on thirty-five. They sat and listened as she explained the Trust's offer, and when she'd finished they both said at the same time, "Take the job, Mummy."

"You're bored to death here," Sarah added, "we know you are. You need some mental stimulation. We'll be fine."

Matthew had laughed and said, "And I quite like the idea of a governess."

"As long as she's fun and looks like Mary Poppins," Sarah added.

By the next morning, after an unsettled night, Bella

had decided that the twins were right, it was the kind of challenge she needed.

Now, she sat in her office thinking over her intriguing conversation with Edward Lockton. He was known the world over as a collector of fine art, but, to her astonishment, not only had he offered her, free of charge, a set of Jack Marlowe pastel sketches and paintings 'which only a handful of people have seen', he had also suggested she should share with the world the collection of portraits which she and Stephen had been given by Jack when they'd moved into Butterfly Cottage.

"But how do you know about those?" Bella had asked Lockton.

"I have my sources, Mrs. Mainstay. I have seen them with my own eyes and they really are spectacular."

"But when did you see them?"

"Before you did, but I knew that Jack wished you and your husband to have them."

"You knew Sir Jack?"

"In another time and place, yes, our paths crossed."

"But who will ever believe they're Marlowe originals? They would need accreditation and that would be impossible to acquire."

"Mrs. Mainstay, if the Trust organises an exhibition of my collection along with your paintings then that will be enough for most people. Of course, the 'Marlowe experts' will never accept them as genuine, but who cares? The world should see them and judge for themselves."

"I don't know. Your offer is most kind and the idea is certainly intriguing, but…"

"If I offer to pay for and arrange the exhibition, with your help, *and* put my name to it, would that persuade you?"

Bella was hovering around saying yes, but her doubts persisted.

"They would have their own separate viewing room and the exhibition would be billed as 'The Jack Marlowe Private Collection'," Lockton continued. "I would assure there would be no authentication issues flagged up by the gallery, nor any toleration of so-called experts decrying the works as forgeries. They are *not* forgeries. Your paintings are by Jack Marlowe, as is my collection, whatever questions and eyebrows they raise. I will personally authenticate them - because only I can."

To convince Bella, Edward had sent her scans of his collection. When she'd pointed out that the sketches were not signed he told her, "Oh yes they are. If you look extremely carefully, within the strands of hair of each sitter is Jack Marlowe's tiny signature accompanied by the date they were drawn."

Bella had increased the size of each sketch on her laptop, and sure enough, there were Jack's signature and the dates, almost invisible to the human eye.

"But it says they were done in 1955," she'd emailed Edward back.

"Of course it does," he'd replied, "and you especially should not be questioning that."

It had been a hard sell to the Trust Committee, but in the end the fact that the offer came from the highly regarded Edward Lockton persuaded them to allow Bella to go ahead. There was also the certain commercial benefit of organising the exhibition to fit in with what would have been Sir Jack's hundredth birthday. Armed with the committee's approval - which she insisted was emailed to her immediately - Bella called Edward and agreed to his terms.

The exhibition would have to be ready in just a few months, but Bella felt sure that at least one of the London galleries would jump at the chance. She got to work contacting all the gallery chairs and committees, preparing herself for the Trust's most controversial event yet.

Chapter Forty-Eight

On the first day of December 2062, the queue for the opening of 'The Jack Marlowe Private Collection' was the largest The Royal Academy had ever seen. It stretched right down Piccadilly and comprised a wide range of ages.

Teenagers who had studied Marlowe's paintings for their History of Art exams; art connoisseurs who had long been fascinated by the oft-told rumours about the unauthenticated works; and those who had read articles and seen documentaries about Sir Jack. They all chatted excitedly in anticipation of what the exhibition would reveal.

The press and TV had been agog at the public interest the event had created, tickets selling out within hours of coming online, inspiring YouTube influencers to create popular discussion platforms about Jack's work. The makers of a BBC Four documentary had tried to contact Edward Lockton at his apartment in New York, to ask him if he would be interviewed about his gift to the Marlowe Trust, but they only got as far as his personal assistant, who breathily told them in her best *Some Like It Hot* voice,

"I'm afraid Lord Lockton is currently unavailable for comment. I'm so very sorry. Goodbye and have a nice day."

Marilyn's final task for Edward had been to book the top floor suite of The Savoy for the duration of his stay in London. He'd first stayed there in 1897, when the Prince of Wales had invited him to attend his mother's Diamond Jubilee celebrations. Although a triumphant day for Queen Victoria, Edward had been struck by how sad she looked at that evening's enormous banquet in the palace. He'd asked Bertie why.

"It's called the one deep, irreplaceable love, Ed," Bertie had replied, winking and nudging his friend as he added, "something neither you nor I will ever be cursed by!"

Now, over a hundred and fifty years later, he sat in the Academy's Courtyard Café, sipping his latte and watching the excited crowds moving through the entrance to the exhibition. Edward tapped a number into his mobile and smiled as the voice of one of his favourite people came on the line.

"And how are you settling in, my boy?" he said. "I do hope Marilyn is looking after you."

He chuckled at the reply.

"That is very good to hear. I hope you will be happy in the best apartment in the world. Farewell, and please give my love to Miss Monroe."

Edward finished his coffee and walked towards a side door, where he showed his VIP pass and slipped anonymously inside. He almost salivated at the thought of seeing the expressions on people's faces, as they witnessed scenes from a time-traveller's adventures.

Chapter Forty-Nine

The AI Beatles were giving a great performance of 'All My Loving' in the specially redesigned events area on the first floor of Imagine Heights. It had been the first song The Beatles had performed on American TV in February 1964, and was thought by the creators of this historic show to be the perfect opener.

The concept was incredible, using the latest A.I. technology and multi-audio mixing and layering, it combined cleaned-up and colourised archive performances by the group with period interviews to create what looked like a live on-stage documentary of The Beatles. When it premièred that night, with a three-month residency before 'The Long & Winding Road' world tour began, Lawrence sat in his front row seat transfixed. John, Paul, George and Ringo looked as real as the day he'd watched them recording in Abbey Road back in 1963. The memory created an emotional mixture of the excitement he'd felt standing in the control room of Studio 2, along with the acknowledgement that Charles was no longer by his side to enjoy it. He silently dedicated the evening to the son of the man who had made his presence there possible.

As the group launched into 'We Can Work It Out', Lawrence thought back to the afternoon in 2016 when he'd received that life-changing call just a few months after Charles' death.

"Good day," a man's voice said, "I want to say first of all how sorry I am for your loss," before adding, "you must miss Charles."

Lawrence wondered if it was someone from the estate agent who was selling Charles' apartment.

"Who is this?"

The caller apologised and said, quite casually, "I am Edward Lockton, Charles´ father."

Lawrence nearly put the phone down, but then remembered something Charles once said: 'My father's also a time-traveller, and I think he's been watching me for years'.

And, as the caller chatted away about Charles, it became clear that this could only be Lord Lockton Senior. He knew too many intimate details, too many childhood anecdotes Charles had told Lawrence, for it to be anyone else.

"I currently reside in the second half of 21st Century New York," Edward told him, "but, as you know, I was born in a suburb of London in 1861."

"Charles told me you'd deserted him and his mother in 1907," Lawrence said, realising it sounded like a rebuke.

"Indeed I did," Edward replied, sounding not at all rebuked.

"Why at that point, when Charles was just a child?"

"For several reasons, but mainly because a detective friend of mine had got himself into a spot of bother, silly boy, and while I was not in any way involved nor implicated, it was likely the police may make things difficult for me and my family. So, after ensuring that Charles and his mother were financially secure, I took my leave and travelled a hundred and sixty years hence, where the incident would be lost in the mists of time – pardon the pun."

His laugh was just like Charles', a whoop of joy.

"But I am actually in your time-space right now, just down the road, in fact. I'm staying at the rather delightful

Druidstone Hotel. I wanted to visit Charles before he passed this mortal coil, and I must congratulate you on Bridesview, an exquisite house."

"You were in my house?"

"Yes, only briefly, you were downstairs banging a few dishes around, and I crept in to have a few last words with Charlie boy. We made our peace at last."

"Charles always thought you were watching him."

"I kept an eye on him. Of course I did. He was my son. Just occasional visits now and then, to make sure all was well with the dear boy. How was meeting Cliff, by the way?"

"You know about that?"

"Of course. There's a delightful apartment in Abbey Road which I've occasionally stayed in. I was passing the studios one morning, on my way to an excellent eaterie in St. John's Wood village, when I saw you and Charles nattering on the steps with Sir Cliff and his rather drab-looking producer."

Lawrence remembered how distracted Charles had been just for a moment, as though he'd seen something or someone. He shook his head at the madness of it all.

"Now, young Mr. York," Edward said. "I have an offer to make. You need to blow the cobwebs of grief and loss away. But it will entail one more time-travel. Interested to hear more?"

Now here he was, utterly beguiled as The Beatles performed 'All You Need Is Love' on the One World broadcast, followed by them visiting the Maharishi in Bangor and then being interviewed about the death of Brian Epstein. This was followed by home movies of them wandering around the Maharishi's retreat in

Rishikesh, laid against the sonic backcloth of George's beautiful 'The Inner Light'.

It created a virtual reality peek into those halcyon days for every member of the audience, all of them – except one – being too young to have been around at the time. For them, this was musical history being recreated; for Lawrence these were his teenage memories.

The concert had ended with, of course, 'The Long and Winding Road', and Lawrence watched misty-eyed as the bearded McCartney sat at the grand piano, singing the song which had become a world anthem. With the rest of the audience, he sang along with tears streaming down his face.

Lawrence joined the hordes milling out of the arts centre chatting excitedly at what they'd just witnessed, and then peeled off for the elevator to his apartment. As it soared to the top floor, he couldn't wait to tell Marilyn all about it.

Chapter Fifty

After Marilyn had brought Lawrence his usual nightcap of Scotch on the rocks, he sat and watched the lights across a hundred miles twinkling through the panoramic window. It seemed an odd place to call home, in a city he´d never thought to visit, but as he watched a small plane float across the sky and remembered watching the UFO with Charles in Little Haven, he reflected on how lonely he had become at Bridesview, before Edward had called him with an offer he couldn't refuse.

A few months after Charles had passed away, Tee had also succumbed. She'd developed pneumonia from what had started out as an itchy cough, and finally slipped peacefully away as he and Suze had told her how lovely the ocean looked that evening, sharing reminiscences of their journeys around Pembrokeshire together.

Suze had decided to sell up and return to London, telling Lawrence during their final lunch together at The Galleon, "I've loved it here with Tee, with you and Charles nearby, but I hope you'll understand that I now need to hear roomfuls of laughter, rather than my own silence."

During his occasional chats with Suze on the phone, the noise of another party at her Great Titchfield flat in the background, Lawrence wondered if he should also go back to London, but his heart no longer lay there. He put Bridesview on the market, sold the Consul to a classic car dealer, and began to plan a grand tour through Europe. Then 'the Lockton Magic' arrived in his life once more and offered a much more amazing adventure, one which, almost fifty years into the future, had introduced Lawrence to a whole new crowd of friends, the movers and shakers of The Big Apple arts scene, keen to include him in every exclusive shindig the city had to offer to the rich and interesting.

One December morning in 2080, Marilyn found Lawrence in the screening room, having passed away as he was watching his favourite movie, *A Hard Day's Night*. It had been his own personal marking of the hundredth anniversary of John Lennon's death, which had taken place just three blocks away from Imagine Heights.

In her statement, broadcast on all the American TV channels on the morning of Lawrence's death, Marilyn said just a few words, "Mr. York was a true gentlemen. He was always so kind and generous to me. But, as everyone knows, gentlemen prefer blondes."

Lawrence had bequeathed the apartment to the Museum of Modern Art, instructing them to open it to the public, allowing everyone to experience the breathtaking views and Edward's astonishing art collection. He also stipulated that the live-in curator and tour guide must be Marilyn, who should be cared for and maintained to the highest technical standards, all paid for from Lawrence's vast wealth he inherited from Edward when he took over the apartment.

Marilyn absolutely loved showing hundreds of people around her beautiful home each week and became as famous as the apartment itself. She always ended her tour with a rendition of 'Diamonds Are A Girl's Best Friend', which delighted the visitors as much as having seen the wonders of the apartment's treasures. *Time* magazine made her Personality of The Year, resulting in people from all over the world flocking to see what all the fuss was about. Marilyn, of course, was in her element.

Chapter Fifty-One

One morning in early March, 2116, Travis Taylor woke with a start. His wife Carla was still slumbering peacefully beside him, while he was covered in sweat. He'd had a feverish night full of odd dreams, one of them featuring a man with grey curly hair standing before a large canvas on which he was painting a group of people who Travis didn't recognise. One by one they all turned to face him and said,

"Good morning Travis, all will be well."

He sat up in bed and looked at the vintage cream Bakelite ´Teas-made´ clock he and Carla had bought at a car boot sale the previous Sunday. It was five-to-five, and as he lay against the pillow waiting for the cheerful 'ding' of the alarm, he began planning his day.

He was a coder and designer at Nature Games International, whose first release, *Save Endangered Species*, had been a huge hit the previous year. It had come with a free hologram of Sir David Attenborough, which appeared when purchasers opened the game on their laptops and smart phones.

Utilising a piece of BBC footage from the 2020s, when Sir David had benignly explained why so many species of wildlife needed humanity's help, the hologram had been particularly fascinating for youngsters who had read and watched films about Attenborough in history lessons. Now they could see him standing in their bedrooms, their sitting-rooms and their kitchens as he explained why caring for the Earth, its oceans and skies, was 'more important than ever.'

Travis was currently working on a new game, *Save Mankind*, which was expected to be even more popular than the Attenborough one, featuring as it did Queen Elizabeth The Third. In it she explained how 'mankind must share ideals, generosity of spirit and consideration for every race, creed, sexual persuasion and belief, and care for our environment as well as each other.' Travis was very excited that it was he who had suggested the idea and, with his team of four enthusiastic students on a year's work experience, had put together the coding and design for the hologram.

The Teasmade struck five o'clock and, putting on his 'Save Mankind' onesie NGI had created for the upcoming marketing campaign, Travis went downstairs, made a strong espresso and, yawning as he drank, opened his emails on the laptop. The first one in his Inbox quickly woke him up. It was from his landlords, a consortium of companies based in Dubai which had bought several blocks of flats in and around London over the last few decades. Their round-robin email was informing all their tenants in the Tooting building that it was due to be sold and turned into luxury apartments. It meant that they would need to vacate the premises in one month to allow for renovations to begin. As he'd sat before his laptop, reading and re-reading the email, Travis broke down and cried.

Travelling into central London each day was already taking him and Carla more than two hours during rush hour, and they rarely got home before nine o'clock at night. They'd eat a takeaway while watching a couple of old episodes of their favourite '90s TV series, *Friends,* before Carla began an hour of study for her upcoming exams to become a Professor of Arts & Textiles, which her college The Slade had sponsored.

Their rent was extortionately high, as all rentals in and around London now were, and the thought of having to find something cheaper further out in the suburbs, adding even more journey time, filled Travis with dread.

He decided to let Carla sleep for another half-an-hour, before he'd have to give her the bad news. He made himself a bowl of fruit muesli, adding slices of banana and some strawberries from the fridge, and opened the next email. It was from someone called Josephine Mainstay from The Marlowe Trust, informing him that 'the contents of the attached letter may be of interest to you'. Travis was sure it was either a spam or a begging letter for cash, and was about to delete it when Carla unexpectedly walked in and asked what he was looking at.

"It purports to come from something called The Marlowe Trust, and has a letter in an attachment which this Mainstay woman says could be of interest to me," Travis told Carla. "I'm going to Junk it."

"Hm, wait a minute…" Carla said, leaning over her husband's shoulder and reading the email. "The Slade is actually linked to that Trust. It contributes to the running of many courses at the college, including mine. It's started up a lot of careers in art and design since it was established by Jack Marlowe in the 1990s."

"There you go then," Travis said, holding his finger over the 'delete' key. "The spammers have obviously done their homework and are trying it on."

"No, don't delete it," Carla said, gently pushing Travis' hand away from his keyboard. "If it was a spam using my association with The Slade, then the email would have been sent to me, not you, and I've heard of Josephine Mainstay. I actually met her four years ago when she came to do a talk at the college, asking for students to create pieces of work to help celebrate what would have been the 150th anniversary of Jack Marlowe's birth. My textile based on some of his portraits was included in the exhibition."

"Who's Jack Marlowe?"

"He was a portrait painter, really amazing artist, he and his wife set up the Trust together and it's still going strong. I had a really lovely chat with Josephine. I told her about you and what you were doing at NGI and she seemed really interested. She's the granddaughter of the lady who ran the Trust until Josephine took over. I think the email's genuine. Go on, open the attachment. Our firewall can zap it if it's hostile."

"True, okay, here it is…"

Carla read the attached letter out loud:

Dear Mr. Taylor,

My name is Josephine Mainstay and I run The Marlowe Trust from my office here in Covent Garden. You may be aware that a bungalow in Turnham Green, 'Butterfly Cottage', where Jack and Ginny Marlowe lived for many years, is now owned by the Trust and has been given a Grade 2 listing by Historic England.

As background for you, the listing means that Butterfly Cottage cannot be structurally altered in any significant manner unless given written consent by us, which is only occasionally given, usually for family requirements.

The parkland behind the bungalow is also now owned by the Trust which has allowed us to amalgamate wildflower meadows - something dear to Lady Marlowe's heart - into the landscaping of the grounds. Many of the plants benefit from the wide spray of water issuing from *what is now known as the Happy Dolphin fountain, and there is also a sizeable butterfly sanctuary, where one had been in the 19th and early 20th centuries, cared for by a curator employed by the Trust.*

Sir Jack's wish was always that the bungalow would be the home of people who are not only connected to and involved in the arts but who are somehow linked, by family or friendship, to him or his wife.

Jack Marlowe had no siblings, and both his parents were only children, so we began extensive research of the Taylor side of the family, which has led us to you. It was also in part due to a conversation I recalled having with your wife, Carla, four years ago when I was visiting The Slade.

Lady Marlowe, who never had children of her own, and was also an only child, was a third cousin twice removed of yours, going back to your great-great-great grandfather, Kenneth Taylor, who was the brother of Ginny's father, Andrew. Another interesting connection is that your great-grandfather, Karl Taylor, once ran The Marlowe Trust before my grandmother took over.

The fact your wife is studying at The Slade, where Sir Jack also began his career, adds to our keenness that you should be offered this residency of the house where the Marlowes lived until 2047, when my grandparents were given it by Sir Jack. My grandmother lived there until her death at the age of eighty-seven, since when the Trust has carried out all the work in the surrounding areas as I mentioned.

Now, please understand, there is nothing forcing you to become the latest inheriting resident of Butterfly Cottage, which this letter invites you to do. If you decide to decline our offer then we will do more research to see if we can find someone else to be the recipient of this free lifetime residency of the bungalow.

However, should you wish to take up our offer, then please ring me on the number below to set up a convenient time for you to come into the office and discuss it further.

I hope to hear from you,

Best regards,

Josephine Mainstay

Carla stared at the screen then at Travis.

"Good god, Travis, this could be our manna from Heaven."

Travis chuckled and picked up his mobile.

"It can't do any harm to go and see this lady. I'll call her to fix an appointment. When's best for you, Carla?"

Chapter Fifty-Two

The George The Seventh Hall on the South Bank was packed as the 2120 British Academy of Video Games Awards was coming to a close. Elena Simmons, the Cultural Director of BAVGA was about to give the Academy's most prestigious award, The World Enhancement Trophy, to that year's lucky recipient.

As Miss Simmons ended her short speech she said, "And now, it is with great pleasure that this year's World Enhancement Trophy goes to a young man who has advanced the preservation of endangered lacewings with his utterly stunning video game, *Save Our Beautiful Flying Friends*. Ladies and Gentlemen, please put your hands together most warmly for Travis Taylor!"

Travis kissed his wife Carla, stroked the cheek of their four-year old son Jack, and leaned over to shake the hands of his special guests that evening, Josephine and Bernadette Carlin-Mainstay, at whose recent wedding Travis had been Best Man and Carla their Best Lady.

When he walked on stage, the audience stood and cheered, while behind him the screen showed clips from his astonishing piece of work. As butterflies wove through three-dimensionally accurate woodlands and fluttered around perfectly recreated summer wildflowers, Travis took his award from Miss Simmons and went to the mike.

Looking proudly at the gleaming award, which was in the shape of a computer keyboard with the letters BAVGA forming the top line of the keys, Travis said, "I want to dedicate this to my wife, Carla, who, with her incredible talent for recreating 3D images of the natural world, has helped me come up with this new video game. The fact that kids and adults all over the world are getting to know – and help save – these radiant creatures with the help of *Our Beautiful Flying Friends* is really the best prize I could imagine."

He held the award to his chest, and, his voice breaking slightly, he said, "But to now get this, the Academy's finest acknowledgement, is truly the icing on a delicious cake. I'd like to finish by also thanking The Marlowe Trust, especially Josephine Carlin-Mainstay. Because of their incredibly generous gift of Butterfly Cottage, I have been able to fully realise the beauty and the frailty of the short but fruitful lives of these amazing creatures, which my wife and I have the pleasure of seeing and walking amongst every day of our lives. Thank you so much."

Travis held up his award, blew a kiss to Carla, then to his son, and finally miming a hug for Josephine and Bernadette, he left the stage to tumultuous applause. As the images on the screen continued, one of the butterflies, a Painted Lady, appeared to fly out into the auditorium and up into the rafters. It fluttered around as people looked up and gasped at the colours and design radiating off its wings, then moved through a tiny glint of light and disappeared off into the night sky.

Chapter Fifty-Three

A single spaceship, 'Time Traveller', floated in darkness, en route to Neptune. The ship's camera had, for the past twelve years, been taking several close-up images of the planets it floated by, beaming them back down to Earth. After entering deep space, the plan was that the ship's journey would continue into parts of the Universe no-one has ever seen before.

Inside the large capsule, in a perfectly recreated version of his art room in New York, sat Edward Lockton, playing chess in his favourite leather armchair with Jack Marlowe. They are billions of miles from Earth, into a beyond they cannot begin to guess at. As Edward declared checkmate, he sat back and smiled at the man who had become his friend and fellow adventurer.

The two men had known each other across many decades, but it was when they ran into each other in November 1954 in Cimiez, a neighbourhood of Nice, that their friendship blossomed and brought them to this moment.

After living under the alias Jackson Cairnforth, Jack had left his apartment in King's Court and taken a time-slip back one year to attend the burial of his old friend, Henri Matisse. While there he had visited Alice's grave, situated next to the resting place of Alfred Van Cleef, who had created Alice's favourite perfume in 1896 with his father-in-law Salomon Arpels.

He had been making his way back to the cosy pension he was renting down the road, when Jack saw approaching him a familiar figure in a long cape, black fedora hat and swinging a silver cane. As they met at the narrow crossroads, the old man removed his hat and bowed grandly.

"Jack Marlowe, how delightful," the dandy-ish old gent said.

"Edward," Jack replied, shaking his hand, "very good to see you."

Lockton put his head on one side.

"I am eating at Le Bon Goût this evening, just down the road from here, would you care to join me? I'd like to discuss a plan I am hatching, over a splendid Beef Wellington and a fine Chablis."

The two men had a hearty dinner in the eaterie's Jasmine-scented garden, chatting about their various trips through decades and centuries and the fascinating acquaintances they'd made. As they sipped an excellent Pommeau de Bretagne brandy, Edward told Jack about his plan to time-slip almost two-hundred years from Nice to French Guiana, 'where I will become the oldest man in space'.

"I know from what I've read and researched that in 2140, France intends to send a volunteer member of the public into deep space, a journey which would provide the French Space Agency, CNES, with the data and images to make them the biggest and most forward-looking Universe explorers in the world."

He lifted his finger.

"But! The proviso is that the volunteer must be aware and wholly accepting of the fact that they will never return to Earth. It is a one-way ticket. I love that idea. Imagine, a time-traveller literally journeying through space into... well, who knows?"

"How do you know they'll accept you?" Jack asked him. "You have many talents, but you are certainly not a trained astronaut nor a space scientist."

"None of those things matter. What you have to understand... or maybe you already know... is that by the 22nd century I am a celebrated time-traveller. As are you, Jack. Our reputations are the stuff of dreams to many people. They will not be able to resist my suggestion."

He sat forward in his chair.

"Especially if I am accompanied by the legendary Jack Marlowe."

He toasted Jack and could see the sparkle of intrigue in his dinner companion's eyes.

"It sounds fascinating," Jack said, "but I still don't see how we could possibly be considered suitable. The logistics surely make it impossible."

"Normally yes, but in this case the ship will be directed throughout its entire journey by a small crew of A.I. astronauts on board who will ensure our safety and will be there to deal with any issues which may occur en route. Is it a risk? Of course? Is it an irresistible risk? Without question!"

He studied Jack for a few moments, swilling his brandy around his glass.

"Am I sensing the idea is attractive to you, Jack? I mean, what were your plans after Henri's funeral? To travel to somewhere else in time? Spend who knows how long looking out at an ocean you've seen many times before, or perhaps sitting, for the umpteenth century, in the Parthenon or the Coliseum, staring out at an endlessly changing landscape and contemplating - what?"

"Truthfully, I haven't really decided..."

"Then come with me! Join me in this journey, literally into the unknown. Now that is something neither of us have experienced for a very long time. Imagine the rush of delight at discovering something entirely new – and seen exclusively by us."

Jack stared at the table for a few moments, not saying a word, until he lifted his glass, tapped it against Edward's and said, "Oh, for heaven's sake, why not?"

"Here's to the heavens!" Edward said, throwing back his head and laughing. "Wherever and whatever they may be."

As Edward had predicted, when he and Jack arrived at the headquarters of CNES in Paris, they were welcomed as heroes. Jean-Pascal Metiér, CEO of the space agency, personally greeted them.

The three of them posed for press photos before he took them on a tour of the enormous complex, finally taking them into the inner sanctum, where the vast to-scale model of the spaceship sent shivers down Jack's spine.

"You will be perfectly catered for by the AI crew, Einstein and Turing," Metiér told them, "cocooned in a delightful living space of your own design, in a synthesised Earth's gravity. You will feel as if you are sailing on an ocean on a fine day aboard the best luxury cruise liner. All you will be asked to do is to keep a daily contact with Mission control, give occasional interviews for the world's media, and enjoy the journey. The rest will be entirely up to us."

"Er - silly question probably," Jack said, "but what about food? How is that provided?"

He was imagining reconstituted sludge from toothpaste-type tubes, the kind he'd seen on TV as a teenager watching missions to the Moon.

Metiér smiled.

"Regenerative organic cell culture, Sir Jack. Don't worry it's all in hand."

He grinned at Jack and Edward.

"You certainly won't starve, gentlemen!"

Metiér then explained that CNES would use the 1997 Cassini mission trajectory method for Time-Traveller's journey, which, he told them, was still the most effective for planetary exploration. It was known as 'Venus-Venus-Earth-Jupiter Gravity Assist', where Time Traveller would orbit the sun before making the first Venus fly-by six months after take-off, giving them the thrust the ship needed to move off into a larger orbit. They'd then do the second Venus flyby in May 2142, followed by a quick Earth fly-by two months later, which would provide the final boost towards Jupiter and beyond, each planet's orbital momentum being transferred to the spacecraft, which accelerated as a consequence. They would pass Jupiter sixteen months later, and four years after that, they would reach Saturn, then onwards to Uranus and finally reaching Neptune in October 2152.

"And, will we lose connection with Control once we go beyond Neptune into deep space?" Jack asked him.

"We are not sure. The ship has been fitted with the most up-to-date systems which may, possibly, allow us to stay in touch for at least some of the time you are in deep space. But, the rest, as they say, is in the hands of Fate itself."

"I can't wait," Edward said. "What an adventure!"

The Ariane 300 Time Traveller took off on September 5th 2140 amidst a flurry of social media fascination, and, as the years had passed, both Edward and Jack had been amused to see how Metiér had aged, while they appeared to be a little younger than when they'd set off. Edward considered that, by the time they'd explored deep space, they could be strapping young blades again.

"Ready for the return journey," he said.

"But there won't be a return journey," Jack had replied.

"Nothing – as we both know, Jack – is ever a given."

One of the highlights early on in the mission had been when Time Traveller had received a communication from the Armstrong-Aldrin Centre, which had been built on the surface of the Moon by a team of androids. It had begun as just a few heavy duty shacks but had now grown into what was an enormous complex. The first long-term team of human astronauts had arrived in July 2069, marking one hundred years since a man first stepped onto the Moon. Now inhabited for several months at a time by a large group of scientists, astronomers and botanists as well as their A.I. assistants, it was the first stage of reaching out into the possibilities of establishing future communities on Mars and beyond.

As Time Traveller was gliding past the Moon, the large screen over the mock fireplace flashed into life and there was the AAC team waving and smiling at them.

"We just wanted to wish you guys bon voyage and safe travel," the team leader Rocky Savoy said, surrounded by several nodding heads and thumbs-ups.

Edward was particularly fascinated to hear about the 'Radeon Protector Shield', which NASA had invented to prevent the inhabitants of the complex suffering radiation poisoning when they were outside on the surface of the moon.

"It's like having an umbrella of atmosphere above us," Rocky told them, "and it means we can wander outside without the encumbrance of space suits. It really frees the mind and allows us to truly take in the beauty of being up here."

Before the connection started to fade, Rocky held up the print of a painting, the one Jack had done when he and Ginny had been visiting the Impressionists in 1863.

"I was given this when I was a kid by my parents," Rocky told Jack. "They knew I wanted to go into space, and they bought me this to show me that nothing was impossible. That's your legacy, Jack, and yours too Edward. Nothing, absolutely nothing, is impossible anymore."

***

Jack had spent a lot of the time sketching the planets they passed, capturing the marble effect of the storm circles on Jupiter and its Great Red Spot; the pale yellow Saturn and its rings of ice crystals, rock and dust debris; the opaque light blue of Uranus, its cloud cover creating a featureless surface, and finally, the freezing cold Neptune, 'with the strongest sustained winds of any planet in the solar system', Metiér had told them as they were approaching the dazzlingly aquamarine giant, four times larger than Earth.

Jack would do a high res scan of each sketch and then send it back to Control, who forwarded the scans onto The Marlowe Foundation, as it was now known. The Foundation had their own plans for them, based on a request by Jack before he embarked on this mission beyond his lifetime.

In one call to Mission Control, Jack had complained that they weren't doing fly-bys of every planet en route to Neptune, which meant he couldn't sketch each planet in the solar system.

"Unfortunately, fly-bys of Jupiter, Saturn, Uranus and Neptune are the only ones possible for your trip," Chief Communications officer, Sascha Kalinsky, told Jack. "It's all about orbital trajectories, Sir Jack."

Jack smiled wryly at the camera.

"I suggested to Einstein that it would be great if we could orbit each planet, but he explained that –"

Sascha finished Einstein's point, "- that it would take you literally hundreds of years to do so."

Both of them laughed at Jack's confessed naivety.

"And, I know you're a time-traveller, Jack, but unfortunately planets don't come with the convenience of time-portals."

"As far as you know," Jack said.

Sascha grinned.

"Hm, maybe one day we could investigate that."

A particularly poignant stage of the journey had occurred when they were passing Saturn. A short alarm signal had sounded, giving Jack and Edward the cue to share precious cargo with outer space. Jack opened a drawer in the wall and retrieved Verity's sculpture of Alice and a sketch he had done of Ginny shortly after they'd met, while Edward took out a photo of Charles which he'd secretly taken when his son had been walking down King's Road in 1948 on his way to see Carol Reed.

They carefully placed them into a cavity in the wall and stood back.

"Sail safely, my darlings," Jack said.

"Bon voyage, my son," Edward said, kissing his fingers and placing them on the photograph.

The two men watched as the portrait, the photo and the sculpture shot out of the side of the ship to begin their silent journey into Saturn's orbit, joining the millions of dust particles floating endlessly around the planet. Jack smiled when he saw Verity's sculpture glinting briefly in the light of the distant sun, like a final wink of farewell.

One of the things Edward particularly looked forward to was when Einstein and Turing would join them for a chat, Jack and Edward relaxing on the two Gustav Stickley rocking chairs Edward had specifically requested. One evening, Edward began waxing lyrical about Marilyn when Einstein said, "We know Marilyn rather well."

Edward replied with a gentle rise of his eyebrows.

"Oh, yes, we do," Turing continued. "We have had extremely amusing conversations with her. She's quite a lady."

They explained that there is an inbuilt global communication network between all A.I. robots, which helps them work as a team when necessary.

"Don't you recall Marilyn telling you that she often had interesting chats with your refrigerator?" Turing asked Edward.

"Well, yes, but I thought she was joking," Edward replied.

"Of course not. The parts that had been used for some of the older Celebrity Assistance robots were eventually re-programmed to create intelligent household appliances. The technology hasn't really changed since the days of Alexa in the 21st century, much more sophisticated but basically the same idea."

"So, Edward," Jack said, chuckling, "your A.I. PA was chatting merrily to your TV and dishwasher, and you had no idea!"

A few evenings later, as Jack was discussing Pointillism with Turing, who suggested that the 'colour coding' of Seurat's paintings was similar to how a computer worked – 'lots of ones and zeros compared to a mass of painted dots of opposite spectrum colours' - the screen over the fireplace fizzled into life.

The blurred picture gradually cleared and Edward gasped. It was Marilyn, sitting in the Imagine Heights apartment wearing the outfit Marilyn Monroe had worn when she sang 'Happy Birthday, Mr. President' to Jack Kennedy in 1962. Edward's dear old friend smiled a scarlet lipstick-smile and giggled delightfully. Jack could have sworn there were tears welling up in Edward's eyes.

"Marilyn!" Edward shouted. "It's so wonderful to see you."

"You too, my Lord. And Sir Jack, what an honour to finally meet you."

"I've heard a lot about you, Marilyn," Jack said.

Marilyn gave a sharp intake of breath.

"Einstein! Turing!" she shouted. "How are you guys?"

The two robots, in perfect synchronisation, said, "We're great, Marilyn. Lovely to see you again."

"I hope you're looking after my Lord and Sir Jack, boys?"

"They are perfect hosts," Edward said, "and their cooking almost – *almost* – matches yours, Marilyn."

Marilyn threw back her head and giggled. It was a

sound Edward had missed. She then coughed lightly, settled herself as though for a screen test and, adopting a serious expression, said, "Okay, guys, I've been asked by Mr. Metiér to tell you that everyone, around the world, sends you our love and thanks for making this ground-breaking journey. Maybe one day it will allow us to find new homes beyond the stars. Stay safe, my friends, but most of all, stay happy. I wish I could be with you. Farewell."

She blew a kiss at the camera and, reaching above his head, Edward caught it.

The following day, thousands gathered in Trafalgar Square for the unveiling of the stone and steel statue of Sir Jack Marlowe and Lord Edward Lockton, showing the two global heroes shaking hands and looking out at the unknown. It had been created by Virginia Alice Carlin-Mainstay, great-great-great-granddaughter of Harry and Hannah and recently engaged to Jack Taylor, the cousin many times removed of Ginny Marlowe.

Virginia had recently graduated with a First from The Slade, having especially delighted the examining board with her essay, *The Amazing Sculptures of Verity Braintree*. She could not have known that millions of miles above her, Tee's sculpture of Alice was now floating in space, alongside Jack's portrait of Ginny and both of them accompanied by a photo of the man who had, centuries earlier, lived in the manor which had once stood just yards away from Virginia's home, Butterfly Cottage.

In the Tuileries Garden near The Louvre in Paris, sitting in two of the thousands of specially arranged

seats on the Grande Allée, with its view of La Place
de La Concorde and the Arc de Triomphe, were Albert
Rothwell and his daughter, Lake, watching the final
broadcast of Time Traveller's journey on a giant screen
which straddled the Allée.

The fact that Edward and Jack had chosen CNES for
their final journey together, along with Jack's love of
the Impressionists, indeed his personal friendships with
the likes of Cézanne, Matisse and Monet, had made the
time-travelling explorers the darlings of the nation.

Many of those there were dressed in exact replicas
of Edward's outfit, others in various outfits featuring
the motif of a rainbow butterfly. All of them carried the
goody-bags which had been handed out as they arrived,
bearing the image of Jack's first painting of Ginny which
now hung in The Louvre, beside the Mona Lisa. It was
acknowledged, along with Da Vinci's masterpiece, as
one of the most important and intriguing works by the
Grand Masters of portraiture.

As they watched the spaceship disappear into
darkness, everyone stood and applauded, cheered,
whistled and cried out the phrase which was now on the
lips of every French citizen, "Jack et Edward, maîtres du
temps et de l'espace!".

Lake turned to her father and said, "Do you think
they know?"

"What? That they are, like us, Eternals? I am sure
Edward does, and, no doubt, he will have informed Jack
that he too is one of our select few."

"Then why has Jack aged so much more than we
have? Even Edward looks younger than Jack by several
years."

"Because of love, my dear," Lake's father explained.

"Jack fell in love and stayed for most of his life with Ginny, and they aged together in real time. Unlike you and I and Edward, who have remained free spirits, untethered by deep emotions which bring occasional heartbreak, we are not anchored by a yearning to stay with one special person. We have been freed of the fast aging process by constantly moving, constantly searching and finding new spaces - alone. Jack will not age any more, he has become the ultimate wanderer, perhaps even beginning a backwards aging process... so I have heard anyway..."

Lake watched her father smile to himself and nodded.

"Perhaps, one day, they will return?"

"I have no doubt about that," Albert replied.

They stood up, Lake linked her father's arm and they joined the exiting crowds, the buzz of excited conversation filling the air.

A few minutes later they had reached Lake's limousine, the A.I. chauffeur, looking uncannily like Jim Morrison, stepping out to open her door.

"Thank you, James," Lake said to the gorgeously dishevelled driver in white blouson and leather trousers.

She was about to get in when her father said, "I hope you don't mind, my dear, but I'll join you later. I have an appointment to keep..."

"Veronica?"

"No, a different time-slip. I am en route to have lunch with Jim and Esther Mainstay. They're very excited about their weekend guests who they want me to meet."

"And they are... ?"

"I'll tell you all about it when we next meet up. I believe we're due to have lunch with Marilyn quite soon?"

"Yes, she's putting on quite the banquet for us, by all accounts. Don't be late."

Lake pecked her father on the cheek and got in. As her limousine pulled away, the strains of 'Riders On The Storm' floating from the driver's window, a group of people wandered by, all of them carrying the bags with Ginny's painted image smiling out at a world she could never have imagined.

"Yes," Albert said to himself, tipping his hat at the passers-by, "I'm looking forward to seeing you again, Miss Taylor. If only you could have witnessed these scenes today."

He wandered off down the Grande Allée and, turning into the Allée de Castiglione, disappeared.

And Jack's sketches of the planets? They, of course, went off into deepest space with Jack and Edward, but the scans he sent down were auctioned at Sotheby's in New York. They fetched $300 million, bought by a private collector, Norma Jeane Mortenson. The money went to the Marlowe Foundation who used it to support struggling artists around the world, paying for their tuition, materials and helping them set up exhibitions and promote their work.

A few days later, Marilyn stood before her latest group of visitors and cooed, "And now, ladies and gentlemen, I have something extra special to show you!"

She licked her lips, blinked her widening eyes several times before moving towards the red velvet curtain which covered one wall of her viewing room. Pulling it open with a flourish, Marilyn beamed across at the gathered crowd who gasped at the framed and perfectly-lit prints of Jack's planet sketches.

"I don't know where Sir Jack or my great friend Lord Lockton are now," Marilyn said breathily, "but I think you would agree with me that the world is a better, more fascinating place with endless possibilities because of those two gentlemen. Wouldn't you say, folks?"

As the room filled with applause, Marilyn covered her mouth with her finely manicured hand, bobbed down in her skin-tight diamanté dress, and blew a kiss to them all.

THE END

Acknowledgements

I would like to thank Rick, Rachel, Sam, Rich, Kate and Emily and the rest of the team at Fisher King Publishing, for their fabulous work in turning the Word document of my first novel into a real live book.

They've been there for me ever since FKP published Incidents Crowded With Life, the first volume in my trilogy of memoirs, in 2018.

It's always a joy working with them and the results are always fantastic. Holding the actual printed book in my hands, after many months of sitting at my pc hoping inspiration arrives, is never less than wonderful.

I'd also like to thank my husband Neil for his patience, support and advice whenever an idea in my head begins turning into a fully-fledged story. When I've finished a book, he reads each one before suggesting amendments which are always spot-on – even though I may baulk at the changes initially!

Finally, thank you to all of you who have bought this novel, physical or on Kindle. I always appreciate your thoughts and comments when you've read any of my books. I'll be interested to hear what you think of Across My Dreams With Nets of Wonder.

John Howard

John Howard

John Howard grew up in, Lancashire, England, training as a classical pianist from the age of seven. John first performed his own material at a college charity concert in March 1970 and for the next three years he played at universities,

 folk clubs and Bolton's Octagon Theatre where an early incarnation of Iron Maiden asked John to be their lead singer! He declined the invitation.

In 1973, while playing at London's Troubadour he was spotted and signed by then Head of Pop at Chappell Music. By the end of the year, John signed to CBS Records and was commissioned to write and record the theme song, Casting Shadows, for the movie, Open Season.

John's debut album, Kid In A Big World, produced by Tony Meehan and Paul Phillips, and featuring Rod Argent and Bob Henrit, was recorded at Abbey Road and Apple studios through 1974 and launched in February the following year with a concert John gave at The Purcell Room for radio, press and TV luminaries. Two singles from the album were released, Goodbye Suzie and Family Man. John's album, Can You Hear Me OK? spawned the single, I Got My Lady.

John performed in fashionable London clubs such as April Ashley's Knightsbridge AD8, Morton's of Berkeley Square and Company, but this new stage in his career was brought to a sudden halt when he was involved in an accident in which he broke his back.

After a long period of recuperation John met Trevor Horn

with whom, in the summer of 1977 he recorded his single, I Can Breathe Again, released in February 1978 on Ariola Records. The backing band comprised what would later become the nucleus of Buggles and The Art of Noise – Geoff Downes, Anne Dudley, Linda Jardim, Louis Jardim and Bruce Woolley. Over the next few years John made more singles with Trevor Horn, and with Steve Levine and Nicky Graham, and recorded several tracks with the late Chris Rainbow.

Through the 1980s and '90s John carved out a career in marketing and A&R at various record companies, working with Elkie Brooks, Maria Friedman, Connie Francis, Hazell Dean, Sonia, Gary Glitter, The Crickets, Lonnie Donegan, Madness, Barry Manilow and Sir Tim Rice. He even found time to write the occasional song for other artists and in 1992 Des O'Connor recorded John's Blue Days for his Portrait album which received a silver disc for 100,000 sales.

In 2001, after retiring to Pembrokeshire with his partner, actor Neil France, John began performing again, at local pubs and in the piano bars on cruise ships. And then something amazing happened… Kid In A Big World was re-released, got five star reviews in the music press, reviving John's recording career with new record deals, a career he still enjoys today.

John's amazing life is documented in an acclaimed series of books that are at times hilarious and deeply moving while being a reminder of how life was in the last decades of the twentieth century :

Incidents Crowded With Life

Illusions Of Happiness

In The Eyeline of Furtherance